PLIGHTS

To Faye.
Happy Birthday !!

Also by B. Pine

The Draca Wards Saga

Familiar Origins

Plights

The Imperium Saga

Tales of the Council of Elders (Jeffa's Tale)

The Draca Wards Saga

PLIGHTS

By

B. Pine

SILVER
LEAF
BOOKS

HOLLISTON, MASSACHUSETTS

PLIGHTS
Copyright © 2013 by B. Pine

Cover Art by Eimi Pinero

First printing February 2013
10 9 8 7 6 5 4 3 2 1

ISBN # 1-60975-049-7
ISBN-13 # 978-1-60975-049-7
LCCN # 2013931832

Silver Leaf Books, LLC
P.O. Box 6460
Holliston, MA 01746
+1-888-823-6450

Visit our web site at www.SilverLeafBooks.com

To my son Justin.
Chasing your dream is not a walk in the park.
It is a triathlon.

CONTENTS

Prologue

Chapter 1: Wards of the Tueri

Chapter 2: The Angel's Chosen

Chapter 3: Revelations

Chapter 4: The Will of the Penta

Chapter 5: Headmaster Schemes

Chapter 6: Springtime

Chapter 7: Dragons and Monsters

Chapter 8: Caster Trial

Chapter 9: Terra's Ward

Chapter 10: Necare

Chapter 11: Morning

Chapter 12: A Concert and a Fire Spell

Chapter 13: Setbacks

Chapter 14: A Spellcaster Discovered

Chapter 15: The Son of Aoiyama

Chapter 16: Vitalia's Ward

Chapter 17: Prelude to War

Chapter 18: The Princess-Heir

Epilogue

PLIGHTS

Prologue

Avre could not take his eyes off of the beautiful white-haired girl sleeping in his bed. He had found her unconscious and alone in the middle of his favorite grove where he would often set traps for beavers and mink. He had not been able to wake her, so he had carried her to his single room cabin to rest and warm up. It was a treat to watch her sleep, sprawled out upon his bed wearing only a light white sundress.

She was a tiny little thing, maybe one third of his twenty-stoneweight frame, with her smooth milky face. She was no child, though. Avre reached over to touch her hair, but stopped when he noticed her stir slightly. He wondered why her hair was white. She couldn't possibly have been born that way. The young woman's head turned, and Avre almost gasped as her eyes opened. Her eyes were as white as her hair!

"Where am I?" she whispered.

He had to be careful. No mistakes. Her strange eyes did nothing to detract from her allure. With a little charm and a little luck... "Ya'ar somewhere safe," he said.

She sat up and looked around. "Did you bring me here?" She sounded like she was from one of the coastal countries.

"I sure did. Found ya half-dead not too far from here. What happened t' ya? Ya'ar eyes and hair, they're all white! Who did that t' ya?"

She touched her hair. "You should not have helped me," she said.

Avre wanted to laugh. As if he could pass up an opportunity to have a female guest in his lonely home. Now all he had to do was make sure she stayed for a while. "The Creator would strike me down if I allowed a beautiful young lady such as ya'arself t' die. I'll get ya some tea." He stood up.

"No, thank you. I am fine."

"I find that hard t' believe." He headed over to the stove.

The cabin door crashed open just as Avre picked up the kettle. He dropped it back on the stove and spun around. "What the..." he gasped at the sight of the man intruding into his home. His white hair and eyes were identical to his lovely guest, but he looked considerably older.

"There you are, Poli," the intruder said, stepping inside the cabin. "I am shocked you made it this far. How you escaped the spirit barrier eludes me, but no matter. Your flight ends here." He did not even acknowledge Avre.

Were these two part of some spiritual cult? "Oh, sir! I know ya must've been worried, but ya'ar daughter is well and safe. I'm about t' give her some tea. Would ya like some ya'arself, sir?" Avre picked up the kettle once again and poured water into the teapot. He was not going to chance angering this man.

"He is no father of mine," the girl said. "And I am not going anywhere with him."

The white-eyed man turned to Avre. "Who are you, man? Well, Poli, have you finally found your ward?" He threw his head back and laughed.

Avre set the kettle down with a bang. The girl had spoken. Whoever he was, the man had no claim on her. And he dared make fun of Avre right in his own home! It mattered nothing that Avre had no inkling of what he was laughing about.

"Now see here! Ya better get out of here, before ya get hurt!" Avre marched over to stand beside the bed. The sight of Poli's soft skin as she swung her legs over the side of the bed strengthened his resolve. He was not letting this opportunity slip away without a fight.

The white man only laughed harder. "Poli, please come on, before this poor silly man gets himself hurt," he choked out between peals of laughter.

The girl gave Avre a worried look. "Don't ya worry none, girl. I'll take care of this lout." Avre reached under the bed and pulled out his prized axe. "We'll see who gets hurt, old man," he growled.

The man stopped laughing. "Poli, I know that breaching that barrier has weakened you terribly. All I have to do is pick you up and carry you back. You would be stubborn enough to let this human die?" he asked the girl, walking slowly toward them.

"Remember the Pact," the girl replied. Her warning did not stop the older man from approaching, though.

"Killing him does not break the Pact. Neither does gathering you up into my arms." The strange man stopped right before Avre. He reached for the axe and pulled it out of Avre's hands as if Avre had offered it to him.

"Obitus, stop it!" the girl cried out.

Before Avre could get over his shock, a pale hand latched onto his neck and lifted his stocky frame effortlessly up into the air. The man's white eyes gleamed, and an evil chuckle rumbled out of his lips. Shocked to his core, Avre struggled to get air into his lungs. The girl jumped out of the bed and ran to the door.

As he stared into those achromic eyes, his energy drained away, along with his courage. He could see in those eyes the true power the being before him possessed. Avre whimpered as he realized that his neck was an eyeblink from being snapped. The hand holding him in the air did not belong to a human being. The monster smirked as humiliating tears fell from Avre's eyes and nose.

"Let the human go, Obitus."

Avre looked up. A lanky man stood behind Avre's heroine, red eyes glaring. Avre supposed he should have been taken aback by those unnatural eyes, but all he felt was relief that help had arrived. His captor glanced back and actually growled at the newcomer.

"I'm taking Poli. You can try to stop me if you wish," the red-eyed man said.

"Leave now or the human dies," the white-eyed man roared back.

"Very well." The red-eyed man took the girl's hand, and they both vanished into thin air.

"No! That hibrida!" Avre tumbled to the floor as the monster-man released him. He started to rise, but an iron-hard leg slammed into his soft spot. Avre crumpled back down, and darkness overcame him.

Poli clasped her hands together in relief as the pudgy trapper materialized on the ground before her. "You saved him from Obitus. Oh, thank you, Semino."

Semino shrugged. "He would have been no big loss. Why did you involve this man, Poli?"

"I didn't. Breaching that sphere Obitus had me trapped in was draining. I'm still too weak to even change form. I stopped to rest and fell asleep. He found me and took me to his home. He thought he had rescued me."

Semino snorted. "Right. And I know exactly what kind of reward he was looking to receive. It's amazing how these humans remain in perpetual heat."

Poli smiled. "You sound jealous."

"As if I wish to spend my life bumbling about in an estral fog. How humans evolved this far with such ingrained libido is beyond my comprehension." Semino crouched beside the man and touched his neck. "I suppose Obitus agrees with me. He gave the man's unmentionables a nice pounding."

"Can you make him forget?" Poli asked.

"Yes. But he will be wondering why his nether parts are so sore. Hopefully he can still walk. He has a two-day trek back to his home." Semino moved his hand to the man's head. He laughed.

"What are you laughing about?" Poli asked Semino as he stood up.

Semino looked at her, and his shape began to change. Poli waited calmly as his long limbs stretched and blood red scales sprouted out of his skin. Soon, a winged four-legged serpent stood before her. The serpent extended a claw, and she stepped forward and held on to a talon. Semino picked her up and set her gently down on his back.

"Why were you laughing?" Poli asked again as Semino spread his wings and launched himself into the air.

"I did not think it fair for the poor man to completely forget about his misadventure." Semino's raspy voice was markedly different from his human vocal tones. "He shall have fond memories of you, Poli."

"Semino! You are so very crude!" Poli pounded on his chitinous back as Semino roared gleefully.

"They are the wards?" Poli asked, studying the image of the farseeing spell Terra had cast on Semino's wall.

"You see before you five of the six we have found," Terra replied, pushing her ebony hair away from her pretty human face. "They are growing up together as close friends. Isn't it amazing?"

Three boys and three girls were talking and having fun in a clearing before a quaint little cottage. Poli watched them carry on. She could tell by their demeanor who they were. The wards were all supposed to have a marked contrast to their draconian familiars.

"The small girl with the bow, that's my little one," Semino said proudly, pointing with his claw.

"Of course. The one with the boyish haircut and the sweet laugh," Poli replied. "Not like you at all, Semino."

"Don't be fooled, Poli. Galen seethes with power."

Poli turned her gaze on the tall blond boy. His golden eyes matched those of Semino's tiny ward. "Galen's brother. Reserved and slightly moody. He holds much inside himself. He must be yours, Terra."

"Ben is the most powerful student at the Arcanum College, and his potential has not even been tapped. When he is ready to accept the deeper levels of spellcasting, he will be a force to be reckoned with." Terra's soft voice dripped with as much pride as Semino's booming boast.

Poli scrutinized his face. "He is troubled."

"Normal adolescent angst. He wants revenge for the razing of his home. He also has feelings for the Princess of Syntrea. Love and anger will create conflict in the wisest of beings. His turmoil is understandable, and hopefully temporary."

Poli nodded and pointed to the dark-haired girl sitting next to Ben, laughing at the wrestling match before her. "Princess Jania. She is as regal as Animis is pragmatic. He has done a wonderful job with her."

"More than you know," Terra replied. "One short talk with her and you will be forever impressed. She will be the perfect Queen."

"If she lives that long," Semino muttered. The huge dragon shied back when he noticed the heated looks the two women gave him.

Poli looked back at the wall and smiled. "And that rambunctious youngster wrestling with the tall redheaded girl has to be the famous Rohen." Semino's disgruntled snort confirmed her statement.

"That is him," Terra said.

"He is amazingly good-natured, considering all he has been through," Poli noted.

"The druid who took him in has done much to help heal his soul, and he has found a new sister in Megan and a kindred spirit in Galen. Those three are very close."

"Rohen and Galen are a dangerous pair. No world should have more than one necare alive at a time," Semino said.

Poli ignored Semino and watched Rohen for some time. "Sanguis must not get her claws on him. We cannot take for granted that his familiar will keep him safe, either. The fact that Vitalia marked him means nothing."

Terra nodded in agreement. Semino did not say anything.

"And the redhead is the child druid Megan. Blunt and precocious. She definitely belongs to Caeles."

"He refuses to admit this," Semino said.

"That is no surprise. But it is a fact. Caeles pulled a remarkable feat by removing Megan from the druidic community. They follow Obitus blindly, revering him as their sacred White Angel. Now Obitus wants Megan back under his control. He is urging the druids to get her back to the commune."

"So she will need protection as well," Terra said.

"That will be delicate. The drui are only misguided humans. To confront them in order to protect Megan would be against our tenets of defending all sentient life." Poli sighed. "The wards will have to deal with that threat without our intervention." She noticed the last one of the group, a boy with light brown skin and blond hair. "Is that boy Surian? He has light hair and blue eyes. That is unusual. Wait!" She watched him for a moment. "He is...?"

"He is," Terra said. "Animis confirmed it not too long ago, during a trip the Princess took to Massea. Jamu saved the Princess and her party from an ambush. He is a close friend of the five, despite his origins."

"Incredible," Poli said. "What legends shall spawn from these we watch?"

"The sixth ward is safe and thriving with Silx. Two remain to be found, your ward and Rigare's," Terra remarked.

"Rigare is searching hard," Semino said. "But she will not disclose her progress."

"She does not wish to alert the Debellos. Senui also searches." Poli sighed. "My imprisonment was worthwhile. I have learned much about Obitus and his plans. But it is good to be free once more."

"It is good to have you back," Terra said.

"Your freedom brings relief to us all," Semino agreed.

"Thank you," Poli replied. "Now I shall rest, and once I have recovered I shall search for my ward."

1

Wards of the Tueri

"That son of a mongrel tried to kill my ward! He is going to pay for that." Animis clenched his perfectly manicured hands in frustration.

Terra was grateful that Animis did not possess Semino's famous temper. He had been in a terrible mood since the attempted ambush a few months ago, but he was handling everything quite well, in her opinion. She did not know how she would react if someone had tried to kill Ben.

They sat in Silx's waiting room. Terra grimaced at the surroundings. Silx was almost as bad as Humo when it came to room decor. The gray stone walls were bare, and the black marble chairs that were set before the matching marble fireplace did nothing to cheer the place up. There wasn't even a rug covering the floor stones. At least the floor was clean and polished.

"It is time to reconsider the Pact," Animis said, staring at his clenched fists. "We have to do something about Humo. He is becoming too dangerous."

"Animis, you cannot blame him for what happened to the princess," Terra replied. "He would never try something so drastic. Besides, this is a setback for him."

"Setback or not, he incited this whole thing. It is his fault Jania was attacked."

Terra sighed. Animis was right. His sister Vitalia had informed Terra that the mysterious attacks against Massean troops, attacks which appeared to be carried out by Syntrean soldiers, had actually been arranged by Humo. Unfortunately, no one was able to obtain proof that Humo was behind these attacks. In any case, the failed attack on Princess Jania's travel party only served to restore close ties between the two countries, which had been on the brink of war mere weeks ago.

A young blond girl skipped into the room. "Hello, Terra," she said. "Do you want to see what I can do?"

"I would love to," Terra told her. It amazed her how fast a learner Milina was.

Terra watched the little girl close her sky blue eyes and mumble something very quietly. She clasped her hands together, and a circle of gray light formed beside her. The gray light dimmed, and Terra could see a bed beyond the circle. Milina put her arm through, grabbed a cushion that was on the bed, and pulled it out through the circle. The circle closed back up as Milina laughed and jumped up and down. "Do you know what spell that was?"

"Let me guess. Was that a portal spell?"

Milina squealed in delight and threw her cushion up in the air. "Can your students do that?"

"Only the older ones. That is a seventh-year Arcanum spell."

"Good. That means I'm still ahead of the Arcanum students," Milina stated proudly.

Animis laughed. "Milina, the students who can now cast that spell at Arcanum started there when you were born. Do you understand what that means?"

"Sure I do, Animis. It means it took some mage my whole lifetime to learn a spell I mastered in two months. But I'm eight, so I was already born when the seventh-year students started at Arcanum."

Animis looked at Terra in amazement.

"You are supposed to be getting ready for your bath, you little scamp," Silx said as he walked into the room. "Go upstairs. Kelita is looking for you."

Milina rushed out of the room without another word. Silx watched her run off with a proud smile on his boyish face. His human guise did not appear to be much older than his ward. He sat on one of the cold marble chairs. "Now, all the Tueri are aware that Poli is free from Obitus and his evil brood, so something must have happened for the two of you to be here. What is going on?"

"An Eastern regiment disguised as Syntrean soldiers tried to ambush the Princess of Syntrea last summer," Terra said.

Silx's jet-black eyes widened in surprise. "Your girl?" he asked Animis. The other dragon nodded.

"She was traveling to Trader's Pass on a diplomatic assignment," Terra continued. "The ambush failed, and the attackers were defeated."

"So everything turned out well," Silx said.

"Yes, thanks to a young Surian noble. A Surian with beautiful blue eyes," Terra replied.

"What?" Silx leaned forward in his seat. "A blue-eyed Surian?"

"You digress, Terra. The outcome is not the issue here," Animis cut in. "Terra and Vitalia believe that the Eastern regiment was under Humo's control somehow."

"Humo has stationed Eastern armies on the continent?" Silx asked, alarmed.

"Only very tiny ones, hidden along the coast. There is no proof of this, though," Terra said.

"Vitalia found a document ordering the attack on Trader's Pass a few years ago," Animis added. "The order was written on vellum paper, and signed by a commander called Adfligere."

"Vellum? That material is not easy to obtain in this world," Silx commented.

Terra nodded in agreement. "But Humo has easy access to it. Arcanum has the means to produce vellum paper."

"Have you heard of anyone named Adfligere?" Animis asked

Silx.

"No." Silx scratched his head. "I would remember that name."

"No human would name their child that," Animis said. "It is a celestial word. The name was adopted."

"We know that, but who adopted it?" Terra asked. She turned to Silx. "Please help us. You have ties to all spellcasters outside of Syntrea. If they could just keep an ear open for the name…"

"I'm sorry, but no. I cannot get involved in this. I have Milina to worry about. I won't risk her yet."

"The lives of three wards, maybe more, may be at stake," Animis said.

"Two wards," Silx corrected. "And two necare at that. Why should I worry about two humans who possess the power to slay dragons? Now if you will excuse me, I have to make sure my ward does not weasel herself out of her bath." He stood up and headed to the doorway.

Terra took a deep breath, ready to give her fellow earth dragon a piece of her mind, but Animis shook his head for her to stop. "You are teaching that baby too much, too fast. You should take it a bit slower with her," he said.

"She thinks I am going too slow as it is," Silx remarked. "Besides, I have to make sure she is ready. The Debellos can strike any day. Look at what happened to Rohen. Look at what happened to Galen." He paused at the doorway. "If I come across this Adfligere, or hear anything about him, I will let you know. I promise. But I will not go out of my way to find out anything." He walked away, leaving them alone.

"Why did you mention Jamu to Silx?" Animis asked.

Terra shrugged. "He should know. All of the Tueri should."

"We have more important things to worry about." Animis shook his head. "Jania would be humiliated if she faced Milina in a spellcasting match. You had better find your ward soon, Terra. You will have quite a job getting him caught up with that little girl."

Terra did not answer him.

2

The Angel's Chosen

Megan kept her eye on the arrow as it streaked her way. She stood still as it whisked past her face and through a hole on a deerskin stretched out between two willow trees. She stifled a yawn as a second arrow flew through the hole right after the first.

"I got them both in, Rowy! Did you see?"

"I'm right here, Firefly. Of course I saw. Let's back up a few more paces this time."

"Sure!"

Megan sat at the edge of the riverbank, watching Rohen and Galen practice with their bows. They stood on the opposite bank, shooting at the targets Megan had marked on the deerskin.

She was bored halfway to insanity. They had been shooting for most of the afternoon. Megan's deerskin marks were only big holes now. She wished she had not talked Galen into wrapping her forearm with cotton. The welts the bowstring would have snapped on her arm would have caused her to stop long ago.

She heard someone walking through the grove. "Careful! Shooting arrows!" she called out.

Yar appeared through the trees. "Hello, Megan," he said.

"Yar! I haven't seen you in months. Where have you been?"

She had missed him during the summer break. He had stayed out of sight even after classes resumed for the new school year. It was nice to see his freckled face again.

"Well, I've been, um..." He sounded nervous. "I've wanted to see you, but I've just been too shy."

"Shy? We're friends already, Yar."

"Yes, I know, but still." Yar stared at the ground, but Megan noticed how red his ears were. As she watched him squirm before her, she realized why Yar was acting so strange.

"Meggie," Rohen hollered from the other side of the river. "Bring the arrows back."

"You come and get them," Megan shouted back. She turned to Yar, smiling. "I'm tired of being around those two. Why don't we go for a walk?"

His eyes almost bulged, but a smile quickly swallowed up the shocked look on his face. "Uh, sure," he said.

"I think that was Yar," Galen said.

"We have to make sure," Rohen replied. "I've told you already, Firefly, we need to watch out for each other."

"But..."

He waved at her to be quiet and weaved his way through the trees. Galen followed him. Rohen was right. He did not realize just how right he was.

They are straight ahead, he signaled to her. Go up.

Galen watched him climb up a tree. She could hear Megan talking nearby. She circled around and chose a tree to climb.

She leaned over a branch and peered down. She spotted Yar sitting very close to Megan, with their backs against a thick tree. He had his arm around her.

She had spied a few of the older Scout students when they took girls into the Espies Wood. It was funny to watch, and she loved it when the girls would make the boys stop – quite violently sometimes – but she never imagined she would catch Megan in such a situation. And with Yar, of all people!

Yar leaned over to kiss Megan, but she blocked his face with her hand. "I think we are being watched," she whispered.

Yar glanced around. "Are you sure?"

"We'll see." Megan waved her hand around in a circle.

Galen heard a hiss, and a branch shook at her flank. Alarmed, she climbed back down. She was more than halfway to the ground when she heard the thump of a body hitting the leafy forest floor.

"Rowy!" Galen dropped the rest of the way and rushed over to him. She found him kneeling and hugging his middle.

Megan and Yar walked up. "I knew it," Megan said.

"Meggie, what did you do to him?" Galen asked. "Rowy, are you all right?"

Rohen shook his head and heaved.

"Maybe that will teach you to sneak around intruding on people's privacy," Megan said.

"Ew." Galen stepped back as Rohen threw up. "Was he supposed to get sick?"

"Definitely," Megan answered.

Galen watched Rohen drop to his side and curl up into a ball. "How could you?" she cried out angrily. Megan could be so cruel sometimes. "He was only watching out for you. That was an awful thing to do!"

"Why do you always take his side? You always act as if he never does anything wrong," Megan yelled back.

"Well if you wouldn't do stupid things, I wouldn't have to take his side. You should have grown a brain along with that bust of yours!"

"Take that back!"

"Make me!"

"You are looking for trouble," Megan warned, giving Galen a hard shove.

Galen pushed her back, and soon they were rolling on the

ground, clawing at each other.

"So now you're a proud Papa of three. Now how in the world did that happen?"

Bilin smiled at Clay. It was a wonderful surprise to see his cousin here. "Rohen and Galen needed someone to care for them until they could apply for Espies. I couldn't turn them away."

"You could never say no to anyone," Clay said. "That's why you would always get stuck helping Theira with her errands."

They both laughed.

"Well, I'm glad I didn't say no to those two," Bilin said. "They have made my life quite interesting."

The front door opened. Yar stood at the doorway, looking hesitant. "Druid Bilin?"

"Hello, Yar. I haven't seen you in quite some time," Bilin said.

"I know. I came to see Megan, and…" He gulped. "I think you should come see," he finished anxiously.

It never failed. Every time the three of them were together… "Come on, Clay," Bilin said. "You can come and meet my children."

He sighed when he saw them, but it was not as bad as he had expected. He had seen them doing worse. He glanced at his cousin. "There they are. Aren't they something?"

Clay nodded slowly as he watched Galen and Megan wrestle. Rohen crawled weakly toward a tree, heaving. "How do you get them to calm down?" he asked Bilin.

"I just put them to sleep," Bilin said, holding his palms out. Soon the three of them were stretched out on the ground, sleeping peacefully. "We should let them rest for awhile. Let's go eat." He put his arm around a dumbfounded Yar. "Come join us, Yar."

"So once the Penta heard of your heroic actions during the ambush, they decided to approve your Confirmation. From what we have heard, you defended the Princess of Syntrea during battle, saved several lives, and helped solve a mystery plaguing two countries. You have made the commune very proud, Megan."

Megan could hardly believe what she was hearing. Druids had to have years of experience before a Confirmation would be allowed. She smiled at Yar. He grinned at her proudly. Galen and her father were also smiling, but Rohen was not. He scowled at her, his gray eyes promising a cruel form of retaliation. Megan met her brother's glare with a defiant one of her own.

"News travels fast," her father remarked.

"News of that scale does travel fast," Clay replied. "The Penta wants me to bring Megan back, so we can give her the recognition she deserves. She needs to know how heroic her actions were."

She frowned. The school year had already started. "I can't go now," she said.

"She's right," her father said. "She has classes she needs to attend."

Clay looked disappointed, but he nodded. "I understand," he told Megan. "Next summer break, then?"

"Next summer," she agreed.

Megan walked along the riverbank, holding on to Yar's hand. It was dark, but she did not use her nightvision. It was nice to walk in the dark with Yar.

"I'm sorry about what happened earlier," she said. "But maybe now we can go back to where we left off."

She felt a familiar tingle play up and down her arms. Before she could react, Yar released her hand and crumpled to the ground.

"Yar! Are you all right?" Megan dropped to her knees beside him and shook him hard. "Ro, this is not funny! Keep Yar out of this!"

She heard footsteps, and the prickly feeling on her skin grew stronger. She was about to yell at Rohen again when it hit her. Rohen's psychic ability never made her skin tingle.

The footsteps stopped, and Druid Clay suddenly stood over her. "Yar will be fine," he said, pulling her to her feet. "Come on, Meggie. We have to go."

"Go where?" She tried to pull her arm away from him, but he would not let her go. The tingle spread to her back.

"Back home. I have to bring you back with me, no matter what." He pulled out a piece of rope with his free hand.

"No! What..." Her arms pressed themselves against her sides, and her legs stiffened. She could not move. "Let me go!" she yelled.

"Quiet!" He pushed her to the ground and began to bind her hands behind her back.

She tried to cry out again, but her tongue suddenly swelled up and filled her mouth. Panicked, she tried to think of some way to get Clay away from her. She had water and earth right before her. If only she could clear her head before he put her to sleep as well.

She heard a thump, and Clay fell on top of her. She looked up. A pair of red eyes gazed down at her.

"I should hit you on the head, too, for making me sick like that," Rohen's northern accent reached her ears a heartbeat before her eyes could make out his face in the dark. He rolled the druid off her back and helped her sit up.

Clay suddenly grabbed Rohen's arm, but a small boot kicked his hand away and stomped down on his neck. Megan noticed Galen pull her arm back at an angle. She tried to say something, but all that came out was a grunt.

"Firefly, no!" Rohen threw his arm to the side, but Megan

heard the twang of a bowstring. Terrified, she switched to her nightvision.

Galen's arrow hit the ground right next to Clay's ear. Rohen had pushed her arm to the side just in time.

"Why did you stop me?" Galen asked Rohen. "We have to kill him."

"No!" Megan managed to croak out.

"We can't go around killing druids," Rohen said.

"Why not?" Galen pulled out another arrow.

"No, no, please," Clay begged. "I'll just go and leave, and we can all forget about this." He gasped for breath as Galen pressed down on his throat.

"You are overreacting," Rohen told Galen as he snatched her bow away. "Stop it!"

"Fine!" Galen pulled her foot up off the druid's throat and kicked his temple hard. Clay jerked and lost consciousness.

The tingle faded. Megan's tongue shrank back to normal, and her hands and legs moved once more. She threw her arms around Rohen. "That was so close. Thank you."

Rohen pushed her away. "Get off me, you witch! I'm still angry with you." He looked over at Galen, who was waking up Yar. "Look at the mess we are in now. We need to figure out what we are going to do."

"We can't tell Daddy," Megan said. "He will never believe us."

"We can't just let him go," Galen said. "He tried to take Meggie away, and I don't think he will give up. He might even try to hurt her."

"No, Cousin Clay would never hurt me. He is like my stepfather; why would he…" She trailed off as her eyes met Rohen's. Maybe she should not have said stepfather.

"What did he do to me?" Yar mumbled. Galen pushed him up to a sitting position.

"He put a sleep spell on you," Megan explained. "I couldn't

warn you in time to—" The tingle returned, painfully strong this time. "Not again," Megan groaned.

She looked around, but she did not see anyone nearby. Galen and Rohen stared at her. She looked down at Clay.

The druid's eyes were open and swollen. His mouth was also open, and she could see warm foam bubbling from his nostrils with her nightvision.

She reached down to feel for a pulse that she knew would not be there. She pulled her hand away from the dead druid's neck. She could not remember ever feeling so afraid.

Obitus growled furiously. He should have made the druid's death more painful, but he did not want to alarm his Chosen any more than she was already. All the damned druid had to do was to get the girl to come back. What the hell had made him decide to kidnap her? Now Megan would never want to return. And she had those two necare protecting her on top of everything else.

He had to admit he was afraid of those two. Especially the girl; she was developed. It probably happened when she faced Gravesco. There was no doubt in his mind that it was Galen who killed the mighty red dragon. Animis and Semino were still bound within the Pact, and the barren aftermath of the terrain could have only been the result of Draca magic. He wondered what would happen when the boy's powers developed. The base instinct of necare was to kill those like them. It was only an instinct, and could be easily overcome, but no living Draca had ever witnessed a human necare, much less two.

Obitus turned away from the farseeing spell. He needed to plan something to get that young druid back, but not now. He had other things to do, and he had slept way too long. He decided to see how his other young projects were coming along.

3

Revelations

Jamu threw the door to his room shut. That damned princess! It had taken him all day to convince her not to hold a ceremony for him at the palace. Just because his father wanted him to have his highblood status known did not mean that he would appreciate his son calling attention to himself. Now the girls who loved to watch Rohen train his troops and practice with his swords would probably be drooling over him this year as well. He could just hear them cooing about the Surian noble who saved Princess Jania's life, like one of the heroes in those romance stories girls loved so much.

He smiled at that thought. That might not be such a bad thing. Rohen did not yet appreciate the pleasure of girls, and Ben was too enthralled with Jania to notice anyone else. That would hopefully change by this year. Girls were fun to be around. Sometimes.

Jamu noticed the full moon poised right outside his window. It was time. He missed the original meeting, but he was sure his father would understand. He had been on an important trip at the time.

He quickly changed his clothes and jumped into bed. He had removed the scant furnishings the Academy Tower had provided when he moved in and asked his sister to send him his belongings from Sur. It always felt like home when he was in his room. He only wished it would not get so cold in the winter. He threw a thin silk sheet over himself and closed his eyes. He was so tired that it did not take him long to fall asleep.

The misty astral fog surrounded him. He looked up to see his father sitting high up on a cloud, watching him proudly with his kind brown eyes.

"Father!" Jamu jumped up to stand beside the cloud throne. He dropped to his knees and grabbed the hem of his father's heavy robe. "Honored I am to see you, Aoiyama."

"No formalities here, my son. Hug me." Aoiyama opened his arms, and Jamu embraced him. "Much honor you have brought to House Aoiyama, my son."

"You have no one to blame but yourself," Jamu replied as he released Aoiyama and stepped back.

"Foreign, you speak." Aoiyama smiled at him and ruffled his hair. "Your eyes, your hair. Conspicuous, are they?"

"No, Father. The barber has made comments, but he thinks it is because I am Surian. Difficult, it is, for him to groom me."

Aoiyama laughed. "Good." He felt Jamu's face. "No beard?"

"Not yet."

"Grow, it may not."

"Easily hidden, that can be." Jamu took his father's hand and kissed it. "Disappoint you I will not. Worry not, please."

"Disappoint? That you cannot possibly do. Prouder of you I could not be if you were my true blood."

Jamu pressed his father's hand against his chest. "I wish I were your true blood," he whispered.

"A foolish wish, that is," Aoiyama said. "A reason, there is, for you to be walking this world. And my love for you could not be greater, even if your blood were mine."

Jamu let his tears well up and fall out of his eyes. Nothing was shameful in the astral plane.

"No tears, Jamu. Wary you should be. Bad things approach and ready for them you must be."

"I thank you for the warning, Father."

Aoiyama stroked Jamu's face again. "Caution is all I ask. Now, listen you must as to what to do next."

Jania heard voices on her way up to the Arboreum. She recognized one of the voices and rushed on. Her mother was up there.

She reached the vast indoor garden. "Mother," she called out, running over to her. She hugged her and gave her a big kiss. It was not often that she was able to do that.

"Oh, Jania, darling!" The Queen hugged her back warmly. "Go, please," she ordered her retainers. "I want to be alone with my daughter."

Everyone left, quickly and quietly. Queen Luce guided her over to her favorite seat. "I am happy you came to see me. We do not spend much time together anymore."

"I know, Mother. I'm sorry." Jania sat down and took hold of her mother's soft white hand.

"Don't be sorry. You are the Heir to Syntrea's throne, and a mage in training. I wouldn't have it any other way. I don't know if anyone has told you this, but you are going to make a great Queen."

"Jamu told me the same thing back at Trader's Pass." Jania sighed. "It sure doesn't feel that way."

"He did? He is the Surian boy you spent the day arguing with, isn't he?"

"He's the one." The stubborn ingrate who had thrown her plans for a celebration back in her face. They had even yelled at each other at certain points. Just thinking about their argument gave her a headache.

"He would make an excellent mate for you. Maybe you should

consider arranging a courtship with him. It would be easy, with you both attending the Academy."

"Mother!" It was embarrassing to hear her mother speak about such things.

"Jania, it is time to consider these issues. You are almost an adult. Nobles much younger than you have married."

"We don't need those kinds of unions anymore," Jania said, looking away. She did not want her mother to see the look on her face.

"We might. Look how close we came to war with Massea. Ties with Sur may be vital in the near future. Jania, as Queen, you must be open to such things."

"Mother, Jamu…" She looked at her mother, and wished she hadn't.

The Queen gave her a knowing smile. "There is someone else, isn't there?"

Jania looked out the glass at the city below and said nothing.

"You know, my marriage to your father was arranged. I was being courted by someone, a rich landowner from Canas that I was quite fond of, but when a prince comes knocking at your parent's door, it is hard to turn down a date with him. I was not the happiest bride there ever was, but I was willing to give your father a chance. I was lucky. He is kind and friendly, and now I would lie down and give my life for him. I am sure he would do the same for me, but love was not the reason we married."

Jania watched the people live their lives below. She knew many would kill to trade places with her, but they didn't know. No one knew how valuable freedom was until they didn't have it anymore.

"Your father also loved another."

"What!" Jania turned to her mother in shock. "Why didn't he marry her?"

"She did not have the bearing to handle herself as Queen, at least that is what your grandmother says. She was of noble blood, but the Queen did not approve at the time. After the wedding, your father told me about her, and after a long talk, I told him I would understand if he wished to...keep in touch with his dear friend."

Jania saw the pain in her mother's eyes. "How could you live with something like that?"

"The peace and happiness of the king seemed more important to me than my life and marriage. I did not care much for him at the time anyway, so I felt relieved that I would not have to put up with his advances. His mistress could not stand the arrangement, though. She drank something she shouldn't have, and after your father was done mourning, he began courting me. A small date here, a few hours alone there, he did everything right. And we have an amazing young lady to show for it." Queen Luce moved closer to Jania and put her arm around her. "Now tell me about this person who has managed to take hold of my daughter's heart."

Jania leaned against her mother. She was tired of keeping her feelings to herself, anyway.

Galen sat between Rohen and Megan, rubbing her eyes. She could not stop crying.

"Gayly, you have to stop crying," Megan exclaimed. "You are driving me insane."

"You are driving me insane, too," Rohen said. "I'm tired of waiting for Widow June to show up. I'm going back to the Academy."

"Ro, Daddy said to wait for her to come. We need to make arrangements. With Daddy gone, we need to decide if we are still coming over here on the weekends or not."

"Why did he have to go?" Galen asked, sniffling. They had told Uncle Bilin what happened with Druid Clay, and fortunately he had believed them. Unfortunately, he had to go take the druid's body back to the commune. He probably wouldn't be back until the following spring. "Why can't we just bury him here?"

Megan and Rohen ignored her. Rohen stood up. "You two can decide what to do and let me know," he said as he walked away.

"Ro! You can't just leave! We have responsibilities. Oh, to hell with you." Megan put her arm around Galen. "Come on, Galen, please stop crying."

Galen rubbed her eyes again and managed to stop. "What should we do, Meggie?"

"Let's start straightening up. Do you want to keep coming here?"

"Not without Uncle Bilin here."

"Neither do I. We will tell Miss June."

By the time the widow arrived, the house was spotless.

"I'll take care of the cottage while Bilin is away. Don't you girls worry about a thing," June said. The three of them sat in the sitting room drinking tea. "But I still would like to train you two. You both still have much to learn about elemental powers. Tell me, have either of you experienced anything new?"

"I can feel magic when it is being used," Megan said. "I can feel it when Gayly uses elemental energy, and when Ben casts spells, and even when Daddy uses spiritual magic."

"That is interesting, but I don't think that has anything to do with elemental magic," June replied. "How about you, Galen?"

Galen hid her face behind her teacup as she shook her head. Widow June did not know about her psychic powers. Telling her that she could read her brother's mind at times was not a good idea.

"So neither of you have heard each other's thoughts yet?"

Galen choked on her tea. "What? Elemental magic lets us read each other's minds?"

June nodded. "No one knows why. But some believe that energy currents being shared at some point create a certain kind of connection between two minds wielding elemental magic."

"I thought...I have to let Ben know." Galen rushed out.

She laughed out loud as she ran back to the Academy. She felt as if she had been let out of a cage. She would still have to be careful with her psychic abilities, but she could communicate with Ben without worrying about being caught and sent to the Sanatorium. Maybe this might convince him to come over to Widow June's farm someday and practice using his elemental powers. They might even be able to read minds with Megan as well. Too bad Rohen didn't have elemental powers. It would have been fun for the four of them to read each other's minds.

4

The Will of the Penta

Bilin watched silently as the Penta chanted the funeral dirges for Clay. The five druids paced around the blazing pyre and tossed vervain into the fire as they sang. A boar roasted on a rack above the pyre, so that the essence of the deceased druid would be absorbed into the meat of the boar from the purifying fire and everyone could receive a part of his soul.

Bilin could not wait to leave. The whole attitude of the commune made him uncomfortable. The Penta seemed to be more upset about Megan not accompanying him than at Clay's untimely death. People had muttered when he had decided to sleep in one of the guest cabins instead of staying with Dena at the temple, as he usually did. And after asking about her daughter once, Dena had avoided him the entire three days he had been here.

He sat down with the others once the chanting stopped. He folded his hands together and began to pray.

"I wish you had not chosen to stay at the cabins," a familiar voice whispered in his ear. "Keep praying. Don't move."

Bilin kept his head down and his eyes closed.

"The Penta has been very intent on bringing Megan back here. This news about her heroism at Trader's Pass is just an excuse. I think I know why they want her. Come see me tonight, please."

Bilin kept pretending to pray until someone placed a dish of roast boar into his hands. What the hell was going on?

It was very late when Bilin reached Dena's quarters. The door was unlocked.

Dena sat in the dark in her dining area. "Sit down and listen to me," she whispered.

Bilin groped for a chair and sat down. He knew better than to cast a warding spell. That would undoubtedly attract the Penta's attention.

"The Penta believes that Megan will be the white angel's Chosen. They want Megan to return as soon as possible, so she can receive the angel's marking," Dena murmured.

"What? That is not the way it is supposed to happen," Bilin said.

"They blame you for upsetting the path of destiny. No, Bilin, let me finish!" She jumped up and grabbed Bilin's arm before he could reach the door.

"I have to get back to my children." Bilin pulled his arm away from Dena's grip.

"They are watching the entrance. They are not going to let you go."

Bilin stopped at the door. "So they are going to try to persuade me to bring Meggie back." It was not a question.

"By any means." Dena grabbed his arm again. "Bilin, you have to keep our little girl away from here. I don't know what is going on with her, or whether she is worthy or not, but I won't allow her to be forced into anything against her will. I would die if I ever saw her spirit broken."

Bilin looked at Dena. She sounded desperate. This was not the same woman he had left five years ago. Dena would never doubt the Penta's motives or decisions. "What did they do to you,

Dena?"

"I lost my daughter because of them! I will never forget what they did when they questioned her about the White Angel. You must hate me for not interfering." She wiped tears away from her eyes. "We have to sneak you out of here somehow."

"I don't hate you, Dena." Remembering that day made his blood roil. But he couldn't hate Dena. "Don't worry about me." He cupped her face with his hands. "Don't worry about anything right now." He leaned forward and kissed her. His tiny tranquility spell set off as his lips touched hers. "Why don't we just enjoy the evening?"

"All right." She smiled and relaxed, unaware of the spell taking hold. "You can tell me about your children. I didn't know you had more than one."

Bilin stared at the ceiling later that night. Dena slept curled up beside him.

He did not know why June's face kept floating through his mind. He shouldn't feel bad. He shouldn't.

He was with Dena for a reason. He wanted her involved as little as possible, and he did not want her tied in any way to his unwanted departure. He didn't need her help for that.

Very carefully, he climbed out of Dena's bed and dressed. He set a shrouding spell around himself and left Dena's temple quarters.

There was nothing at the cabin he needed that could not be replaced. And his traveling gear, along with Trust, waited for him at the bottom of the cliff. Bilin thanked the heavens above for deciding to leave Rohen's horse foraging around at the bottom of the canyon instead of risking the climb up with him. If he set a fast pace and took a few shortcuts, Trust could get them back to the Academy just before winter settled in. He only hoped the horse had not encountered a wolf pack.

He reached the wall at the edge of the canyon and pushed the hidden stone away so he could crawl through the opening to the ledge where Megan had hidden so many years ago. Time went by so fast. He reached back and pulled the stone back in place.

Even with his nightvision, he could barely see anything. He shuffled over to the edge.

They might chase after him. Heaven only knew what the will of the Penta was these days. What he did know was that whatever they wanted was not in Megan's best interests. He thought about what Mage Terri had told him about the Tueri and the Debellos. He may not be able to protect her from every danger she would have to face, but he could protect her from this. He said a quick prayer and jumped off the ledge.

He let himself fall for a while before spreading his arms out. His descent slowed considerably. He waited patiently as he drifted down, hoping he wouldn't land in the river. It would be a mighty cold night if he did.

On the ledge, one of the shadows shifted, and a pair of glowing red eyes appeared. They were visible for only an instant; after a quick glance around, the eyes disappeared into the darkness. The shadowy shape remained, however. It shifted forward, and slipped over the ledge after Bilin.

5

Headmaster Schemes

Humo walked over to the Espies compound. It was time. He had put this off for too long. Galen's name was spoken more and more often. The little brat held the top ranking score for her age group, and her aim with the bow was on its way to becoming legendary. If he continued to avoid her, people would begin to wonder about his lack of interest in the Academy's young phenom.

It shouldn't be so bad. Terra had masked her powers, so he should not feel the dreaded emanations that always reminded him of Gravesco's demise. One quick visit and it would be over and done. Then he could move on to more important matters.

He was amazed, and enraged, by his own apprehension. Why did she threaten him so? He was a dragon. She was a tiny human whelp. He could end her life with the thrust of a claw. And yet here he was, avoiding the girl while he tried to delegate her demise to incompetent peers. No more.

He found the second-year Espies cadets at the main yard of the scout's college, testing their paces. All scouts had to learn to walk in a way where each stride was of the same standard length. This was how they kept track of how far they have traveled, and where they should be at any point in time. It helped them with mapping, too. The scout head, Autis, noticed Humo's presence and called the Cadets to a halt.

"Master Humo. It is an honor to have you visit us," Autis said, walking over to him and bowing his head.

"I came to see our famous girl scout," Humo replied pleasantly. He spotted her. "It pleases me to have such an excellent student at the Academy. Can you come here, please, Galen?"

Galen skipped over and gave him a small curtsy.

"I would love to see what everyone is so impressed about. Can you shoot some arrows for me?" Humo asked her.

Someone handed her a bow and some arrows. Galen walked over to the archery range and strung the bow. She took out five arrows and shot them quickly, one after the other. When she was done she unstrung the bow once more and set it down on the ground. "Come and see," she called out, waving him over. She had a high-pitched, babyish voice.

He walked over to the target area. The arrows were in a perfect circle around the small center ring.

"That is amazing, Galen." He walked over to her. "Walk with me. I would like to have a word with you." He took her hand and led her away from Espies.

He fought back the urge to snatch her up by the neck and squeeze. His position as Academy Headmaster was too valuable to risk. He could not kill her now, but he could neutralize the threat she posed.

He waited until they were out of earshot before speaking. "Galen, do you know who I am?"

"Yes. You are Headmaster Humo," she answered brightly.

"Right, but do you really know who I am? What I am?"

She looked puzzled. "You are the Academy Headmaster. You are in charge of all the colleges. You make all the important decisions, and you tell everyone what to do."

"Right." He looked down at her. She didn't know. "Are you afraid of me?"

She looked back at him. Her eyes were open, trusting. "No. Not at all."

"You should be."

It was fun, in a way, to see the change in her expression. "Why?"

"Like you said, I am in charge here. If I wanted to expel you, there is nothing you could do to stop it from happening."

He saw the fear. It was just a flicker, but a seed was planted. Just a little more fuel, and... "Just imagine what would happen if you were expelled. Druid Bilin would be so angry, and Rohen would fall into disgrace with a ruined reputation because he sponsored you. Would you be able to face them if you were expelled?"

Galen shook her head no.

"Your brother would be ashamed of you. And where would you go? Back to Stony Forest? It would be a very long trip for a little girl. No one would be able to take you."

She looked terrified now. Humo smiled at her, enjoying himself immensely. "All I would have to do is announce it. So you see, you should be very afraid of me. Your life is in my hands, at my mercy. And so are the lives of your loved ones. I could do the same to any one of them. So now are you afraid of me?"

She blinked back tears as she bit her lip and nodded.

"Now go. And remember what I said." He watched her run off.

To think he had been afraid of that tiny hatchling all these years. He should have done that a long time ago. Galen would be a good little girl from now on. Chuckling, he turned and headed toward Arcanum Tower. Now to work his charms on another young girl.

"I can't believe Master Humo would say that to you!" Rohen exclaimed. He paced back and forth before Ben's bed. Ben wiped tears off his sister's face.

"He's wrong, Gayly. I would never be ashamed of you," Ben said. "And I would never abandon you. Neither would Druid Bi-lin."

"There is nothing you can possibly do to make us ashamed of you," Rohen added, kneeling before her. "You have made us all nothing but proud."

"But all he has to do is say one word and my life will be ru-ined," Galen said. "And there's nothing I can do about it." She was trying very hard not to cry again.

"Did he say he wanted to expel you?" Ben asked her.

"No."

"Listen, you shouldn't let him scare you. As long as you are a good student, he will not want you to go. You are a very good scout, and that is what the Academy needs. All you have to do is stay out of trouble and not get Master Humo angry," Ben said. "Why don't you lie down and rest for a bit? I hate to see you upset like this."

"Ben is right, Firefly," Rohen said, sitting on a stool at the foot of the bed. "Everyone loves you, and no one wants you to leave Espies."

"Keran does," Galen said.

"Don't worry about Keran. He can't do anything to get you expelled. Now lie down and close your eyes," Rohen ordered.

She complied. Rohen watched her as she dozed off. Humo must know about her. Why else would he terrorize her the way he did?

"You seem upset."

Rohen looked over at Ben. "Of course I'm upset. Aren't you?"

"Very. But it is heartening to see that there are others who care about my sister." Ben had a strange look on his face.

There was more he wanted to say, Rohen could tell. "What is it, mage?" he asked.

"I never thanked you for passing up the trip to Trader's Pass with Jania."

"No, you didn't."

"I should not have asked you to do that. I apologize."

"You don't have to." Rohen looked back at Galen, recalling the dream she had told him two summers ago. The three of them had been standing with Jamu. Except for Jamu, they each held a stone. He knew Galen shared his destiny. But he was not so sure about Ben.

"How can I ever repay you for everything you have done?"

"What?" He looked back at Ben. "What the hell are you talking about?"

"We are all here because of you. We are all friends because of you."

"Because of me?"

"Jamu told me about your first day at Espies. He would have run away if it were not for you."

"He only thinks that."

"I almost ran, too. When Mage Terri dragged me to the owl banner, I panicked. Then you spoke up, you invited me to meet with you later on, and everything seemed all right."

"You are making things bigger than they are, Ben."

"No, I'm not. You have brought us all together. Think about it. Jamu, Megan, Jania, even Hedi and Jai, in a way. And then there's Galen." Ben looked at his sister.

Ben was right. Rohen's heart began to pound as he realized. They were all friends because of him. And they were probably all in danger because of him. Galen certainly was.

"Ro, are you all right?"

Humo was a dragon, and an evil one. There were seven others like him. There were also eight good dragons.

"Ro?"

Eight humans were supposed to help the good dragons save the world from the evil dragons. But the evil dragons could convince the humans to help them, instead. "I'm fine, Ben. I'm just thinking about what you said."

"Did I say something to upset you?"

"I just realized something." Galen might be able to defend herself if need be, but what about the others? What kind of danger was he getting them into by being friends with them? What about

Megan and Bilin? He looked at Ben. In Galen's dream, he had a black stone.

"You don't look well, scout."

"I don't feel well." It was not a lie. "I'm going to go rest for a while. Would you like me to take Galen back to her cabin?"

"No, I think I'll have her sleep here with me tonight."

"All right." Rohen took one last look at Galen and left. He went over to his room and climbed into his own bed.

His friends might very well be in danger, and it was all his fault. Galen had already caught the attention of the Headmaster. He had all but threatened the people she loved. And Sanguis had done the same to him. How long before she actually started harming his friends, his family?

He pulled his hand away from his face and saw it was wet. He had not realized he was crying. He scrubbed his eyes. It was stupid to cry. All he had to do was make sure nothing happened to any of his friends. If he could fight a dragon, he could certainly keep his friends out of danger.

Jania pushed her books away and dropped her head down on her desk. The spells were so much harder to study this year. Studies were taking up much more of her time, and keeping her mind focused on her classwork was hard, especially when she would start thinking about her trip last summer. She hoped things would improve. She was already planning for a trip back to Trader's Pass next summer.

Someone knocked on her door. "Who is it?" she called out.

"Headmaster Humo. May I speak with you, Princess?"

Jania stared at the door incredulously. The Headmaster had never visited her before. This was a surprise. She went to the door and opened it.

It was strange to see the Headmaster standing at her door carrying a tray with a pitcher and some cups. "Oh, good," he said. "I was afraid I might be calling a little too late."

"No, this is fine, Master Humo." She opened the door and waved him inside. "I have discovered that fifth year mage students do not sleep much."

Humo chuckled as he set the tray down on her desk. "You will be rewarded tenfold," he replied. "But right now, I think you deserve to take a little break and have a drink with me."

The fruit juice was refreshingly cool. She drank an entire cup without stopping. "Please excuse my manners," she said as she poured herself some more. "I had no idea how thirsty I was."

"Don't worry about me," Humo replied. "As you sate yourself, allow me to tell you why I'm here. I want to tell you how proud I am of how you handled the attack on your traveling party and the events afterward. I cannot wait to see what you will bring about once you are Queen."

Jania finished her second cup. "I thought you were against the monarchy, Master."

"You can call me Humo here, and yes, I am against a monarchic government for Syntrea. But seeing who is next in line for the throne, I am beginning to have second thoughts."

Jania set her cup down and stared at Humo. She had learned a long time ago that sometimes the best way to handle things was to just keep quiet and wait. Silence made people uncomfortable.

It seemed to work this time as well. Humo gave her a smile and a little nod. "All right, I will be upfront with you. As an Arcanum mage, you will be the most powerful person to ever sit on the throne of any country in our known history. You will have weapons and resources no other ruler has had. And your friendship with the Surian boy is a gem for you. Sur is a spectacular military power."

Jamu again. If she wasn't careful she just might wake up married to him one morning.

"You also have an inner strength that your father lacks. You know what I'm talking about. I know you have not approved of many of the things he has done lately, and I am willing to wager that you find certain aspects of his character, how should I say this?" He scratched at his thin beard. "Shaky, perhaps?"

"I don't find anything lacking in my father, and I will support any and all decisions he makes," Jania said, calmly but firmly. Her opinion of her father was none of his business.

"Loyalty. The best character a leader can possibly have," Humo said. "I would never rise against the King, despite what the Senate will have you both think. I cannot change my stance against the monarchy, either; it will make me look indecisive and hurt my reputation. But I want you to know this; I want you on that throne. You are the best thing that has happened, and probably will ever happen, to Syntrea. If you ever need advice on anything, or even just some emotional support, please know that you can always come to me."

Jania stared at him, stunned. He was offering her his support?

"I will not take up any more of your time." He stood up. "Just remember that you cannot believe everything you hear or read. Trust your heart, and you will always make the right choice. And remember, you have an ally right here." He walked out and closed the door behind him.

Jania looked at the books she had pushed aside. There was no way she was going to get any studying done after that conversation. She stood up, locked her door, and began to change into her nightclothes.

He was right about not believing everything she heard and read. But could she believe him? After the terrible declaration he had made about psychic abilities? No one had ever explained to her why her father had allowed Humo to do such a thing. Did the King have something to do with the whole conspiracy? Would he have something to gain by it?

She did have friends she trusted. She had Ben, and Rohen, and Jamu, and even her cousin Nelsen. But they had about as much worldly experience as she did. Jamu was very wise, but his country was so different. Many of his ideas and beliefs were simply incomprehensible to her.

She needed someone who could guide her. She thought of Animis and their secret lessons. Animis was too concerned about getting her psychic powers developed to even bother worrying about her becoming Queen of Syntrea. And she had no idea where he was. She had not seen him since he left her at Trader's Pass.

She climbed into bed. Animis often told her not to condemn a person based on a few actions. Humo was a good Headmaster. The Academy took good care of its dwindling students, and its reputation was known worldwide. Maybe it would be a good thing to listen to Humo's advice. At the very least, he could show her things from a different point of view.

Megan ran toward Somatica's infirmary. Her father was back already! Traveling by horseback sure did make a difference.

She stopped halfway down one of the long straight halls as she saw her father turn the corner. Megan ran over to him and hugged him tightly.

"Daddy, it's so good to see you. Are you all right? You look terrible!" Megan brushed melting snowflakes off his hair. He looked tired, and so much older. "Did something happen to you, Daddy?"

"I'm fine, I've just been traveling hard. How are you?"

"Fine, Daddy. Why are you back so soon?"

"I will tell you everything that happened, once we are back home with Rohen and Galen. But first of all, I want you to promise me something."

"Sure, Daddy, anything."

"Promise me you will never go back to the commune, for anything. Even if they tell you your mother is dead. Promise me, Meggie."

"I won't go, I promise." That wouldn't be a difficult promise to keep.

Bilin took her and held her tightly against his cold chest. If Megan didn't know better, she would have sworn her father was crying.

The scent of the human she had been ordered to follow finally reappeared, flowing strongly into her nostrils. She looked up. A human dwelling loomed large before her. This is where the human lived. She had succeeded!

The sound of young humans approaching sent her scurrying for cover. She found a good spot beside a tree, under a protruding root. She peeked out in time to see two young females run into the clearing in front of the dwelling, flinging snow at each other.

"See if you can avoid this, Meggie," the smaller female shouted, scooping up an armful of snow and hurling it into the air. The snow melted into a thick strand of flowing water. The water wrapped itself around the second female and froze in place, trapping her arms against her body.

"Bah!" the second female scoffed. She clenched her fists, and the ice binding her arms turned into a billowing cloud of steam. The first child squealed as the bigger girl emerged from the cloud. The children chased each other around the clearing and finally into the dwelling.

Finally feeling safe, she relaxed and sent her message. Master. I am here. I have found them.

Her master responded almost immediately. Well done, my pet. Now rest.

How long shall I rest?

Until the spring is well in hand and the weather just begins to turn hot. Remember, sicken the red-haired child before anyone else. She will pass it on to her family, but make sure it spreads to the city and the schools. And make sure the girl becomes so ill that only her mother will be able to save her.

Understood, Master.

Good. Sleep now.

Proud of herself, she trudged off a little distance away from the dwelling. Although she was tired and wet, she had just enough energy to dig a nice deep hole. She climbed in and pulled the snow and dirt down over herself. Her scant black fur was wet and grimy, but it warmed her up nicely. She closed her eyes. The weather would warm up soon enough.

6

Springtime

The dried-up soil in Jesi's newly assigned flowerbed was hard and dense. The lack of use in the past year had clumped up the soil and rendered it practically worthless for gardening. Jesi considered replacing it altogether, but that would take much more work than just adding nutrients and some moss to it. Still, it was clear that her hand-held cultivator was losing its battle against the dried-out bed. She hacked around for a while before finally standing up in defeat.

"I am not wasting all day with this," she muttered to herself as she brushed off her loose cotton pants. It was too beautiful a day to spend sweating over dirt. She looked around the small yard nestled between the new greenhouse and the eastern walkway. Not a single person was in sight. She took a deep breath. It was risky, but she was alone, and no one would question how she turned the bed so quickly. Exhaling slowly, she kept her gaze fixed on the flowerbed. The bright morning sun and late afternoon shade would make it perfect for the sweet woodruff and delicate shiso plants she planned to grow. The soil shifted as she watched. Soon the dry, packed earth turned darker and damper as Jesi blended the topsoil with the loose moist dirt underneath. The bed still needed fertilizing, but the hardest part was over. Jesi smiled and tugged happily at her long blond hair, tied in a tail draped over her shoulder.

"Tisk. That was not spiritual magic you used there, child."

Jesi gasped and whirled around. A slender woman with limp brown hair spilling down her back stood directly behind her. She gave Jesi a smug smile.

"Who are you and where did you come from?" Jesi asked, hoping the woman could not see how frightened she was. If anyone at the Academy found out she was psychic, they would send her off to the Sanatorium in Sevi that same day.

"Now this is quite interesting," the woman continued as if Jesi had not said a word. "You are a Healer student. You can wield spiritual magic. But you used your…"

"Stop!" Jesi cried out. "There is no need for you to make a speech about what you…saw." The woman's eyes were an eerie shade of blue. Jesi frantically tried to think of a way to get herself out of this predicament.

"Oh, do not be afraid, my dear," the strange woman said soothingly. She reached out to stroke Jesi's head. "I do not wish to report your psychic powers. I never tell on my friends."

Jesi stepped away from the woman's reach, but she got her message. "What do you want?" She did her best to sound bold.

"How about we introduce ourselves? We cannot be friends if we do not know each other's names."

"You can call me Jesi." Her fear waned. Despite her weird eyes, the mysterious lady did not appear to be dangerous. And if she was willing to keep her secret, then she was not looking to harm her.

"And you can call me Seanna," the woman replied. Her smile was a bit nicer this time.

"Why do you want me to be your friend, Seanna?"

The woman glanced around, looking a bit nervous herself. Jesi found that odd.

"As you probably know, I am not from around here," Seanna

said, once she felt comfortable enough to speak. "I am not an Academy instructor, but I am a teacher."

Jesi was skeptical. Seanna did not sound very convincing. "A teacher? What do you teach?"

The blue-eyed woman stepped close to Jesi and glanced around again. "I teach a subject that is being unjustly targeted. There is nothing wrong with people with mental powers," she whispered.

Jesi stepped away once more. This was becoming a very dangerous conversation.

"You know I speak the truth. I can feel how powerful you are. You have been honing your psychic powers. And you can use spiritual magic as well! You have no idea how happy I am to have met you." Seanna clapped her hands together gleefully.

Jesi could only gape at the woman before her. How could a complete stranger learn about her deepest darkest secret in a span of just a few moments? She gasped again as a thought came to mind. It was a thought, but not her thought.

I can train you. I can teach you things you cannot even imagine.

Jesi did not feel comfortable with this at all. "What do you want?" she asked again.

"There is a boy here who is a powerful psychic," Seanna said. "He is so strong that it is only a matter of time before he is discovered, and he will be sent off. I cannot allow that to happen to him. And now that I have met you, I cannot, no, I will not, allow that to happen to you either. Being an Academy student is a wonderful privilege, but if you are sent away your time here would amount to nothing."

She was right; Jesi could not dispute that. "Who is this boy?"

"He is an Espies student, around your age. A Northerner."

Jesi gasped yet again. "Rohen?"

Seanna seemed almost excited as she nodded. "Yes, him. So you know him."

"I...yes." Jesi tried to keep her reaction hidden. Megan's gorgeous brother took up most of her waking thoughts, and her sleeping ones, too. Rohen was quite desirable, even the Princess-Heir of Syntrea seemed to fancy him, but that did not discourage her at all. Her shameless crush had put a great strain on her friendship with Megan, but that was a small price to pay. And he was finally beginning to respond to her pursuits. She thought about the kiss he gave her last autumn during the Last Night festivities. "Yes, I do."

Seanna studied her for a moment. She had to be aware of Jesi's crush, but Jesi did not really care.

"Rohen is in denial of his ability," Seanna said after a moment. "I tried approaching him before, and it did not turn out very well. But I cannot blame the poor child. If his secret came out, his life would be ruined. There is no reason for him to trust me. But if you were to become a close friend, he would trust you. He needs a friend who is wise and courageous enough to help him make the choices he should make, and it is obvious that you are the one destined to help him."

Destined to be part of Rohen's life. It made perfect sense to her. She smiled at Seanna.

"I need you to get as close to him as you can," Seanna said, looking nervous once more. "You are very beautiful. I can see you as his girlfriend."

"I can see that, too," Jesi said.

"I love the way you think, Jesi. When I am ready, I will let you know when I shall return. Have Rohen ready for me, and I will take you both and train you the way you should be trained. Now I must go." Seanna held her arms up, gave Jesi one last smile, and vanished into thin air.

Jesi glanced back down at her herb bed. She did not feel like playing in the dirt anymore, but the sooner she finished, the sooner she could go looking for her destiny. She went to go fetch the fertilizer, daydreaming as she walked.

❖ ❖ ❖

Galen sighed and adjusted her backpack. The warm-weather boots she had picked up from the cobbler's shop were becoming heavier with each step she took. She was tired of lugging her boots all over Syntrea's market section, and tired of having to follow Ben, Rohen, and Jamu around.

It might not have been so bad if Megan were with them; the five of them made this trip every spring and fall. This time, however, Megan had to do penance for flattening the greenhouse at Somatica. It was a good thing that most of the plants had survived. However, because Megan never thought before she acted, Galen had to endure a tortuous afternoon on her own. Grumbling, she stopped to readjust her backpack once more.

"Hello, little girl," a whispery voice said.

Galen turned to look. An old beggar sat by a corner leading into a narrow alley. He smiled and offered her his hand.

"I have some candy," he said, scratching his sooty beard. "Would you like some?"

Galen stared. His eyes were a deep bright blue, bluer than Jamu's. Where had she seen eyes like that before?

"Come," the man beckoned with his other hand, then quickly dropped his gaze.

"Galen!" Jamu grabbed her hand and pulled her along. He frowned at the old beggar as they walked away.

"What did he say to you?" he asked her.

"He offered me some candy," Galen replied, glancing back. The man was gone. "He looked familiar."

"You should not take candy from strangers."

"I know that! But why would a beggar offer me candy?"

"You do not want to know the answer to that." Jamu released her hand once they caught up with Ben and Rohen. The two boys stood before the dressmaker's shop, staring at the dresses displayed in the front window. Galen sighed. Ever since Jesi had dared Rohen to kiss her back during Last Night celebrations, the only thing he seemed to think about was girls. Ben and Jamu weren't much better, although Ben seemed to like the Princess very much. It was the fourth time they had stopped by the shop. She knew exactly what they were going to say, too.

"I can't believe the girls are going to wear those skimpy little dresses this spring," Rohen said.

"I can't believe we're going to be able to see them in those," Ben added.

Galen let her pack slide to the ground. "I can't believe you can't think of anything different to say whenever we walk by here," she said. She ignored the dark looks they gave her and glanced at the display. Airy knee-length dresses with thin shoulder straps for sleeves adorned the wooden molds set before the window. She had to admit, the dresses were very pretty.

Two girls approached the shop. "Oh, hello, Ben," one of the girls said. "Looking for something different to wear this spring?"

Ben's face turned red as the girls laughed.

"Actually, we are," Rohen said, grinning. "But dresses are so complicated. Can you help us out? Maybe help us try on a few?"

The girls laughed even harder as they went inside the shop. The second girl gave Rohen a strange look as she walked in.

"Who are they?" Jamu asked Ben.

"Sixth-year mages. They sometimes help us prepare practice spells." Ben frowned at Rohen. "Ro, get that look off your face and let's go."

"We're going back now?" Galen asked hopefully.

Rohen looked at her. "Not yet," he told her, smiling. "We need to do one more thing."

She should complain. Megan would have thrown a fit long before this. "And what is that? Chase after those girls?"

He smiled and took her hand. "Why, buy you a dress, of course."

"What? Like those?" She glanced at the window.

"That's right. It's my gift to you." He pulled her toward the door.

"Ro, this is insane. The dressmaker is going to throw us out."
Ben blocked his way.

"Not if we insist on keeping an eye on Galen. Come on, Firefly." Pushing Ben aside, Rohen opened the door.

Jamu picked up Galen's bag, grinning. "We should at least ask
Gayly if she minds us using her to get in there."

"I don't mind," Galen said quickly. It was better than waiting
outside. And she would get a dress! "But Megan is going to get
jealous."

"Well, she shouldn't have gotten herself into trouble then,"
Rohen said. "Let's go."

Sanguis seethed as she watched Galen and Rohen enter the
shop. What the hell had possessed her to disguise herself as a
man? No young girl would follow an ugly old man blindly into an
alley, unless she was extremely stupid. And Galen was far from
stupid.

She retreated into the alley. Since she had ruined her chance to
take care of Galen, she was going to have to change her strategy
and whisk Rohen away. Rohen and Galen were too dangerous to
remain together. And since she could not persuade Rohen to go
with her willingly, she was going to have to force him. It would be
foolish now to wait for that simpering Healer student to make a
move. Humo was away, preoccupied with something else. It was
the perfect opportunity. She had to do something now.

She changed back to her female human form and walked toward the dressmaker's shop. Hopefully Rohen's shock at seeing
her again would give her the time she needed to make her move.

"Let me see if I have this clear," the sour-faced dressmaker
said. "You are her Academy sponsor, and are paying for the dress.

You are her troop leader, and are responsible for what happens to her off Academy grounds. And you are her brother." She looked sharply at each of the boys as she addressed them.

"We are not letting her out of our sight. We all stay, or we can find another dressmaker," Rohen said. He held on to Galen's hand.

The dressmaker turned her scowl on Galen. "How do I even know she is really a girl?"

Galen bit her lip. She didn't think that was a very nice thing for the dressmaker to say.

"She is a girl, no doubt," the sixth-year mage who had talked to Ben said. "Everyone knows about Galen. Her troop leader made her cut her hair." She looked at Jamu. "That would be you, wouldn't it?" She sounded disapproving.

"I had my reasons." Jamu stared back at her. The girl's stern look melted away, and she smiled at him.

The dressmaker pulled her away from Rohen. "Well, then, let us begin. Perie, measure her, and I will take her back when the other girl comes out." She handed Galen over to a pretty blond girl and disappeared behind a door in the rear of the shop. The girl took Galen's hand and led her to a raised platform flanked by two long mirrors. She pulled out some long strips of cloth and a ribbon marked with ink lines and numbers.

"Please, let me help you with that," Rohen said, taking one strip from her. She looked at him, surprised, then smiled. He smiled back.

As they wrapped the strips around her to measure, Galen watched Jamu and Rohen carry on with the two girls. She wanted to laugh at the uncomfortable look on Ben's face.

"Well, Galen," the mage said to her. "You are a lucky girl, to have these three nice young men looking after you."

If she only knew. "Not really," Galen replied. She scratched a sudden itch on her neck.

Jamu smiled. "A girl cannot have too many escorts," he said.

"But I am sure you ladies have your pick of volunteers."

"Pickings are actually quite slim," Perie replied. She smiled at Rohen. "Sadly, I have no one to walk me home tonight."

"That is a shame," Rohen said. Galen noticed him rub the corner of his eye. "You shouldn't ever have to walk alone."

The conversation faded into a drone as Galen tried to look outside the dirty window. She scratched her neck again. Something was wrong. She could feel it.

Sanguis could not help smiling as she approached the shop. She would kill them all quickly, then grab the boy and leave. A small but smoky fire would make it seem like an accident. It was the perfect chance. She had to take advantage...

A man's shoulder slammed into her own, sending her spinning. Something caught on her ankle, and she went sprawling to the ground.

Galen could barely keep herself from clawing at her neck. Her scar was really starting to bother her. She looked at Rohen's scar as he helped Perie to her feet. She wondered if it was bothering him, too.

She felt uneasy. She was about to tell Rohen about the itch on her neck when the back room door opened and the mage who had given Rohen the funny look walked into the room.

"What are you doing in here?" she asked Rohen.

"We're getting Galen a dress," he replied with that annoying smile of his.

"He's being a great help, too," Perie said, putting her hand on Rohen's arm.

The mage noticed Perie's hand. Her face darkened.

Galen looked from Rohen to Perie to the mage, her itch forgotten. This was going to get interesting.

"Oh, dear, my Lady has fallen. Allow me to help you up."

Sanguis snarled and her hand shot up to crush the man's throat. It froze halfway as she noticed a pair of blue eyes, identical to her own, staring down at her.

"Don't touch me! Get off! Thief!" Sanguis shouted as she tried to break away from the man's grip.

Animis smiled at her. People stopped, looked, and hurriedly went about their business. No one wanted to become involved with a Royal official.

"No, my Lady, I'm no thief. Dearest Heaven, I sure have upset you, haven't I? Come, I shall give you a ride to your home, my Lady." Animis pulled her toward a nearby carriage. Sanguis felt talons dig into her skin-covered arm. She had no choice but to follow him.

Galen jumped as she heard a woman cry out for help outside. She ran to the door and stepped outside before she realized what she was doing.

A Royal official was leading a woman away. He must have assisted her; yet watching them walk away together made Galen feel more uncomfortable than ever. She ran her thumb absently along the scar on her neck.

"Looks like everything turned out all right," Rohen said from behind her. "She really gave me a start."

"Rowy, I feel something," Galen whispered to him.

His eyes glinted, and he gave a tiny nod. "As I said, everything turned out all right." His voice dropped to a whisper. "Rub your left eye if it gets worse."

Galen closed the door, and Rohen took her by the arm. "Let's finish your measuring." He looked over at the two girls glaring at each other. "Quickly."

"Well, well. Now what am I going to do with you?" Animis asked as he seated himself opposite Sanguis inside the carriage. He closed the door, and the carriage began to move.

Sanguis did not answer him. She gave him a cool stare and waited. She would react depending on what he chose to do.

When Animis realized she was going to stay quiet, he continued. "You have broken the Pact we made to not attack each other directly. You are open to attack from any of us, and your own allies do not trust you. You are, I suppose, a renegade Debellos."

Sanguis pushed away the fear she felt and held her gaze steady on the human face before her.

"I can kill you right here, right now, with no consequences." Animis leaned forward. "But that can be avoided."

"What do you want?" Sanguis asked.

"I want you to find a human for me. His name is Adfligere."

Animis must be desperate. She snorted. "No human would have a name like that. You are just looking for an excuse to spare my life, aren't you?"

Animis had always been a calm and patient dragon. That was why it was so surprising to Sanguis when he grabbed her by the throat and squeezed her windpipe shut.

"You will find this human for me, or I will hunt you down and slay you myself. Is that understood?" He released her and sat back in his seat.

Sanguis gave him an evil look before phasing away.

"I can't believe they started fighting like that," Galen exclaimed. "Did you see how angry the dressmaker was?"

"She almost threw us all out," Jamu said. "That was some smooth talking, Ro, to get her to calm down and not fire Perie."

"I'm just glad she didn't stick one of those needles of hers through my heart," Rohen said.

"I'm surprised she didn't," Ben said, shaking his head. "I wish we could take a trip over here once, just once, and not get into some kind of trouble."

"What do you mean?" Rohen asked. "We didn't get in any trouble. We rarely get in trouble. Well, maybe once or twice."

"Per week," Jamu added.

Galen laughed. The itch on her neck was completely gone. She felt much better.

"Why don't we get something to eat? It's early, so the taverns shouldn't be crowded. There's one over there," Rohen said, pointing.

"Sounds good," Ben said. "Let's go."

The tavern's great room was cozy, with two fireplaces providing light and warmth. A kind old lady waved them over to a set of benches by the street window where the four of them could sit with a table between them. Galen sat back and closed her eyes. It felt good to be off her feet, with her bag off her shoulders.

"Stay away from the mages, please," Ben begged Rohen. "They can do some nasty things to you if you make them angry. Aren't the Healer girls enough for you?"

"Why do you think that I am interested in every girl I talk to?" Rohen asked. "I don't want a girlfriend, and I can only kiss one girl at a time."

"That is not exactly true," Jamu said, grinning.

"Do not give the Northerner any ideas, Jamu," Ben said. He turned to Galen. "This is why you should stay away from boys."

"I can't," Galen said. "I'm the only girl at Espies."

"Well, just think about these guys when some boy comes around wanting to kiss you," Ben replied.

"Sounds like girl troubles," the woman who had greeted them

said. "Here, have some of these." She set two bowls of strange brown strips on the table. "We have stew that is almost ready. Would you all care for some?"

They all nodded. Galen reached for one of the strips as the woman walked off. "What are those?"

"Fried noodles. They are good. Try some," Jamu answered.

She took a bite of the noodle she held. It was very tasty. "This is good." She popped the rest of the noodle into her mouth.

"Jania said that you contacted the Casters about taking their Trial test. When is it?" Rohen asked Ben.

Ben frowned. Galen wondered why Jania's friendship with Rohen and Jamu still bothered him. She remembered how upset he had been when Rohen told him that Jania had asked him to escort her to the palace whenever she went to spend the weekends there. That was only a few weeks after Ben had apologized to Rohen for asking him not to go to Trader's Pass with her.

"Next month," he replied. "I just turned fifteen, so I am finally eligible."

"So how does it feel to be an adult?" Jamu asked.

"It doesn't feel like anything," Ben replied. "I feel the same way I felt last fall."

Galen scooped up a handful of noodles and crammed them into her mouth. She loved the way they crunched.

"I can't wait until I'm fifteen," Rohen said.

"I can," Jamu replied. "My father wants me to consider a courtship once I turn fifteen. He says that as a Surian highblood, it is necessary for me to consider potential Syntrean ties."

"Who did he have in mind?" Ben asked.

Jamu stared at Ben. He did not reply.

"You cannot be serious," Ben exclaimed.

"It would be a political alliance, not a romantic endeavor," Jamu said.

"Would you have to marry her?" Ben asked.

Jamu shook his head. "No. But during these times, with the

East threatening the mainland, it will give both countries a good excuse to help each other out. And it is only a consideration. I have to talk to Jania about it."

"King Raimo has probably suggested it to her as well," Rohen said.

"Probably. But I do not have to worry about that until I am fifteen," Jamu said.

"How wonderful," Ben muttered, shaking his head. He reached for some noodles. "Galen, you ate them all!"

Galen gulped down her last mouthful. "Sorry," she said.

The wind gusted through the back courtyard of Arcanum, whipping Jai's short bobbed hair about. Her classmates waited anxiously for her to cast her spell.

Jai lifted her hands up in a stopping motion and carefully sang out an intricate incantation. Her tongue stumbled slightly over one verse, and she saw Ben flinch from the corner of her eye. Undaunted, she finished the spell and lowered her hands, waiting. Except for the wind, everything was still and quiet.

"I don't think it worked, Jai," Ben finally said. "The spell should be revised. It is too old."

"It worked, Ben. I felt the energy. The spell flashed right through my head. I should have been able to stop the wind," Jai replied. "And how can a spell be too old?"

"Repeated copying over time can alter the spell. And I heard that little stumble while you were chanting. You probably messed it up." Nelsen shook his head in disappointment.

"Don't be silly!" Jai frowned at him. "It takes a lot more than that to corrupt a spell." The wind died down. "See? It worked," Jai said.

"I'm not so sure about that," Hedi replied, pointing to the far side of the courtyard. "Look over there."

A dark funnel rose from the ground. The six mages watched

warily as it thickened and darkened.

"What in the world is that?" Nelsen gasped.

"It looks like a swarm of bugs," Ben replied. Hedi and Jania groaned.

"What kind of bugs are they?" Seth asked, squinting at the swarm.

Jai scrutinized the funnel. "They look like..."

Before she could finish her sentence, the bugs streaked into the air and flew away from the tower, out of sight.

Galen stared at the painted target as she strung up her bow. Rus, Cyen, and Laren, her three troopmates, stood beside her. Keran, her old troopmate who was now part of Rohen's group, stood with his troopmate Sprit a few paces away.

"Three shots in the inner circle, and we win," Rus said. "You have five arrows left, Galen. This match is won."

"It's not a real match, only practice," Sprit spat out. Keran glowered at Galen.

She ignored her two opponents. Keran was very good, but Sprit was more of a handicap than anything else. Of course, Keran would find a way to blame their loss on her instead of his partner. She just had to make sure this was decidedly won and get all five of her arrows well within the circle. It would not be hard. "Give me the arrows."

Laren handed her five arrows. She tucked four of them under the strap behind her back and notched the remaining arrow. The wind was quite strong, but she knew how to compensate for that. She pushed all thoughts out of her head and aimed.

One arrow after another thudded close to the center of the target. All five of them were well within the circle.

"All right, Galen!" Rus jumped up and down. Laren grinned and clapped his hands.

Galen looked at Keran, waiting for one of his nasty remarks.

He was not looking at her, though. His face had a puzzled look on it. Galen heard a strange sound.

She turned to see what Keran was looking at, and saw a dark cloud rushing toward them. "What is that?" she asked.

No one answered her. They were too busy covering their faces from the onslaught of tiny flying bugs.

Jamu watched as Autis moved little wooden pegs around a map set on the display table. Something did not seem right with the scout head's strategy for encircling an enemy encampment.

"Remember, it is not what it is on the map that is important, it is what the enemy believes is around them that is important," Autis said, as if he could hear Jamu's thoughts.

"What if they call the bluff?" Rohen asked. "The gaps between scouts are too wide to be safe."

"It is all about deception," Autis answered. "The gaps would be unexpected, right? How would the leader of the surrounded group react to signs of an army closing in on them? How many choices would he have?"

Jamu shook his head. It was a nasty game of double guessing. "There is still something not right about the deployment," he said.

"Well, can you think of what it is?" Autis frowned grumpily at him, but that did not mean the Scout Chief was offended by Jamu's question. Jamu looked back at the map.

The door to the room opened. Carl, one of the third year cadets, peeked inside.

"Chief? May I interrupt?"

Autis sighed heavily. "What is it, boy?"

Carl stepped inside and stared at the floor. "Something happened to some of the second year cadet troops. Jamu's entire troop, and some of Rohen's, some bugs got all over them, and they are all a mess."

"What?" The entire class asked in unison.

"It's true. They are at the archery range." Carl looked up at Autis. "They have ticks and other stuff all over them."

Jamu stood up. "I will go and check," he said.

"I'll go with you," Rohen offered.

"No need, Ro. How bad can a few bugs be? With your permission, instructor?"

"Go check on your troops, Jamu," Autis said.

Jamu followed Carl to the archery range. What he saw there made his jaw drop.

Rus, Laren, Galen, and Cyen were gathered at one corner of the range with Keran and Sprit, picking ticks off each other. They had paired off, Rus and Cyen, Galen and Laren, and Keran and Sprit. Other scouts stood watching, keeping well away from the infested group.

"Dear Heaven," he exclaimed as he reached the seven cadets. "How did this happen?" He grabbed hold of Galen's head and examined her scalp. Lice crawled all over her hair.

"Jamu, you should stay away from us," Galen said, squishing a tick she had just pulled off Laren's ear. "You might catch lice."

Ticks ringed Cyen's neck and bordered his ears. "That does not answer my question." Jamu still could not quite believe what he saw.

"We were having a match with Keran and Sprit, and this cloud of bugs just flew right over us. It hit the side of the cabin over there, and the bug cloud just disappeared. But the ones that got on us stayed," Rus said.

"Are we in trouble?" Galen asked timidly.

"No. Do not worry, I will get you all cleaned up." He patted Galen's back comfortingly and smiled, but he fumed inside. Those idiot mages. You would think they would at least come out and see what kind of damage they caused. "Galen, Laren, you two come with me."

He noticed them all stiffen and lower their heads. They knew he was angry. He did not care, though. Grabbing Galen and Laren by their hands, he marched off toward Arcanum.

Ben went over the spell once more. "You may have changed a key word when you stuttered there, Jai," he told her, adjusting the lenses on his face. "There are a lot of nuances in many of these verses."

"I didn't stutter, and I did not change any of the words," Jai said. She leaned over Ben's shoulder to look as the others crowded around. "Maybe it was the way I moved my arms, or the way I was facing."

"I don't know, Jai," Jania said, running her finger over one of the lines in the book. "Ancient spelling can be rather tricky when it comes to proper pronunciation."

Jai mouthed the words silently. "No, it had to be something else," she insisted.

Ben noticed someone turn the corner of the tower. He looked up, and so did everyone else.

"I knew you mages had something to do with it!" Jamu stormed over to them, dragging Galen and Laren along. Ben stared, stunned. He had never seen Jamu so upset. His friend stood right before them, holding on tightly to the hands of his two troops. Ben noticed small things crawling on Galen.

"Who is responsible for this?" Jamu pushed Galen and Laren forward. Ben gasped as he realized the things crawling on Galen were ticks. He felt Jai release his shoulders as she stood.

"I am," she said.

Jamu fixed his deep blue eyes on her. Ben heard Jai gulp behind him.

"My entire troop, and half of Rohen's, were attacked by your little conjuration. They are covered in ticks and lice now. Look!" He pushed Laren and Galen forward again.

"Gayly, are you all right?" Ben stood up, but Hedi and Jania kept him from going over to check on her.

"I'm all right, I guess," she replied, scratching the back of her neck. "You should stay away."

"She is not all right!" Jamu did not take his eyes off Jai. "She is infested with parasites. And so are five other scouts. The number will probably grow, too, if something is not done."

"I am sorry! I miscast a spell. I did not mean to do this. I apologize," Jai said, but Jamu's expression did not change. Jai threw her hands up. "What do you want me to say, Jamu?"

"Being sorry does not take care of the problem," Jamu replied. "I want you to fix this mess you caused."

"Fine," Jai snapped. "I will go and see if the Healers have a solution for this. Where do you want me to meet you?"

"You need a Healer's help for this? Why are you casting spells you cannot control?" Jamu asked.

His tone annoyed Ben. "Accidents happen, Jamu. There is no need to be rude."

"Let him be as rude as he wants, Ben," Jai said coldly. "Tell me where you want me to meet you."

"At the archery range," Jamu replied. He turned and waved for Galen and Laren to follow. The three scouts left.

"What the hell is wrong with your friend?" Jai asked Ben.

Ben shrugged. "Those were his troops who got infested. He has a right to be angry."

"It's actually sweet of him to concern himself so. Did you see how he was not afraid to be near them? He doesn't care whether he catches lice or not," Jania said. Ben heard the admiration in her voice.

Jania's words seemed to deflate Jai. "I suppose. Let me go see if Somatica has anything for conjured bugs," she said, walking away.

"I'll go with you, Jai," Ben stood up and followed her.

"Thank you Ben, but you don't have to come with me," Jai said.

"My sister has a nest of bugs in her hair. I have to go and help her," Ben replied. He pulled his lenses off and slipped them into his pocket. If Jania had any more compliments for Jamu, he did not want to be around to hear it.

"I guess I can't blame Jamu for getting so upset at me," Jai said.

"Don't let him get to you. As soon as this is all fixed, he will probably even forget it was you who caused it. He's more upset at the situation than anything else."

Jai nodded. "I hope so. I don't think I would like him to stay angry with me."

"Wait for Ro outside and tell him and Chief Autis what happened," Jamu called out to Carl. The boy nodded and ran off. Jamu crushed a tick crawling up his arm. "Do not worry," he assured his half-naked cadets as he pulled off his own shirt. "Some pesticide and a good shower will fix you all up, and probably me, too." He scratched behind his ear.

Galen squirmed and scratched. After endless picking, most of the ticks were off the boys, but there was no way Galen was going to take her shirt off out here.

"What has happened here?"

Galen stiffened and spun around. She knew that voice. She did not think she would ever keep from cringing whenever she heard it.

Humo's face stared down at her, his black eyes boring into hers. "Looks like you crawled under the wrong bush, girl," he said, a slow cold smile creeping onto his face.

Galen shook her head at him and stepped back behind Jamu. Humo's gaze turned from her to her troop leader. "Well?" he asked Jamu.

"Master, the mages miscast a spell, and a few cadets were infested with ticks and lice," Jamu explained.

"Oh, the mages miscast a spell. And how would a scout know

about a miscast spell?" Humo glowered down at Jamu.

Galen held on to Jamu's waist and stared up at Humo fearfully. Jamu had erred; he criticized the mages to an Arcanum graduate. What was Humo going to do?

Jamu did not back down. "I approached some of the mage students and they admitted responsibility."

Humo's black eyes narrowed.

"Master Humo, Jamu is correct." Jai ran up and placed herself between Humo and Jamu. "I tried a windstop spell." She laughed nervously. "It was the strangest thing, Master. I stumbled over one word, and the wind did stop, but then a swarm of ticks and lice appeared. We were trying to find out what happened when we discovered what happened to the scouts, so I went with Ben to Somatica..."

"Windstop is a fifth year spell," Humo interrupted sternly. "What year are you?"

"Fifth year, Master," Jai hung her head. Humo stared at her thoughtfully.

"Find out what happened, and send me a written paper explaining the miscast. Windstop is an old spell. Times change, and spells sometimes need to be modified." Without another word, he whirled around and disappeared.

Galen let go of Jamu's waist and allowed herself to breathe again.

Jai's shoulders slumped in relief, and she handed the basket over to Jamu. Galen noticed Ben approaching.

"That was dangerous, talking to Master Humo that way," Jamu said to Jai. "Are you insane?"

"The Headmaster has a soft spot for Arcanum students," Jai replied, running her hands through her shoulder-length hair.

"You did not tell him about me barging over there, either." He rummaged through the basket. "Thank you."

"If I wanted you in trouble, I would not have cut into your conversation with him." Jai pointed into the basket. "These can be used all over the body. Druid Bilin said to use it twice on each of them. This cream is for the hair. Leave it on for an hour, and then use these combs. The cream should be used for three days, in case of eggs. You should use it, as well."

Ben walked up, carrying another basket. Jai reached over and took Galen's arm. "I'll take care of Galen. Ben has her things."

Ben handed the basket to Jai. "I'm going to find Galen some clothes," he said. He blew Galen a kiss as he headed to the cabins.

"Thank you, Jai," Jamu said, smiling down at her.

Jai blushed. Her eyes traveled down to Jamu's bare chest. "You are very welcome. Come on, Galen."

Later that evening, Galen and Jai walked across the Mall, heading back to Espies. Galen's wet hair stuck to her head and face. She wore her new blue sundress. It felt strange walking around in such a loose, light dress. It was like walking around with only a towel wrapped around her, and her legs felt exposed. It didn't feel bad, though.

"Galen, I am very sorry for what happened today," Jai said. "I should have been more careful."

"That's all right," Galen replied. "Everyone makes mistakes. And if Jamu is not angry with you anymore, then I shouldn't be, either."

"You really think he's not angry?" Jai asked hopefully.

"I know he's not. You saved him from Master Humo. He's not going to forget that." Galen looked down at her dress. Ben had burned her other clothes. "I'm going to have to get new clothes."

"I will come for you tomorrow. We'll go get you some new clothes," Jai promised.

Galen grinned. "That will be great!"

The two girls skipped the rest of the way to Espies. They walked up to Galen's cabin, and she knocked quietly on the door.

Jamu opened it. "There you go! I had a feeling I was missing a scout." He ruffled Galen's wet hair as she walked in. "Please come in," he told Jai.

Galen noticed Keran and Sprit bunked down between Rus and Laren. Sprit made faces at her. "What are they doing here?" she asked.

"Moreus wants us quarantined," Jamu explained. "In the evenings, anyway, until we are sure there are no eggs. If there is an outbreak, then the cabin will be burned and rebuilt."

"That's a little extreme," Jai said.

Jamu shrugged. "I doubt it will happen. It is only a precaution."

Galen sat on her bed and began unpacking the bag she carried. "Ben burned my clothes," she said. "He only let me keep this dress."

Keran and Sprit clapped their hands. "Ben sure knows how to handle women," Keran said.

"No more of that," Jamu told the two boys. He turned to Jai. "Jai, I want to apologize for the way I acted today."

"No, you don't have to," she replied.

"Yes, I do," he insisted. "Would you mind going for a walk with me? It is a nice evening, and the trees are just beginning to flower."

The cabin became very quiet.

"No, not at all," Jai said after a moment.

Jamu smiled and opened the door. Jai waved at Galen and walked outside. "Behave yourselves," Jamu warned everyone, walking out behind her.

The cadets all looked at each other in amazement. Galen counted to ten, then jumped off her bed and ran to the window, followed by the others. She grinned as she saw Jamu and Jai walk into the woods.

"That's too bad, Galen," Keran whispered in her ear. "It seems you are not Jamu's favorite girl anymore."

Galen's grin slid off her face. Suddenly Jamu's interest in Jai did not seem all that exciting to her anymore.

7

Dragons and Monsters

Sanguis lounged against a tree, waiting for Rohen to ride by on his way to the druid's cottage. The stubborn boy would not be too pleased to see her, so she knew that he would be happy to do the exact opposite of whatever she suggested to him. A few chosen words, and he would be in that little hussy's arms in no time. She could not hold back the smile that crept onto her human face. Intellectually, those two humans were no match for her. They had no chance.

"What are you smiling about?"

The snarling voice behind her tree was unmistakable. Her smile vanished as she turned to face Animis, who stepped around the tree and grabbed her shoulder.

"Animis, I am so glad you found me." That blasted Tueri was not going to make her lose her composure again. She was ready for him.

"Then that means you have something for me," Animis replied.

"I have been—"

"Before you waste my time with some contrived story, let me say that I have seen you snooping around the Academy, and I know that Rohen is approaching. I have no interest in what it is you are trying to do, so if you wish for me to leave you alone, whatever you have for me had better be satisfactory."

Sanguis shrugged his hand off her shoulder and reached into a fold of her long narrow skirt. She pulled out a scrap of paper and handed it to Animis.

"That map shows the current locations of three hidden armies close to Trader's Pass. Two are just north of the Massean border and the third is farther south, in Syntrea."

Animis glanced at the map, then back at her. He did not look pleased.

"Is this it? This is all you have for me?"

"That is more than plenty," she shot back. "But if you wish to be greedy, I have a bonus for you. There appears to be a hibrida hibernating around here, somewhere near the cottage where Rohen lives."

"Worthless information to me!" Animis grabbed her shoulder again and shook her. "Get out of my sight! And find something that will actually help me!"

Sanguis snarled at him. She could not fight him and win. Rohen was approaching, and even if she could hold her own against the stronger dragon, she was sure the boy would be all too willing to lend Animis a hand. Disgusted with herself for flapping her jaws about the hidden mongrel she had sensed, she phased away. She could always have a talk with Rohen some other time.

Animis landed lightly in the midst of the ragtag group of filthy soldiers. They babbled on, oblivious to the towering half-dragon standing in their midst. Animis studied their garb. It was Eastern gear, but the unhealthy, unsanitary men could not possibly be from the East. Eastern soldier uniforms were made of much better quality, and were kept clean and mended, but that was something Gravesco had always maintained. Now that the mighty red dragon was dead, had the Eastern fighting forces deteriorated as much as their promising civilization? It would be the ultimate travesty if it were so, despite its detestable founder.

He spotted the largest tent and made his way there. A couple of men stood guard at the entrance, but that did not mean that there would be anyone inside. The day was too perfect for any human to stay cooped up in a stuffy tent. He walked inside, still in his smaller dragon form, still unseen by the humans around him.

He was right. Not even a servant child. The place was quite messy, but Animis was sure it would not take him long to find something useful. He switched to his human form so he could fit comfortably in the seat behind the worn wooden desk nestled in the corner opposite the unmade bed. He singled out the most ornate box stashed underneath the desk and set it up on the desktop, popping it open easily with just a thought. He peered inside expectantly, and growled in frustration at his discovery.

Scorched scraps of vellum lay scattered atop a small stack of blank vellum sheets. Animis picked up a piece, frowning as it crumbled between his fingers. This particular officer had some scrap of intelligence. Now if Animis could only find out the real name of the commander he was serving.

Aminis began to close the box, but something caught his eye. There appeared to be a torn sheet tucked under the blank ones. He grabbed a corner with his thumb and forefinger and pulled it out.

It was a map, torn lengthwise. The piece Animis held showed the mainland coast, with the main cities clearly marked and labeled. Animis held it close, noticing a few smudges marking certain places on the coast between Syntrea and Trader's Pass. Animis was convinced the smudges were placed there deliberately. He noticed a compass circle on the bottom of the sheet, and smiled in triumph. The compass design was only used by one mapmaker. And Animis knew the crotchety old human personally. He had stubbornly refused to switch office quarters with Animis, claiming his dark little cubby was the warmest place in the castle.

He stood and rewarded himself with a nice stretch. He shoved the map in his coat pocket and phased away.

Galen set her feet carefully on the branch and stood up slowly. She glanced down. Jamu watched her from the ground, studying her form as she balanced herself on the uncomfortably thin branch. A light breeze blew, but it was not strong enough to make the branch sway. Her thighs burned as she did her best to keep from pressing down too hard on the branch. Jamu's face gave her no indication as to how well she was doing. She straightened her legs and locked her knees. She waited for her troop leader's approval.

Jamu finally nodded. "The branch did not even move. No one would have noticed you. That was very good, Galen."

Galen grinned proudly. Jamu rarely gave compliments to his troops, other than saying 'good enough.' She jumped off and landed lightly next to him.

"Your legs are the key to stealth," Jamu told her. He gave his thigh a pat. "If you can balance your entire weight on one leg and shift your stance all around without falling, you do not need much else to move about quietly through any terrain."

"Really?" Galen held her left leg up. "Is that an Espies lesson you learned?"

"No. I learned that on my own."

"Oh. Well, I agree." Galen arched her back until her hands touched the ground and threw her legs up to end up in a handstand. "How about all your weight on one arm?"

"If you have to walk with your arms, then I suppose that would be so," Jamu replied with a grin.

Galen lifted one arm. "Would you like me to try standing on that branch again? Or do you want to teach me something else?"

"I do not have much more to teach you. While the rest of your troopmates are still finishing their written exams, I am stuck babysitting you because you were done with testing almost an entire day earlier. Now stand up. I do not feel comfortable talking to your feet." Jamu tugged at her boot to make her lose her balance, but Galen easily pulled her foot away from him.

"I'm sorry. I didn't know I would be in your way," Galen said as she set her feet down on the ground and righted herself.

"You are not in my way. I was joking when I said I was stuck babysitting you." Jamu glanced up as a sudden gust made the branches above them wave about. "It is quite breezy today. Get your bow and we will get some target practice out of the way. The wind should give you a bit of a challenge."

Galen bit her lip. Ever since her talk with Humo, shooting arrows made her a bit uncomfortable. But that was not the only reason why she hesitated.

Jamu frowned at her. "What is it?"

"I left my bow at home," she confessed, her eyes fixed on her boots.

"Galen! You are always supposed to have your weapons ready to use. That does not sound like you at all, to forget your bow."

Galen swallowed hard and forced herself to look up at her troop leader. "I was worried about other things, but that was thoughtless of me. I am sorry." Espies scouts did not cry. They admitted their mistakes and faced their penalties with courage. But it did not help that Jamu always seemed unusually harsh with his punishments. She looked straight into Jamu's blue eyes, waiting for the rest of her scolding.

Jamu's frown did not go away. "Your troopmates are lucky. They will end up with no cabin cleanup duties this week."

Galen nodded and let her gaze drop. She would have rather done extra training, but Jamu knew her well enough. Cabin chores were less grueling than running two leagues twice a day, but it took more time, and her penalty was also a sort of reward for the others, which meant that they would not feel compelled to help her avoid making the same mistake again, unlike other punishments where the entire group was affected. Jamu saved those for different types of infractions. He was very clever with his punishments.

"Well, since we have the rest of the afternoon free, and we have nothing better to do, I suppose we could go to the cottage and get your bow. We will still have time for a few rounds of target practice," Jamu said as he ran his hands through his hair. "I would prefer that to a haircut today."

"Oh, Jamu, thank you!"

"You still have to do chores this week."

"I understand." Galen turned to go.

"Wait! If we cut through the thick part of the woods, we will come out behind the cabins and closer to the front gates. Follow me." Jamu turned and jogged off the opposite way. Galen ran to catch up.

Jamu made his way easily through the thick growth. Scouts did not venture often through the dense part of the wood, except for advanced trials and occasional trysts by the older scouts, who would usually end up being watched by other scouts. Galen had never been in this area before, but it was still easy passage for her. Jamu moved as quietly as Rohen, but he was just a bit more careful, just a tiny bit slower. A thought came to Galen's mind.

"Try to catch me," she called out to Jamu as she ran ahead. She dodged trees and shrubs without making a sound. She slowed down enough just to hear Jamu rustling about behind her, and dashed off once more.

The clearing opened up before her without warning. Galen stopped as her feet hit hard ground. She gaped at the cobblestones beneath her feet. She stood on a paved circle, at least ten paces across. She turned to see Jamu jog into view. The surprised look on his face must have mirrored hers.

"Did you know about this?" she asked him.

"I did not." Jamu walked to the center of the circle. "And the height of the weeds growing through the cracks tells me that not many people do."

Galen looked around for other clues that would tell her a bit about this place. A few trees had pushed their way up against the edge of the patio in some places, but that was all she noticed.

"It appears to be an old sparring area," Jamu said.

"What makes you think that?"

"The pavers edging the circle." Jamu pointed. They are different in certain places. The pattern looks like our sparring circle by the archery range."

Galen walked over to Jamu to take a closer look. "I see. I would have never noticed if you had not pointed it out. You are so smart, to figure things out like you do!"

"It has to do with how you think, not how smart you are," Jamu replied. "We must move on if we want to get some shots in before supper."

"Sure." Galen followed Jamu out of the clearing. She kept quiet and close to him as they made their way out of the wood.

"Why the sudden change in mood?" Jamu asked her as they walked through the massive front gates on their way to the cottage. "You wanted me to chase you. What happened?"

"I thought I might end up in trouble again, and it seems like I have been getting in trouble a lot," Galen said. She took a deep breath. It was something she really wanted to know, and now seemed as good a time as any to ask. "Jamu, are you still glad to have me in your troop? You do not want to trade me or send me away, do you?"

"I am very surprised that you would ask me that," Jamu said. He turned his head to look at her, but did not stop walking. "You do not get punished any more than your troopmates, and you are top ranked. You are in no danger of being cast out, and you are my most skilled troop. Why do you worry?"

Galen did not know how to answer him. She kept up her pace beside him, looking straight ahead.

"I will let you know something, but just this once," Jamu said when he realized Galen was not going to say anything. "I am amazed by your progress. You learn quickly, you are brave and tough, and you never hesitate to help your troopmates when they need it. You are a troop leader's dream, and I am so very proud of you."

Galen felt her face get hot, and she couldn't help smiling. But before she could say anything, Jamu kept talking.

"I am disappointed that you cannot see this yourself," Jamu continued. "If nothing else, the scoring system should tell you plainly where you stand among your peers. Have more confidence in yourself, little Gayly, because you are quite exceptional, and I am not going to tell you this again."

It was such a relief to hear Jamu's words. Getting expelled from the Academy seemed much less of a danger now. "Thank you, Jamu. You are the best troop leader ever!" She felt so much better she decided to bring up another subject, a subject she had not dared bring up before. "And I am sure you are going to be a really nice boyfriend."

"What?" Jamu stopped walking this time. "Have you been talking to Jai?"

"No, but you sure have," she teased. It was true; Jamu's visits to Arcanum were becoming more frequent as of late, and Jai had even stopped by the cabin twice after the bug incident. Galen was sure she was visiting Jamu in his room at the Tower as well.

Jamu hesitated, a thoughtful look on his face. "If I tell you something, do you promise not to tell anyone?" he asked.

"I promise," Galen said. She did not bother to hide her excitement. "Are you going to ask her to be your girlfriend? Is that what you want to tell me?"

Jamu nodded, a big grin on his face. "You are the only one who knows. What do you think?"

"I think..." A surprising twinge of jealousy pricked her. Her smile died. She could not lie to him. "I think I am going to miss you."

"Gayly, you should not feel that way." Jamu put his arm around her shoulders and gave her a squeeze. "Nothing is going to change. I will spend just as much time with my troop and my friends. The only difference is that Jai will be around a lot more. And you will always be my star troop, and a dear friend. No matter what. Now let us go get your bow."

Galen smiled. "Of course. All right, I will run to the trees. When I get there then you can try to catch me again."

"All right. I hope you hide better than you run, though!"

Galen closed the door to the cottage behind her, bow in hand and her quiver strapped to her back. "I'm ready. Let's—" she jumped as a black blurry streak shot out of the trees behind Jamu and streaked across the front yard. "Jamu, did you see that?"

"I noticed something out of the corner of my eye," Jamu said as he glanced around. "I had a feeling there was something nearby. Where did it go?"

"Behind the well." Galen strung her bow and pulled out two arrows.

"I will flush it out. Be ready." Jamu crept over to the well. He was still a few steps away when a strange black animal jumped into view, landing on his arm and knocking him to the ground before dashing out of sight into the forest.

"Jamu!" Galen dropped her arrow and ran over to her troop leader. "Are you all right?"

"Yes." He stood back up before Galen could reach him, but he looked shaken. "What the hell was that?"

"It moved so fast I could not tell," Galen replied as she checked his arm. There was a welt on his shoulder, but the skin was not broken. Galen gulped in relief.

"It did not hurt me," Jamu said. He looked angry. He pulled out his knife. "I think we will substitute target practice with a tracking session. We need to find out what that thing is."

"As you wish," Galen said, readying her second arrow. "So do you want me to stay behind you?"

"No. You make less noise than I do. You track it, and I will stay out of sight. Go." Jamu disappeared into the trees.

Galen wasted no time. She ran off, quickly finding marks of recent passage. She had no idea what she was hunting, but the blurry thing did not look too friendly. At least it wasn't a giant lizard. She was tempted to reach out and sense for it, but it was too risky with Jamu nearby. What would he do if he ever found out about her mental powers?

She was completely unprepared for the attack. All she saw was a black splotch appear in front of her, and suddenly she was on the ground, weaponless with something fierce on her face, scratching at her head. She grabbed the thing and hurled it aside. It felt clammy and leathery in her hands.

She heard a strange hiss. She rolled onto her feet and searched for the animal that attacked her. Something strange darted about in a zigzag pattern, moving so fast Galen still could not recognize what it was. The blur leaped at her once more, but Galen was ready for it this time. She lunged forward to try and grab it in mid-jump.

She missed. The thing plowed into her, knocking her down again. The mystery creature stopped on her chest, and Galen finally got a good look.

A furless fox with an inky black hide and horribly long fangs snarled at her. It raised a clawed leg to slash at Galen, but hesitated, swinging its head to the side in alarm. Galen punched the thing off her chest and sat up.

Jamu appeared, knife ready, using the base of a tree trunk to launch himself at the black thing. He tried to go for its neck, but their quarry was too fast, and the knife sailed harmlessly through the air. The animal took off again, Jamu close behind. Galen spotted her bow and quickly retrieved it. She pulled out yet another arrow and followed. She walked slowly, making some noise to let

Jamu know where she was. She knew he would do his best to circle around and drive the thing her way.

It did not take long for her to hear movement. She held her
bow up, arrow notched and ready. She had to be quick and sure if
she hoped to make her target. She had never seen an animal move
so fast. She saw a flash of black…

Her arrow flew off before she realized. She heard a thunk, then
all was quiet. Galen waited a moment, holding her breath and
wishing she had held her shot. She had not seen Jamu. She could
have shot him. What if she had? "Jamu," she called out softly.
"Jamu?"

Her troop leader emerged from the brush, holding the foxlike
creature by the tail. He looked disgusted. Her arrow stuck out of
its nearly hairless chest, and its neck gaped open. Jamu had slit its
throat.

"Are you hurt?" he asked her.

Galen felt her scalp. "It scratched me, but I am all right," she
said.

"It appears to be a sick fox. A very sick fox," Jamu said. "It is
likely contagious. We should bury it. Right now."

Galen nodded. The thing was hideous. "I will get Uncle Bilin's
shovel," she said.

Jamu nodded. "I will wait right here. Give me your jacket to
wrap this thing in," he said.

Galen pulled her jacket off carefully and gave it to Jamu before
running off. She fetched the shovel, and Jamu wasted no time. He
quickly dug a deep hole and tossed the carcass in, along with his
spring cotton jacket. He covered the hole and tossed some leaves
and sticks over it to conceal the area. They quickly returned to the
cottage, where Jamu washed his hands. Once he was done with
his hands, he checked Galen's head and hands.

"No cuts," he said. "But I think it would be best if you wash
your hair and face now."

"Sure. I will go get some more soap." Galen opened the door

to the cottage.

"Do you think you can find some of that tincture Megan uses to clean wounds?"

Galen hesitated at the entrance. "I know where she keeps it. But you told me that you were not hurt."

"I am not hurt, but I would like to make sure this welt is clean. It is beginning to look like a scratch." Jamu examined his shoulder once more.

"Do you think we can catch whatever disease that thing had? Is that why you buried our jackets with that thing?"

"Yes, it could make us sick, that is why you need to wash up. As long as we are clean, we should be fine. We soiled our jackets trying to catch it, and covering that pest with them should keep any scavengers from digging the thing up. Now please hurry, it is getting late."

Galen rushed inside to fetch the soap and the tincture. Once her hair was clean, she took one of Rohen's old Espies jackets and handed it to Jamu.

"That was unnecessary, but thank you. Remember, you should shower as soon as we get back to Espies," Jamu said as he donned the light cotton jacket.

"I will," Galen promised as she put on the jacket she had found for herself. They headed back to the Academy, walking quickly in order to be back in time for the early supper session. The afternoon breeze was quite cold on her freshly washed head. She hoped no one would ask her why her hair was wet.

"Galen," Jamu said as they emerged from the trees and reached the meadow leading to the Academy.

"Yes?"

"Let us keep this little adventure between ourselves."

"All right. But aren't you worried about that thing? If it was a sick animal, what if there are more?"

"If there are more then we will say something. But I do not think we will see another one, and I do not care to explain what we encountered if we will not see it again."

"I understand. I really don't feel like telling anyone anyway."

Jamu grinned. "We think alike. I knew there was a reason why I like you."

Galen grinned back.

"So, Caeles, what do you make of that?"

Animis kicked aside the brush covering the freshly made grave. His white haired, white-eyed companion stooped over the site, his white robes hovering off the ground.

"That thing was too small and weak to be one of Abeo's creations," Caeles said. He held his hand over the grave, palm down. After a few moments he stood up. "I think I know who did this. But it is of no concern, really. It has been slain properly, so it will not revive, and I do not sense any others nearby. You would know if there were a swarm of them."

"Who do you think did this?" Animis asked.

"I would rather not accuse anyone without irrefutable proof," Caeles answered. "And there is really nothing to worry about. The children solved this problem quite nicely, I should say. Thank you for informing me of this."

"Caeles, wait!" Animis reached for the older man's arm, but Caeles vanished before Animis could grab hold.

"Pompous dragon!" Animis glanced back down. Caeles was right, despite his evasiveness. The thing was gone, with no involvement of any dragon. He had better things to do than hover around a grave. Animis turned and left, deciding to walk for a bit.

8

Caster Trial

Ben laced his pant legs snugly against his calves and slipped his low-cut suede boots over them. He straightened up, picked up his books, and walked out of his room. His mouth was dry, and his fingers quivered as he walked down the hall to the tower entrance.

His outfit was soft and comfortable, but it only accentuated the importance of this day. The doors to Arcanum Tower stood wide open. Ben hesitated at the entrance. He was so nervous that he doubted he could make it to Arcanum Tower without getting sick, let alone pass the Caster's Trial.

He spotted his friends gathered in the middle of the flagstone court, and his hands stopped shaking. He smiled. Of course they would not let him go through this alone.

His five classmates were there, and Rohen and Jamu and Yar. And of course Galen. Even Megan and Druid Bilin were there. They all looked happy and excited to see him. Ben ran down the Tower steps to join them.

Galen hugged him. "You look so different wearing that!" she said, running her hand up and down his sleeve. "So soft. I have never felt anything like it. What is it?"

"It's a secret material the Casters make out of cotton," Ben explained. "It does feel nice wearing it." Jania, Hedi, and Jai moved up close to feel his shirt.

"Can I borrow it when you're done?" Rohen asked, watching the girls run their hands all over Ben.

"Why? You never had a problem getting girls to paw you." Ben jumped as a hand grabbed his rear. "Hey!"

"The girls are right," Jamu said. "That really is nice and soft." Hedi and Jai giggled.

"All right, everyone, Ben needs to go to Arcanum." Druid Bilin handed Ben his mage rod. "Ben, this is from all of us. We asked Mage Nin to spell-charge it. There are twenty stun spells in it now."

"You did this for me?" Ben was touched. He took the rod from the druid and held it before him.

"Why not?" Jania asked. "Not many Arcanum mages get to try to pass the Caster Trial. You deserve it."

Ben smiled at her. It made him so happy, seeing her among his closest friends. She definitely had a place in that group, even though she probably did not realize it.

"It is a momentous occasion," Bilin agreed. "Are you ready?"

"Almost," Ben said. "They gave me some material to help me prepare. I memorized some of the allowed spells, and I have a slight idea what I will be facing. I just need to choose who I'm going to take with me."

"You have to take someone with you?" Jania asked.

Ben nodded. "Just as armies rely on Casters to protect them, Casters rely on soldiers and fighters to protect them, too. Part of this trial is to determine how well I can work with others. So I need a companion. It cannot be another mage."

"That is strange," Megan said. "So who are you going to take?"

"I'll go," Rohen said.

"So will I," Jamu added.

Ben recalled his trip to Stony Forest last summer and quickly made his decision. "Thanks guys. I'm touched by your offers, but I want my sister to be with me," he said.

"Yes!" Galen shouted, jumping up and down. "I'll go get my bow." She raced off.

Rohen frowned at Ben, but said, "I have my old sword I can lend her. I'll go get it." He ran after Galen.

Ben looked at Jamu. "Can I?" he asked him. Jamu was her troop leader. It was only right to ask him.

"Are you sure about this, Ben? Maybe you should take someone you will not be so worried about." Jamu did not seem pleased with the idea.

"I'm sure," Ben replied.

"All right. She can go."

"Thank you," Ben said as he began walking toward Arcanum. "Thank you all."

"You would have done it for any of us," Jai said, taking his arm and walking with him.

Jania took his other arm. Ben looked straight ahead, hoping she could not see the look on his face.

"So how are you feeling, Ben?" Caster Nate asked, sitting across from Ben in the fifth-year Winter Room. The room was big but dark, and not as warm as the other student study rooms in years past. In the springtime, though, it was a lovely place to study, with the big desks set next to the bright airy windows. Ben was alone with the Caster mage; everyone else had been shooed off, and now they waited for Galen to arrive to begin the Trial.

"I'm a little nervous," he admitted.

"That is normal. You are handling yourself very well, Ben. When I went through the Trial, I was shaking in my boots the entire time." The battle mage smiled at him.

"The Trial has not started yet," Ben replied. "We shall see how well I still handle myself when it does."

Caster Nate threw his head back and laughed. Ben liked the good-natured Caster. He made Ben realize that Casters were people too.

Galen's head poked through the doorway. "Ben?"

Caster Nate looked at her, surprised. "I did not even hear you approach," he told her. He turned to Ben. "He will be your companion? He looks rather young for something like this."

"She, Caster Nate. This is my sister, Galen. She is the highest ranking second-year Espies student, and a sharpshoot-level archer. She is only eleven, but she is a lot tougher than she looks."

Caster Nate stared at Galen. "You are the Galen of all those peddler stories?"

She nodded.

Caster Nate looked skeptical. "If that is your wish, Ben. Galen, I apologize for thinking you are a boy. Come on in. Did you really do what the stories say you did?"

"I don't remember much about all that," Galen replied as she walked in. "I don't mind you mistaking me for a boy. It happens a lot."

Ben noticed Rohen's old sword strapped to her hip. It was a good size for her. She took a seat beside him on the couch.

"All right, we can begin now," Caster Nate said. "Galen, you will serve as witness as to what is spoken here. Will you hold Ben's answers close to your heart?"

"That's a witness vow," Ben said to her, noticing the confused look on her face. "Say you will."

"Oh. I will," Galen said quickly.

The battle mage gave her an approving nod and turned his full attention on Ben. "Now, the first and most important thing. Why do you want to become a Caster?"

"To fight the Eastern Armies."

"That is a rather vague answer."

"Eastern soldiers killed my parents and destroyed my home. I want revenge for what they did."

"Revenge is a hollow purpose. Your goals and aspirations have no substance."

"Of course they have substance! This is not about getting even. I can't do anything to the ones who hurt me. My sister already took care of that." Ben glanced at Galen. She stared back at him, chewing her lip. "What I want is for the attack on my village to be the East's fatal mistake. If I can play a part in destroying the Eastern forces, then all of those who died at Edgewood did not die in vain."

Nate said nothing for some time. Finally he asked, "Are you willing to give up your life for this?" He gave no sign of how he felt about Ben's answer.

"Absolutely."

"Everything and everyone you have here, and anywhere else, you will leave behind. You may never see them again. Are you ready to accept this?"

Ben looked at Galen again. They had spoken about this. "Yes," he said. He thought of Jania, and felt a pang of regret.

"Very well, then." Nate pulled out a scroll and opened it before him. He mumbled as he read through it quickly. "Hold hands," he ordered.

Ben reached for Galen's hand. He could feel his fingers shaking once more.

"Let us go," Nate said.

Ben released Galen's hand and looked around. A grassy plain stretched out as far as the eye could see, meeting up with a pretty blue sky at the horizon. Fluffy clouds dotted the sky.

"Is this real? There's nothing here," Galen said.

"I am here," Nate said from behind them.

Ben and Galen spun around. Nate smiled at them. He wore a golden robe, and he held a scroll in his hand.

"This scenario is magically created, and each spell you cast will be guaranteed the effect you expect, as long as you cast it properly. The dangers are real, however, so you can get hurt, and possibly killed, so be cautious." He handed the scroll to Galen. "Your companion carries important papers. The purpose of this Trial is to get her to the outpost to deliver those papers. If she dies, loses her papers, or cannot continue for any reason, you fail. If she reaches the outpost with her charge, with or without you, you succeed. However, this is not just a pass or fail test. You will be scored on how you handle yourself and the way events turn out. Your rod is an acceptable weapon for you to carry, so you will be allowed to use it. Best of luck to you." Nate raised his hand in a small wave and disappeared.

Ben looked around. He had no idea which way to go. "Well, here we go. I hope you ate something before we left."

Galen was down on one knee, stringing up her bow with a grin. "We're going to make a great team, Ben, don't you think?"

"Galen, do not take this lightly. We will be facing real danger here."

Her smile faded away. "I know that," she said, standing up. She dropped the scroll inside her quiver and drew the opening snugly around her arrows. "Which way do we go?"

"Good question." Ben considered the spells he had memorized. Two direction spells and one locate spell. He also had one tremor spell, one fog spell, one fireball spell, one bind spell, two phasing spells, and a teleport spell, the most powerful spell in his head. Should he find out where the outpost was, or where he was?

"I'll cast a direction spell to find out about the terrain. Do you know how to map?" he asked Galen.

She rolled her eyes and pulled out a pencil and a tiny paper tablet, bound with wax on one end.

"All right, that was a silly question," Ben muttered. "Let's get to work."

A short time later, Ben examined his sister's handiwork. It was just the way he saw it in his mind. He hoped the magical scenario did not change the terrain during the Trial.

"So what do you think?" Galen asked.

"Very well done. Trace a copy of it, so we can each carry one." Ben took off his lenses and tucked them into his pocket.

"Good idea." She tore the paper with the map off the tablet, tucked it under the next sheet of paper and carefully traced out the markings.

"All right, this is what we know," Ben said as Galen worked on her copy. "We are on an island, and north is that way." He pointed. "The outpost is straight west from here, but there is something in the way."

"It's probably a hill," Galen said.

"It could be a river, or a lake, or a jungle," Ben said. "How do we proceed if we don't know what we are going to face?"

"We wake up each morning not knowing what we are going to face. It's called life, Ben. You know, you worry too much." Galen stood up and handed Ben one of the maps. "We will figure out what to do once we find out. Now let's go see what it is."

Ben frowned at her back as she walked off. She was becoming way too uppity for her age. He followed her, wondering how Jamu managed to keep her in line. She was a good one to talk about worrying too much.

They walked for a while with Galen at the lead, doing her scout thing. Watching her made Ben feel better. She was enjoying the trek, wary but unafraid.

"You seem to be having fun. Can you tell me if we've made any progress after all the walking we have done?" He stopped. Even with comfortable boots, his feet felt achy and swollen. He looked at Galen's boots. "Are your feet all right?"

"Why wouldn't they be?" Galen looked back at him and stopped.

"I'm just looking out for you."

"Oh. So your feet hurt, huh?"

Ben gave her a flat look. "Have we made any progress, scout?"

"Yes, we have. I think you were right about there being water between us and the outpost. We should also expect company from the south. Listen."

He did. "I can't hear anything."

"I can. There is a group of riders heading this way."

Ben felt his stomach clench. "So what do we do?"

"Whatever you decide to do, mage. It's your Trial."

He fought down the urge to choke her. She was right, after all. "Well, how about some suggestions?"

"There's not much we can do." Galen kicked at the grass. "The grass is not tall enough to hide in, and there's no other type of cover. We cannot outrun them. All we can do is head west until they catch up with us."

"Then let's keep going." He looked around as Galen pulled her bow off her back. Everything looked exactly the way it did when they began walking. However, there was an oppressive feeling in the air that was not there before. He pulled out his rod as he followed his sister. The thin wand felt woefully inadequate for what they might face. He glanced at the small sword at Galen's hip. His father's cherished longsword came to mind.

"I wonder what happened to Papa's sword," he wondered aloud.

"I hid it," Galen said.

"You hid it? How? When?"

She slowed her pace. "After you helped me escape from the wagon, I went back to the village, but I don't remember much. I had the sword with me when I left, but when…by the time I found you, it was gone. But I knew it was safe. I know it is safe."

"Do you know where it is?"

"Um, not really." She stopped. "There they go," she said, pointing.

A cloud of dust rose just beyond the horizon. This time Ben was able to hear a slight rumbling.

"That is a huge army coming at us," Galen said. "Are we supposed to fight them?"

"We're supposed to get you to that outpost," Ben said. "How we do it doesn't…" He was shocked by the sudden crackling feeling that danced up and down his arms. "Galen, behind you!"

A rider blinked into view behind Galen, bearing down on her. She tried to dive out of the way, but the rider grabbed the collar of her tunic and hauled her up onto his mount. The rider raced off in the direction of the advancing army.

"Gayly!" Ben raised his rod, but the rider flew off his mount before he could fire a stun charge. The horse staggered to its knees. Galen grabbed the horse's neck and seated herself on the saddle. She coaxed the horse back to its feet and rode back over to Ben.

"We might be able to outrun them now," Galen said as Ben jumped on behind her. "What do you think?"

"I think we should try," Ben replied, glancing south. The dust cloud was much bigger, but Ben still could not make out any riders. He felt the strange tingle on his arms once more. It was magic energy! He could feel when magic was being used.

"Galen, go!" One, two, three riders appeared out of thin air as Galen kicked their horse to a run.

Ben wrapped one arm tightly around his sister's tiny waist and held the other out to his side, rod in hand. He hung on with his knees as the horse dodged and weaved through the three riders. Ben threw one stun charge at the closest rider, and Galen gave the horse its head. The terrified horse bolted.

"What the hell is this?" he shouted in frustration. "Casters are not supposed to run away from their enemies. They are supposed to fight large armies."

"That can be arranged, Ben," Galen shouted back. "All I have to do is turn this horse around. Is that what you want?"

Ben stared at the back of her head. Even in the midst of peril, she had the nerve to make wise cracks. "You know what, little sister? Someone needs to give you a…"

A sudden blast off to the side made the ground shake. Panicked, the horse screamed and danced around. Galen struggled to regain control, and Ben held tight to her waist to keep from falling. Another blast shocked the horse into running again. Ben closed his eyes and prayed.

He opened his eyes again as he felt the horse slow. A sandy beach bordering a huge lake stretched out before them. Ben couldn't see the other side. There was no sign of the outpost.

"How do we get across?" Galen pulled the horse to a stop and slid off. "I hope you have a boat spell or something."

"I hate to dash your hopes, sister," Ben said, swinging his leg over and dropping to the ground. "But there is no such thing as a boat spell. We have nothing to cross that lake with." He grabbed the horse's bridle and tried to think of what to do next.

He felt Galen's thought push its way into his head. We can move the water.

No. There's no telling what the Casters will make of that. We shouldn't even be thinking at each other like this.

Galen looked down at her quiver. "I dropped my bow when that man grabbed me." She sighed and pulled out her map. "I liked that bow."

Ben looked back. Their pursuers were nowhere in sight. "What happened to the other riders?"

Galen shrugged. "I don't know. Ben, take a look at the map." She held her copy up as Ben fished out his lenses.

He studied the outlines of the area he had not been able to identify. The outpost was located within the lake. Galen ran her finger along the marks outlining the shore. "The outpost cannot be on the lake; we would be able to see it if that were the case. But…"

Magic, being used again. "Gayly, danger."

Galen pulled out her sword as one of the riders appeared, bearing down on her just like the first one. She slashed at the horse's leg, and the rider pitched forward as the horse went down.

A second rider appeared before Ben, swinging a saber. He used the horse he held as a shield, wincing at the animal's scream as the rider's sword bit into its neck. Ben released the bridle and let the horse run off. The rumbling noise returned.

Ben took a quick look back as his attacker stopped and dismounted. He could see the army now. Riders, more than he could count, galloped toward them. He held his rod ready as the attacker approached. He looked like any ordinary man; the scowl on his face was the only sign he was a threat. The sounds of clashing swords told Ben that Galen's attacker had recovered from his fall.

"Gayly, hold on," Ben called out, shooting a charge at his attacker. The man tried to dodge too late. He fell to the ground with a strangled cry, twitching and heaving.

"Ben, stop that army! I can handle this jerk," Galen called out as she parried her attacker's swings. The blows from the much larger man drove her back.

He glanced at the riders, then back at Galen. Stunning the man would not take very long. He raised his rod as she dodged a vicious slashing attack.

She intercepted one swing and used the block as leverage to push herself to her opponent's flank. She spun around and sank her sword into his side just as Ben let loose the charge.

"Oh, hell," he shouted as Galen sank to her knees and arched her back, screaming. Her attacker's scream turned into a gurgle as he dropped lifeless to the ground. Galen wavered for a moment on her knees, then pitched forward and fell flat on her face.

"Gayly!" Ben rushed to her side. How could he be so stupid as to stun his own companion? His little sister, no less. "I am so sorry, Gayly."

Her eyes rolled back into her head, and she struggled to breathe. Her hands gripped Ben's arms tightly. Ben sat down and laid her head on his lap. His mother would whip the skin off his back if she were here.

He watched the army approach. He had to do something quickly. He cast his fog spell. A wall of thick mist formed between him and the riders.

He stood up and tossed Galen over his shoulder. Making sure she still had her quiver, he carried her over to the one uninjured horse. He draped her over its back, and remembered her sword. He ran back to the dying man and pulled the sword out of his side. The man did not even cry out. Ben couldn't help wondering whether they had truly killed that man or if he was only an illusion. He sure didn't smell like one.

Ben ran back to the horse and jumped on. He sat Galen up and set her where he could hold her securely with one arm, her face resting against his chest. He put the sword in her scabbard and looked back. Four riders had made their way out of the fog. Ben cursed and dug his heels into the horse's ribs. Things looked bad, but he had a plan.

It was hard holding on to someone with one hand while trying to drive a galloping horse with the other. "They should train Arcanum mages to do these kinds of things," he said to Galen. "Then if we are in a situation where we have to do this, we won't look like fools."

Galen gave no sign she even heard him. She blinked drunkenly as she struggled to breathe.

"Can you hold on to me, Gayly?"

Her arms slowly encircled him, and he felt her hands grip his shirt. "You are good," he said, easing his hold on her.

He looked back. The riders were catching up fast. But he should not have to go much further, if his guess was correct. And by the way the shoreline turned in, he was confident he was right.

As they rode, Galen began to revive. She squinted, trying to regain focus.

"Come on, scout. Snap out of it. Do you know where you are?" He looked down at his sister.

She nodded. "Where are we going?" she whispered.

Ben was totally unprepared for the horse's sudden stop. Galen flew out of his arms as he pitched forward and over the horse's head. He cried out as he suddenly noticed that the ground was much lower than it was supposed to be.

He fell onto a sandy slope and rolled down. It seemed to take forever for him to stop falling and rolling. He lay still when he finally did, just in case it started again. When it didn't, he sat up slowly, spitting sand out of his mouth and trying hard to make everything stop spinning.

He heard a groan beside him, and turned to see Galen push herself up to a crouching position. "Maybe you should ask Jamu to give you some riding lessons," she said, shaking sand out of her hair.

"Are you all right?"

"I've been worse. Where are your lenses?"

Ben's hand flew to his face. "I need to find them!"

They floundered about in the sand. "Here they are," Galen said, holding them up.

"Oh, good, they are not broken," Ben said, relieved. He put his lenses back in his pocket. He looked up as he heard horses approach.

"They are coming, and I don't have my bow," Galen whined, pounding the sand with her fist. Her expression changed as something caught her eye. "Ben, look!"

He did. The beach extended to the bottom of the steep slope, connecting to a second beach several hundred paces away. And at that beach stood a wooden building.

"That's it!" As he had guessed, an illusion had concealed one part of the lake. "Let's go!"

The riders appeared just as they got to their feet. They dismounted and began to gather stones from the ground.

"We can't get away from them," Galen cried out.

"Sure we can. You go and I'll keep them at bay. Just keep running, no matter what." Ben turned to face the men above as Galen stumbled off.

He reached for his rod, and was relieved to feel it securely strapped to his waist. He could not remember putting it away. Pulling it out, he pointed it at the men as they began tossing stones. He missed a few times, but soon had all of them lying on the ground, motionless.

Grinning triumphantly, he turned to check on Galen's progress. His grin died as he saw her lying on the ground not too far from him. He ran over to check on her.

A nearby stone and her bloody head told the story. He wanted to scream. This was not her Trial. Why was she getting hurt like this?

He looked up at the top of the slope. Riders were lined up at the edge. He looked back at the nearby outpost. There was still one thing he could do.

He dropped to his knees and cast his tremor spell, centering it on the slope. Horses rained down as the entire side of the slope caved in. Ben didn't bother to watch them fall. He had to use the little time he had.

He checked Galen's quiver to make sure the scroll was still there. He reached down and kissed her forehead. "Thank you, little sister," he said. Keeping his eyes fixed on the outpost, he cast his teleport spell. Galen blinked away.

Still on his knees, Ben dropped his head and waited. He still had his fireball spell. He would wait until they came close, then cast the fireball. He would take out as many of them as he could. He began to cast.

He felt himself wavering, and the spell popped out of his mind, spoiled and forgotten. A hand fell on his shoulder.

He looked up to see Caster Nate gazing down at him. They were alone in the Winter Room. Ben stood up to face him.

"You succeeded in finishing the Trial," Nate said. His face and voice were expressionless. "We will contact you shortly with our decision."

Ben walked down one of Somatica's long corridors. He held a warm bag of fried noodles in one hand and his rod in the other. Healer Stanis had insisted on keeping Galen in the infirmary for a few days to see if there were any kind of aftereffects from the stun spell. Stun spells were painful and sometimes lethal, so no one was willing to volunteer to subject themselves to such an attack. Healer Stanis was not going to pass up an opportunity to study a survivor of the powerful spell. He also wanted to take a look at Ben's rod. It took Ben a few days to agree to give it to him.

Jamu and Rohen walked out of Galen's room. Jamu smiled as he saw Ben, but his expression changed to mock horror as he noticed the rod in Ben's hand.

"He has the rod! Duck!" Jamu and Rohen threw themselves on

the floor, covering their heads with their hands.

Ben's own hand twitched. Healer Stanis would just love to have two more subjects to study. But Jania might get mad at him for stunning her friends. "To hell with you," he said, stepping over them. "To hell with both of you."

They sat up, laughing. "You should not bother her right now, Ben," Jamu said, still chuckling. "She is asleep. Healer Stanis has been poking and prodding her all day."

Ben's mouth went dry. Healer Stanis had not found out about Galen's psychic powers yet; she was still here. Even so, Ben wondered if there was a possibility he could stumble onto Galen's abilities by doing whatever it was he was doing with her. "How long does she have to stay here?" he asked, walking up to her door.

"I can take her back to Espies tomorrow," Jamu said.

"You really should let her sleep. She is very tired," Rohen added.

"Let me at least leave this here for her," Ben replied. He went inside.

It was a tiny bare room with a tiny bare window. Galen slept peacefully. The bandage on her head was gone, and the scrapes on her arms and legs from the falls she took were beginning to fade. Healer Stanis wanted her to heal naturally in case Healing took away any of the stunning aftereffects. Ben tiptoed over to the table next to her bed and set the bag and the rod down on it.

"Ben?" Galen's eyes opened.

"Go back to sleep. I just wanted to leave a few things."

"You're leaving?"

"Yes, but I will be back tomorrow. I promise."

"Have you heard anything?"

"Not yet."

"You'll make it. I know you will." Her eyes closed. "I'm fine Ben. I'll be out of here tomorrow."

"I know, but I still worry about you. Sleep well."

Galen smiled, but did not open her eyes. Ben tiptoed out of the room.

His two friends stood waiting for him. "You didn't have to wait for me," Ben said, closing the door behind him.

Rohen grinned. "But we want to take our future Caster friend out for a drink. How about a quick ride to Syntrea?"

"Sounds great," Ben said.

"I don't think I'm going to make it. Nothing went right," Ben complained, draining his mug. He set it down beside the other two he had already emptied.

"From what both you and Galen say, it seems like you handled everything just fine," Jamu said.

"I don't think you have anything to worry about," Rohen said, smiling his girl-snaring smile at one of the servers. She winked at him and motioned him to wait.

"Nothing went as I expected. Magic barely played a part in the Trial. I don't understand." Ben lifted the mug to his lips, forgetting it was empty.

"Magic plays a very small part in war, even for Casters," Jamu said.

"They were testing you for competency under stressful situations. They know you can cast spells already," Rohen said.

"The most important aspect of a leader is the ability to adapt to changing situations. Casters answer to few people, so they must have leadership qualities. Resourcefulness, courage, selflessness, they need to see these things in you," Jamu added.

The serving girl set down three mugs and ruffled Rohen's head. He fished out a piece of candy and gave it to her.

"You are just the sweetest," she gushed, hugging his head to her chest. She smiled at Ben and Jamu before rushing off.

"Where did you get that?" Jamu asked Rohen.

"Jania gave me some. She always does. It still tickles her that I never had any cocoa when I was a child," Rohen replied.

"I should have come to you guys before," Ben groaned.

"I'm surprised you didn't. Casters are warriors, Ben. You should have known that they would test you for more than just spellcasting ability," Rohen said.

"It does not matter," Jamu said. "He did fine. I am sure he scored extremely well."

"Stunning his sister senseless isn't going to help his score any," Rohen said.

"No, I suppose not," Jamu laughed.

Ben drained his mug. "Thanks for cheering me up, guys," he said, banging his mug down on the table.

"Any time," Rohen said, grinning at him. He glanced over Ben's head. "I'll be right back," he said.

Ben watched Rohen walk up to the girl he had given the candy to and follow her through a back door. "It still tickles her that I never had any cocoa when I was a child," he mimicked, mocking Rohen's Northern accent.

"Jealousy does not become you. It is also groundless. Ro has no interest in the princess," Jamu said.

"But Jania seems to have plenty of interest in Ro," Ben replied. He reached over and grabbed Rohen's mug.

"You do not know that."

"You're right. I wish I did know."

"Then ask her!"

Ben shook his head as he emptied Rohen's mug. "I sit next to this girl almost every day, Jamu. How can I ask her something that might make me look like a fool?"

Jamu shook his head. "You are a fool," he said.

Jania knocked on the door to Jamu's cabin. She waited anxiously for the door to open, wondering if Ben would be there. She hoped he wouldn't be, and yet she hoped he would.

Why did her brain turn to fluff every time Ben crossed her

mind? She could not even decide whether she wanted to see him or not. She knocked again, angry with herself. If she really did not want to see him, then why was she standing here?

The door opened, and her irritation melted away. Ben stood at the doorway, looking a little surprised to see her. He smiled as he noticed what she held. "You are too kind, Princess. You shouldn't have."

"And why not?" She smiled back at him. "May I come in?"

"Of course." Ben stepped aside, and she walked in.

Galen sat on her bed next to Jamu. Her troopmates sat on the floor around her bed. They all jumped to their feet once they noticed her. "Hello, Princess," Galen said, smiling cheerfully.

"It is good to see you well, Galen," Jania said, holding up the bow she carried. "Here's a gift to welcome you back."

Galen's jaw dropped as Jania put the bow in her hands. "It's so smooth and shiny," she said.

Jamu reached over to feel the polished surface. "What kind of wood is it?" he asked.

"It's yew." Jania glanced at Ben. He seemed happy that Galen was pleased. "It's supposed to be excellent for bows."

"It is," Jamu said, sounding impressed. "It is also hard to find."

Galen's eyes gleamed as she gazed at the bow. "This is amazing. A yew bow! Rowy is going to be so jealous."

"Is he, now?" Jania laughed. "I'm surprised he's not here. Is he busy?"

"Why? Do you have a bow for him, too?" Ben's tone sounded strange.

Jania looked at him. The happy look was gone from his face. She glanced at Jamu. He stared at Ben, then turned to Jania with a smile and a strange glint in his bright blue eyes.

"Princess, you are always welcome here, and I am not trying to dismiss you in the least, but it is getting late. Would you like me to walk you to Arcanum?" His eyes seemed to be trying to tell her something.

"I hate to put you out of your way." She glanced at Ben. He had a brooding look on his face.

"Ben can take you," Galen said, stroking her new bow. "He was just about to leave when you knocked."

Bless that sweet little girl. "Do you mind, Ben?" Jania asked.

"No, not at all." Ben opened the door. "Let's go, then. Jamu is right; it is getting late. Take care, Gayly."

Jania said her good-byes to the scouts and followed Ben outside.

It really was getting late. The sun was gone, and dusk was quickly darkening into night. There was still enough light to see Ben's face, though. He seemed uncomfortable, yet he walked close beside her.

Her mind raced. She had to know why he was acting so strange. Why would he ask her if she had a bow for Rohen? There was only one way to find out.

"Why did you ask me if I had a bow for Ro?"

Ben actually gulped. "It just came out. I was just...I did not mean to ask that. Forget I even said anything." He turned his face away.

She remembered the look Jamu gave her. "Ben, does it bother you to see me with your friends?"

He sighed. His expression looked like that of a first-year mage caught casting a third-year spell. "I don't like it," he admitted sullenly.

"They are my friends, too," Jania said.

"I know," Ben said quickly. "And I want you to be friends with them. I just feel as if...oh, I can't explain it! I can't help how I feel."

"Well, I am sorry you feel that way." Keep your wits about you. Do not be upset at him because he told you how he felt. "Can I do anything to make you feel better about this?"

Ben was quiet as they walked. Finally, as they climbed the steps to Arcanum Tower, he said, "There is one question I would like you to answer."

"Ask me, then," Jania said as Ben opened the door for her.

Hedi, Jai, Nelsen, and Seth stood waiting in the atrium. "I thought you would never get here," Jai exclaimed. "And Jania is with you, so we're all here. You received a letter from the Casters, Ben!"

Ben rushed over to Hedi, who waved a scrollcase in the air. He snatched it from her with one hand and whisked his lenses on with the other. His hands shook as he unrolled the page inside the leather case.

Jania held her breath as she waited. It seemed to take him forever to read the long page. She stared at his face, waiting for a happy reaction.

There was none. Ben kept reading, and reading. Jania's heart dropped as his face became stony. Finally, he lowered the page and let it drop to the floor.

"Ben?" Jania pressed her hands against her middle tightly. It was painful to see him like that.

Ben took a deep breath and pulled his lenses off. He then turned and threw both the scrollcase and his lenses as hard as he could. His lenses clinked as they landed on the marble floor. Ben turned around and ran out of the tower.

"Ben!" The others ran after him, but Jania just watched as they gave chase. She could not remember ever feeling so awful. Ben had wanted this so much, and he was so smart, so powerful with magic. Why didn't they want him?

She spotted the page he had dropped. She picked it up and began to read. As she read, the pain in her middle sharpened and spread to her chest.

9

Terra's Ward

Ben dipped his fingers into the fountain pool and watched the ripples travel across the water. He wanted to cry, but to cry would only stress the magnitude of his failure. No, it was better not to give in to tears. He was glad his classmates were with him; he would not dare cry around them.

They were all with him except for Jania. They sat around him silently, but their presence alone was more comforting to Ben than any words. He wondered where Jania was. He could see her searching for Rohen to tell him the awful news. Any excuse to see him.

"Did they explain to you why, Ben?" Hedi asked.

Ben nodded. Their reason made it all the worse.

"What did they say?" Nelsen asked.

Maybe it wouldn't hurt so much if he said it out loud. He was about to tell them when he saw Jania walking toward them. She had that damned letter in her hand.

He waited for her to reach them, curious at her determined stride. She walked up to him, sat down beside him on the edge of the fountain, and placed the letter carefully on his lap.

"Ben, you don't have to accept their decision," Jania said.

"You can fight this."

He pushed down the surge of hope he felt. "Their decision is final. They do not want me. How can I make them accept me?"

She pointed at the letter. "They turned you down because you wear lenses. That is the most frivolous excuse I have ever heard. You can demand that they reconsider."

"You want me to make demands of the Casters?" Ben let Hedi take the letter from his lap. "I have been humiliated enough, Jania. I will not make a fool of myself."

"Half of this letter is complimenting you on how well you did," Hedi said. "And then, 'while you performed in an exemplary manner during the Trial, your dependency on vision enhancement equipment leaves us no choice but to decline your request for admittance into our organization.' Did something happen with your lenses during the Trial?"

"They fell off my face once, and Galen and I had to search for them. But that did not affect the outcome at all."

"Could you have completed the trial if you had not found them?" Jania asked.

"Of course! I only need them to read."

"Why were you wearing them when they fell off your face? Did you need them at that point?"

"I did not have time to take them off." He stared at Jania, realizing what she was getting at.

She stared right back at him. "So they had no good reason to turn you down."

"It doesn't sound like it," Nelsen said.

"You should make a fuss, Ben. The Casters get away with just about everything. It's about time someone stood up to them," Seth said.

"I don't know. What good can come of it?" Ben tried to take the letter from Hedi, but she moved her hand out of his reach.

"I'll hold on to this for a while. You look ready to rip this to pieces, and I don't think that would be a good idea right now," she told him.

She was right; he was angry. He could see now what a silly reason they gave him for ruining his dream. He wondered if the others noticed the fountain shake slightly.

"You should take some time to think about this, Ben," Jai said. "Wait until the shock wears off so you don't make any rash decisions."

"No, I have already decided," Ben replied. "I will talk to Mage Terri tomorrow morning and find out how I can fight this."

His classmates were quiet. None of them seemed to disapprove, although Jai looked a little worried.

"I think you are doing the right thing," Jania finally said. "And I will do all I can to help you."

"Thank you." Ben smiled at her. "But what kind of influence can a princess possibly have?"

"Oh, you would be surprised," she replied dryly.

Terra drummed her fingers on her desk, waiting for Ben to arrive. She knew he had received notice from the Casters, so his request to speak with her could only mean that he needed to make preparations to go.

She would not be able to watch over him if he went off with the Casters. Which was exactly what Humo wanted. He even went as far as to write a letter of praise to the top ranking Caster— the Master General—to vouch for Ben. Terra could not believe that Humo would send an unmarked ward away.

Why he would dismiss Ben that way? Whatever his present plans entailed, they obviously did not include the wards. Or was that the way Humo wanted it to be seen?

The knock on the door pushed all thoughts out of her mind. "Come in," she called out, wondering if there was any way she could keep Ben from leaving.

Ben entered. She took one look at his face. Maybe she would

not have to worry about him leaving after all.

Ben walked up to her desk and handed her a scrollcase. "I've been turned down. They feel my lenses are a handicap to being an effective Caster."

Human faces were so expressive. Terra found it difficult to keep hers neutral. "That is terrible. I am so sorry, Ben."

"Don't be. I want to dispute their decision."

"What?"

"I don't think that my wearing lenses is an adequate reason for rejection. I want them to reconsider."

What did she have to do to make Ben want to stay at the Academy? "Ben, that is ludicrous. The Casters do not need a reason to accept or reject anyone. You are lucky they gave you an explanation."

"Well, they should have kept their explanation to themselves." Ben waved at the scrollcase. "You are not going to read that?"

Terra looked at the scrollcase. "No. I don't need to," she said.

Ben's eyes widened. "I came to ask you to help me," he said. He sounded unsure.

Anything else, and she would do whatever it took to help him. "Ben, it is not worth the trouble. You are putting your reputation and character at risk. I am sorry, but I will not help you do that. Accept their decision and put this behind you. Please."

His face was still, but his eyes took on an angry amber shade. "I can't do that," he said thickly. "I have to fight this. I will go to Master Humo if I have to." He picked up the scrollcase and turned to leave.

"Ben, wait." Terra caught up to him at the door. She grabbed his arm before he could open it. "You shouldn't."

"I won't let a few mages decide my future for me. I control my fate, no one else!" Ben pulled his arm out of her grip.

Terra sighed as she warded the room. "No, that is not true." Humo would make her pay, but her choices were exhausted. Ben was every bit as important as Galen, and Rohen, and Jania.

Ben glanced around warily. "Why did you ward the room?"

"I know what you want, Ben. But joining the Casters is not the way. There is another way to get the revenge you want. You must follow the path to your destiny."

"No," he yelled. "I will not follow any path. I will make my own."

She had to do this. If she hesitated now, she would lose the little influence she had on him. She might lose it anyway. "Ben, let us sit down and have a talk. There is much that you need to know."

"Come on, Galen, we don't have much time. Hurry up!"

Galen carefully strung her brand new bow, ignoring Laren's complaints. She took her time getting it ready, but she could not wait to try it out.

"Galen, the ranking trials will start soon. Get your shots in," Jamu said sternly.

"All right!" She pulled out an arrow, notched and drew. The yew was strong, but it flexed smoothly. Galen smiled, amazed at the difference. Promising herself this would be the last bow she ever owned, she aimed her arrow at the target.

A white flash blinded her, and something hot shot through her head. Galen gasped, and her arrow shot into the ground a few steps in front of her.

"What happened there, Galen?" Jamu asked.

She lowered her bow and went down on one knee. The flash happened so fast she could hardly recall what it felt like, but she knew that whatever she felt had come from Ben. And she knew that he had not taken the Casters' rejection well.

"May I be excused? I don't feel well," she said.

Jamu crouched down beside her. "What is wrong?"

"It's my head," she replied. "I just need to walk it off. I will be all right for the rankings." It was not a lie.

Jamu felt her head and peered into her eyes. "Maybe you should see Healer Stanis. You are still recovering."

"I will if I don't feel better," she promised him. "I just need to calm down and clear my head."

"All right. Go take a walk." He patted her on the shoulder and stood. "You know where to find us."

Galen left the archery range, remembering to unstring her bow. Except for staffs, carrying bared weapons around the Academy was against the rules. Bows had to be unstrung. She jogged over to Arcanum Tower.

She pushed open the entrance doors and went inside. She knew exactly where to go. Ignoring the questioning looks of the mages milling about, she found the stairway and ran up.

She stopped just a couple of flights from the top, pausing at the landing. Before she could reach for the door, it opened, and Mage Terri stood in front of her.

She did not seem surprised to see Galen there. Galen bit her lip, waiting for the mage to tell her to leave, but she only gave her a searching look before walking past her and down the stairs.

Galen listened for a moment to the tapping sound of footsteps as the mage descended before moving on. She went to the door across the corridor and entered.

Ben sat on the floor in the middle of the large room. He looked up as Galen stepped into the room and closed the door behind her.

She swallowed hard at his look. It was not anger, not fear, but a combination of both. Ben never got this upset, ever. Suddenly afraid for him, she ran over to her brother and threw her arms around his shoulders.

"Gayly, everything we have gone through, all the people that died, all that, because of the whim of one...dragon!" His arms shot up and squeezed her hard.

Galen felt her blood run cold, but she was not sure why. "Dragon? What are you talking about?"

Ben stood, pulling her up with him. "It's all right. You can tell me now."

Galen stared at him. "Tell you what? What's a dragon?"

"Don't tell me you don't know about them! Semino is one!"

"Semino is a dragon? No!" And yet she had always known, deep down inside, that the kind mysterious man who had helped her long ago and promised to return for her someday was much more than just an ordinary man. She had never bothered to think about it before. But now...

Ben stepped away from her. "That's what Semino was hiding from us. We are wanted by dragons, not people! And they are fighting over us like two wolf packs over a dead carcass! Gayly, why did you let Semino mark you? What if he had been evil?"

"Ben..." Galen began to shake. He was not supposed to know about that. How did he find out? "How do you know about my being marked?"

"How did you know to come here?" Ben asked her.

"I felt something. It felt like..." Her voice fled. It was the same flaring shock she felt when Semino had scratched her head all those years ago.

"Hold my hand," Ben said. "Focus on my mind, and tell me what you feel."

Galen took his hand and closed her eyes. A familiar energy pulsed in his head. She could pinpoint it, in the front of his skull, right behind his forehead. The feeling was unmistakable. Ben was also marked.

Shocked as she was, Galen felt a weight she never knew she had lift from her shoulders. She was not alone. Someone else, someone she loved and trusted, shared her secret now.

"So that's what I felt happen. Who marked you?" she asked.

"Mage Terri," he replied.

"What? No!" She let go of his hand. "She is one? How can that be? What is she doing here?"

"She's here to watch us," Ben said. He tried to take her hand again, but she pulled it away. "And to protect us. Master Humo is a dragon, too. But he is not a good one."

Yet another reason to be afraid of the Headmaster. It was too much for her. She began to cry.

"Don't cry, Gayly." Ben captured her hand this time and pulled her close. "We are safe. Nothing is going to happen to us."

"Is Master Humo like that woman who tried to…wait, that woman! She was trying to mark you, too!" Galen exclaimed.

Ben nodded. "She tried to force me, and Terra…Mage Terri did not. She let me choose."

"Why do all these dragons want to mark us?" Galen asked fretfully.

"There are only eight dragons, Galen. We are already marked by the dragons we chose. And Master Humo is the only bad one we need to worry about right now. We are going to be all right. Believe me."

Galen nodded. "I do, Ben," she said. She hoped Ben made the right choice in letting Mage Terri mark him.

Jania hesitated before knocking on Master Humo's door. She was supposed to be researching for her chemistry project, but she knew she would get nothing done in the state of mind she was in. She felt comfortable now coming to Humo for advice, but she knew he was a very busy man. Hopefully he would have time for her.

She was beginning to enjoy talking to him when things were bothering her, even though she didn't always agree with everything that he had to say. And sometimes his behavior perplexed her. She did not understand why he supported Ben's decision to try to join the Casters after initially stating he was against the idea. He never explained why he changed his mind. She had witnessed his reaction when Ben told him about wanting to join the Casters. Jania still shuddered at the look on the Headmaster's face.

"Come in," Humo called out.

Jania opened the door and walked in. She saw Humo standing out on the terrace overlooking Espies and Arcanum. She joined him.

"I am honored by your visit," Humo said.

"I am glad you are willing to make time for me," Jania replied. "Things have been bothering me lately."

"Is it the report of skirmishes on the northern border?"

"Partly." She had completely forgotten about the recent news since Ben had read his letter. "But right now I'm worried about Ben. The Casters turned him down."

"I had not heard." Humo sighed and looked over at Arcanum. "That is a shame. I'm surprised."

"They don't want him because he uses lenses," Jania continued, a spark of hope sprouting up inside her. "He wants to contest their decision."

"That will be a futile fight."

"It might not be, if you help him."

Humo seemed thoughtful as he gazed at the mage's tower. "I may consider it, if he asks."

Jania was surprised at his lack of candor. "But you seemed so excited about the prospect of Ben joining the Casters. And that was after you were angry with him for deciding to apply. I don't understand."

"There are many things to consider," Humo said. "I was upset at the possible loss of an exceptional student. But fighting his decision would raise too many problems, so I looked at it from a different perspective. To have a connection to the Casters by sending them an Arcanum student is valuable in itself, so I decided to support Ben. Now, with what you tell me, I have to look at it in many different ways all over again. So I will wait for Ben to decide which course he wishes to take, and as long as it is not against the interests of the Academy, I will support him as best I can."

Jania followed his gaze. Some of the carvings were big enough to make out from the terrace. There was one she had not noticed before, an owl in flight, about to strike with its talons. "It sounds so complicated."

"Leadership is complicated, Princess," Humo said. "You must look at everything from a hundred angles."

Just thinking about looking at a hundred different perspectives made her dizzy. "But wouldn't that amount to just second-guessing yourself?" Animis had always told her to keep things as simple as possible. That way no one could corrupt her resolve once she did make a decision.

Humo gave her a pat on the head. "You must see things the way others may see it. That way you know what to expect from your opponents, and anticipate when they are most likely to betray you. As you can see from the skirmish reports, you cannot even trust your own subjects to keep their word."

"I think I understand." She hated Lord Tyron for inciting the Masseans along the Northern border. He was determined to make trouble for her father, despite the King's attempts to appease him. "I wish Father had let me cast a compel spell to make him keep his word not to attack Massean border patrols. He said it was not ethical."

"Well, you will not have to worry about your father's ethics once you are sitting on the throne," Humo told her.

Jania grinned at him. She could learn so much from the Head-master. "You are right," she told him.

The blue ink flowed smoothly into the inkpot from the brass canister Pedek held carefully with his off hand. The last few drops were just enough to fill the pot up to the top-off mark. The old cartographer smiled proudly. Even past his eighth decade, his hands were still steady enough to refill ink without spilling so much as a drop. He placed the canister in a bag, marking it with his favorite pencil as a reminder to order some more blue ink.

The door to his windowless office opened without warning.

Animis, the King's favorite adviser and main tutor for Princess Jania, breezed in, a distracted look on his perfect face. The sheets of parchment and vellum hanging along the walls to dry waved, as if to greet the intruder. Pedek grunted his own greeting, picking up several boxes filled with drawing instruments and walking over to a shelf to put them away. Animis never knocked when he came over for something. Pedek was sure it was his way of getting on the old cartographer's nerves for not convincing him to trade offices.

"I am sure you have had your share of silly questions," Animis said, not bothering to even ask how Pedek was doing. "Here's another one for you. Can you tell who requisitioned this map?" He held up a scorched strip of vellum and smiled.

"That question is beyond silly. It's just plain stupid," Pedek grumbled, snatching the scorched map piece. He looked closely at the design on his compass. His eyesight was as reliable as his steady hands. "Yep. This is one of a bunch that I made for the Academy." He rubbed the sheet between his fingers. "This is the vellum that Humo provided for the order, I can tell."

"I am impressed," Animis exclaimed. "Thank you, Master Pedek."

"Anything for you, pretty boy." Pedek scratched his ear. "Why do you ask? How did this one get burnt?"

"It is a bit of a boring tale. I shall tell you some other time." Animis smiled and gave Pedek a friendly slap on the back of his head.

Pedek blinked his eyes. For a moment, he had forgotten what he was doing. He frowned at the wooden storage boxes in his arms. Strange. He put the boxes on a shelf and pulled out a thin script. His hands might still be young, but it might be best to begin writing his tasks down. If senility was creeping up on him, he planned to be ready to face it head on.

10

Necare

"Come on, Rus!" Galen jumped up and down, cheering her troopmate along as he dashed toward the finish line with Keran at his heels. Rus needed to win this race so they could maintain their top ranking. If Keran won, Rohen's troop would take the top rank. Her jaw dropped as both scouts crossed the finish line simultaneously.

"It's too close to call," Rohen's old troop leader Kal announced. "The race is a draw."

She had never seen a draw. How were Jamu and Rohen going to resolve this one? Ranking was vital to a troop leader's reputation, and Rohen was frustrated at always being second. He was going to do whatever he could to get top rank. But Jamu was not going to concede the race and lose his top ranking without a fight.

Keran gave Rohen an apologetic look, but Rohen smiled and gave him a friendly punch on the shoulder. "That's the way to run a race," he said.

Galen wondered how such a big boy could run so fast. She smiled at Rus, but he only sighed and shook his head. He prided himself on his speed. It didn't matter to him that Keran was a powerful runner.

"Well?" Jamu asked Rohen.

"Well, what? I have a higher score. I'm first ranking." His troops cheered.

"No! Nil scores for draws do not count when ranking is at stake!"

"Jamu is right." Kal walked over to the two troop leaders. Kal had decided to stay at the Academy to serve as an Espies instructor. "You must choose an event to decide who will claim the score."

Galen shared an excited look with Rus. They still had a chance!

"Fine. How does this work?" Rohen asked, rubbing his forehead. Galen bit her lip to keep from smiling. He always did that when he was troubled or trying to think something through.

"The troop leader with the higher score decides on the tiebreaker. It can be an event or a match."

Rohen looked at Jamu and grinned. Galen's heart dropped. She knew what Rohen was going to choose. The last scout to beat him in a sword match graduated from Espies the year before Galen started.

"Get the sparring sabers out, Surian," Rohen said.

"Fine," Jamu answered shortly. He walked over to the barrel holding the wooden practice weapons.

Disappointed, Galen watched her troop leader pull out two sticks. The training yard became very quiet. Jamu and Rohen sparred all the time, but Rohen was the only scout at Espies who was undefeated for almost three years. Even when he was using only one weapon, Rohen was too fast, and he struck hard and often. Megan was the only person who could come close to beating him, and even she had trouble with his upper body strikes. He liked to attack from the sides, pivoting and striking high as he avoided attacks. She thought about Rohen for a moment, and grabbed Jamu's arm as he walked by.

"Jamu, let me fight Rowy. I think I can beat him." Actually, she was quite sure she could.

"Galen, this is no time for joking. Our ranking is at stake here." Jamu frowned down at her as Keran and Sprit laughed.

Galen glanced over at Rohen. He looked amused. "Do you mind, Rowy?"

"I'd be a fool if I did," he replied.

"Galen, you cannot be serious," Jamu exclaimed.

"I haven't let you down yet, have I? I can keep us on top, I know it," Galen said, tugging at his arm. "Please let me spar."

Jamu hesitated. "Is it allowed?" he asked Kal.

"You can choose anyone in your troop as a champion," Kal answered.

"Go, before I change my mind," Jamu said, giving her a little push. Galen grabbed the sparring sabers from him and jogged over to Rohen.

"Ready for a thrashing?" Rohen teased.

"Thanks, but not today," Galen replied. She tossed one of the sticks over to him and took her most comfortable stance. "You can use two sabers, if you like."

Rohen was not the only one who laughed at her remark. She didn't care. They wouldn't be laughing for long.

"I think I will challenge myself today, Firefly. This is for either five points, or a fatal strike." Suddenly the smile was gone from his face, and he stood before her, ready.

She liked sword drills, but standing in front of Rohen, she suddenly felt terribly out of her league. He was so much taller, and his bearing alone was aggressive and intimidating. She set her jaw and waited for his strike. Rohen never bothered with feints.

He did not waste time. A quick step to the side, and his stick was sailing toward her sword arm.

Megan had a move that always disoriented Rohen. He was able to counter it, though, because of her long weapon. Galen had watched the strike and counterstrike dozens of times, and was sure she could imitate it, but she was not sure how it would work with a short sparring stick.

She stepped inside his reach, lunged down, and brought her wooden saber up quickly to block his arm. He tried to pivot out of her way, but her leg was between his from the lunge. She hooked her leg around his, and he fell back. She placed her saber against his heart as his back hit the ground.

The leaves suddenly sounded quite loud as a breeze rustled them about. Galen was as stunned as everyone else. She had not expected it to be that easy. Megan was never able to bring her quarterstaff up in time to keep his arm from hitting her head. And it all happened in a matter of a few heartbeats.

"Rohen is down, and Galen has him under a fatal pin. She has won. Jamu's troop keeps top rank," Kal said numbly.

"What the hell! She tricked Rohen somehow!" Keran's glare made Galen's blood run cold. "You witch! What did you do?" He rushed toward Galen.

"It was a valid strike. Ro was overconfident." Jamu gave Keran a warning look, and Keran stopped in his tracks.

"He's right. Galen countered his first strike cleanly," Kal said.

Galen looked back at Rohen, and her saber dropped from her hand. Rohen's look made Keran's seem like a pout. She stepped back as he stood up. His eyes shone with rage, and his face was splotched with red. Strangely, Galen found his anger...familiar.

"I'm not done with you yet," he said, pointing at her. His accent sounded thick, the way it usually did when he was upset.

"Yes, you are," Jamu called out. "She won the match fairly. The ranking is ours."

"To hell with the ranking. You can have your bloody top rank," Rohen yelled, his eyes never leaving Galen's. "We are not finished. Are we, Galen?"

His anger was infectious. She felt it growing inside her as his eyes locked on to hers. He was not going to intimidate her! "No, we're not."

They both picked up their sabers and faced off.

"Galen, stay defensive," Jamu said.

Her saber flew up to intercept Rohen's before Jamu finished his sentence. Again and again Rohen struck, pressing forward with each overhand strike. Galen's parries could barely keep up. She inched back, trying to find an opening.

She jumped to the side as his leg tried to trip her. She countered with a spin kick. Her heel hit his face, and he stumbled to the side.

She knew Rohen did not lose bearing easily, and that probably saved her from a blow to the side of the head. As his weapon whizzed by her face, her anger flared hotter, and she attacked.

She felt burning rage flow into her arms and legs. She saw herself swinging the sword into the gray soldier's neck, and she knew she had the strength to do whatever she wanted. She struck, high and low, and now Rohen was on the defensive. A blow to the head, one to the ribs, and his silver eyes blazed with a strange light as he parried not quite as fast as she could strike. She took a step forward, then another. Rohen backpedaled, and she aimed her saber at his neck.

She could hear shouts and cheers coming from somewhere far away. Rohen's free hand grabbed her sword arm and pulled her forward. Something hit her cheek, and her feet were swept out from underneath her. She cried out as the ground rushed up and smashed into her face.

She heard a shout, and she knew she had to react. She rolled aside and onto her feet, and once again she was parrying for all she was worth. She held her stick with both her hands to block a surprising underhand swing, and his boot connected with her chest, sending her flying back. She landed on her rear hard.

She struggled to regain her breath as he rushed forward. She did not have time to stand back up before he was upon her again. She blocked his swings, but she could not get her lungs to work, and soon bright spots made it hard for her to see the strikes coming at her. One swing made it through and hit her neck. As she toppled sideways, she noticed Rohen lift his saber up high out of the corner of her eye.

A new sort of energy surged through her and seared her hands. She knew she could make him drop his weapon before he struck that last blow. She turned her head and watched the saber drop. Her hands burned, and she readied herself.

Another saber intercepted Rohen's. "Enough already! What do you think you are doing?" Jamu asked him.

Galen sucked in air as her lungs loosened. The red-hot rage subsided, and she could see Rohen's anger fade from his eyes as well. She let Jamu help her stand, and nodded when he asked if she was all right.

She did not know what to think. What in the world brought that on? What started out as a simple match almost turned deadly. What would have happened if Rohen had struck her?

She looked at the large crowd that had gathered as Jamu led her to the cabins. Her worry turned into fear when she saw Headmaster Humo. He had been watching, and so had Mage Terri. The whole Academy was going to know about this. Grateful that Jamu had stopped them before things spiraled out of control, she took his hand as they walked.

Humo relaxed his jaw as Galen walked off and Rohen led his cadets away. That was close. The Surian had no idea how close he had come to being killed.

He faced the crowd that had gathered. "Carry on, now. It was an exciting match, but that is all it was." He turned to Terra as everyone dispersed.

"Did you feel it?" he asked her quietly.

She nodded. "It almost broke through. Had she lost control..."

"She is dangerous. She must be watched." He waved his head for her to follow. "You will be responsible for doing that. If I see her fighting again with any of the wards, I will find a reason to expel her. And if that happens, you know what my next step will be."

To his surprise, Terra nodded in agreement. "For once we have arrived to the same conclusion. I will watch her closely."

Humo glanced at her, suspicious, but she seemed truly shaken. He could understand. That sudden flaring emanation would unnerve even the most stoic of the Draca.

Jania stood still as the crowd streamed past her. She could not believe what she had just seen. How could two people move so fast, strike so hard, even with wooden weapons, and not kill each other?

She noticed Ben and Jai standing nearby. She had been with Master Humo when the fight began, and when he realized it was not a regular spar, he had phased over to them. She did not have a phase spell in her head at the time, so she had to race out of Arcanum Tower on her own two feet. She had learned something on her way down; when a princess ran as fast as she could, others seemed compelled to follow.

She joined her classmates. "Did you see that?" she asked them.

"Only the part where Ro kicked Galen to the ground," Jai said. "He is such a bully!"

"There was much more to it than that, Jai." Jania looked at Ben. He was understandably upset. "Why don't we go check on her, Ben?"

"No. I don't know what I will do if I find a bruise on my sister," Ben said. "They will come to me once they are Healed and explain, and if it's not a good one, I'll...they just better have a good reason for fighting." Ben walked off.

Jania watched him go. She wondered what was going through his mind right then.

"He is still upset about the Caster thing," Jai said. "I think we should do something for him tonight."

"That's a good idea, Jai. Let's see what we can arrange."

"I can't believe Ro did this to you," Megan said. She pressed her hand gently against Galen's neck as she Healed the bruised muscles. Jamu held a cool wet cloth against her face.

"We were sparring, and it just became a little too intense," Galen replied.

Megan shook her head, but kept quiet as she turned to Galen's face. She couldn't help wincing as Jamu pulled the cloth away from her face. She had been trained never to show a reaction to the sight of a wound, but the fact that it was Rohen who had inflicted this on their sweet little Gayly was just too appalling.

"What did he hit you with?" Megan probed Galen's cheekbone with her fingers.

"I don't know," Galen said, squirming. "But it did not hurt as much as your fingers do now."

"I know. I'm sorry. There's nothing broken; that's good." She began to Heal.

"He hit her with the end of his sparring saber," Jamu said, squeezing Galen's shoulder. "Galen, what in the world got into the both of you?"

"I don't know. Rowy was angry because I beat him, and I was angry because he was angry."

"That makes no sense," Megan said. "Galen, you are starting to act too much like a boy."

Galen bit her lip as Megan took her hands away. "Is Rowy all right?" she asked.

"Worry about yourself right now," Jamu told her.

"Jesi is tending to him," Megan said. She was glad for once that Jesi was so eager to be around Rohen. Megan did not want to even look at his face right then. "Wait until Daddy finds out about this."

The door opened, and Rus came in. "Hello, Megan," he said

politely. "Is Galen all right?"

"She's as good as new." Megan stepped away and helped Galen off the stool she sat on. "Now you can go see Ro, since you seem so worried about him."

"I didn't say I wanted to see him," Galen replied with a frown.

"I don't think you have a choice," Rus said. "Mage Terri has summoned both of you to her office as soon as you are both fixed up."

Megan couldn't help feeling sorry for Galen. She took her hand. "It's all right. People spar all the time. You are both still walking. Why would you be in trouble?"

Galen nodded in agreement, but her face was pale.

Rohen sat hunched on the steps leading to his troop's cabin with his hand on his forehead.

He didn't know what felt worse, the guilt of lashing out at Galen in anger, or the worry that he might have hurt her. Why had he become so enraged? Galen did nothing wrong; a defeat by a junior cadet after a three year streak was stunning, and a bit humbling, but that was not something that would make him lose his temper. Especially not with fellow scouts. And especially not with his little firefly.

He heard the cabin door open behind him. "Rohen, are you all right?" Jesi asked.

Rohen moved aside. "I'm fine. You did a wonderful job with me. I am not even sore. Thank you."

"It wasn't much," she replied, sitting beside him. "I meant how are you inside?"

"That is not doing so well," he admitted. "I should not have done what I did."

"You did the right thing," Keran said, opening the door. "She had it coming. Can you imagine how swollen her head would have become if you had just walked away without showing her she was only lucky?"

"It was more than just luck," Rohen said, standing up to let Keran walk down. "I was careless. I deserved to be beaten." He ignored Jesi's hand on his arm.

Keran shook his head. "You are her sponsor. If everyone had not seen how mad you were at her, people might have believed you let her win. You did right."

"Galen is not defenseless. You both just got a little carried away," Jesi added, rubbing his arm.

Rohen inched away from Jesi's hand. "You are both great for wanting to support me, and I appreciate it. But I really need to be alone right now. I have to see Mage Terri soon." He sat back down on the step and lowered his head.

He let out a tiny sigh of relief as he heard them walk off. He glanced at Galen's cabin. He dreaded facing her, but he had to let her know he was sorry. He would wait for her to come out, and they would go see Terra together.

He had a good idea why Terra wanted to see them. He prayed she had an answer for what had happened. And he also prayed the answer would be a good one.

The door to Galen's cabin opened, and she walked out with Jamu. Rohen stood up and walked toward them, disappointed she was not alone.

They saw him approach and stopped to wait. Surprisingly, neither one seemed to be upset with him. Galen even gave him a tiny smile.

"Firefly, are you all right? I am so sorry; I don't know what got into me." He took her hand.

"It's all right, I am fine," Galen said, giving his hand a squeeze. "Rowy, I'm sorry I made you so angry."

"No, don't be. You did nothing wrong. In fact, you did a great thing. You secured top ranking for your troop. As your sponsor, I am so very proud of you."

"Not as proud as I am," Jamu said. "You are a hero, Gayly.

Now let us go. No need to keep a mage waiting."

Rohen's hopes that Jamu would stay behind were dashed as he took Galen's other hand and began walking. But Jamu couldn't hover around Galen forever. Sooner or later he would catch her alone and they could really talk about what happened.

"Why do you think Mage Terri wants to see us?" Galen asked him.

"It could be anything. She does not really have the power to reprimand us. I think she may want to know what exactly happened. There was quite an audience gathered." Twisting truth became easier and easier for him. He figured it was supposed to.

"Maybe she saw something more," Jamu said quietly.

Rohen gave him a sidelong glance. He trusted Jamu, but...

"More and more students are being sent to the Sanatorium because of psychic abilities they did not even know they had. The way you two fought each other was incredible; your moves and speed were amazing. She might suspect something." Jamu put his arm around Galen's shoulders as she gasped. "I am sorry. I did not mean to frighten you."

Rohen released Galen's hand as she pulled it away from him. "I seriously doubt that," he said. "Healer Stanis would be the one summoning us if that were the case." Why didn't Galen want to hold his hand?

Jamu lowered his head, and his voice. "What really happened between you two?"

"I honestly do not know," Rohen replied.

Galen shook her head. "Everyone believes that psychic abilities lead to violent insanity. Our behavior may have Mage Terri wondering about that."

"We will find out soon enough," Rohen said.

"Autis, is it usual for scouts to spar with such ferocity?" Terra asked the grizzly scout head.

"Not really," he replied. "Unless the opponents have some kind of grudge. Galen and Rohen get along famously, though." Autis seemed quite concerned about the incident. "The looks on their faces, it seemed as though they wanted to kill each other."

"Even the best of friends fight sometimes," Terra offered gently. She did not want Autis to come to any suspicious conclusion. With Stanis doing random psychic sweeps, this made for a very delicate situation.

"And they were both under a lot of pressure," Autis agreed. "Having the ranking of your troop resting on your shoulders after two days of trials can be hard." He cleared his throat. "But I did not come to see you about them."

"Oh. What is it, Autis?"

"Moreus is planning on sending all the graduating scouts to Trader's Pass for their first assignment, but the group will not have any experienced scouts leading them. They will have a regular infantry officer as their leader. You have first-hand knowledge of current events at Trader's Pass. Is there anything going on that I should know about, so I can train these kids properly?"

Moreus must have received direction from Humo. "This is the first I've heard of this."

"I apologize then. I must be overreacting to the importance of this."

"I am supposed to be made aware of any decision involving Trader's Pass. You have a good reason to inquire. Give me some time to find out what is going on, and I will let you know." She held her hand up as he opened his mouth to say something. "And I will not tell Moreus, either."

"Thank you, Mage Terri. One more thing. How can I get my hands on some vellum sheets?"

"Vellum?" Terra's ears perked up. "What for?"

"Moreus asked me to bring him some."

There was a knock on the door. "Come in," Terra called out. She was not sure how she was going to handle this. Rohen knew about the Draca, but she had doubts about Galen. However, Ben did know, and Semino had marked her. She had to know something. She smiled at them as they walked inside.

"That was some spar," she said cheerfully, hoping to put them at ease.

They stood before her desk, staring. They knew not to be taken in by a light tone.

"I will take my leave now," Autis said. "It was a pleasure speaking with you, Mage Terri. I will see you two back at Espies." Rohen and Galen both winced as he closed the door behind him.

"You can ask Mage Les for the vellum," Terra called out after him. She turned to the two young scouts in front of her. "Don't worry about him. He was here for other reasons. I am the one who wants to talk about your little tiff today."

"It was only a spar," Rohen said.

"We just got a little carried away," Galen added.

"You want to believe that, don't you?"

"I would love to believe that, yes," Rohen said, crossing his arms. The sudden change in his tone made Galen start. "But it is obviously wrong. What happened out there, Terra?"

"Rowy!" Galen cried out.

"It's all right, Galen. I don't mind him speaking candidly. Please sit; this may be quite shocking to you. You too, Rohen." Terra waited until they were seated before continuing. "You both have a talent that allows you to tap into a rare kind of power."

"Are you talking about psychic talents?" Rohen asked. Galen gave him a fearful look this time.

"No," Terra said. She hoped Galen wouldn't sick up. She looked a bit green. "This is different. Galen, I know about you and Semino. He is a friend of mine."

Galen's face went from green to white. "I know. But…" She looked at Rohen.

"Rohen is like you. He is marked, too. You don't have to keep your secret from him," Terra said.

Galen hugged her middle and rocked back and forth in her seat.

"Galen, Rohen, I am here to help you. I must warn you about what happened out there. You both have a power within you that could flare out of control if you confront each other in anger. You must not let that happen. Terrible things could happen if it did."

"I promise, it will not happen again," Galen said. "May I be excused now?"

Terra couldn't blame the poor girl for being terrified, but she had to face this. "Galen, you don't have to hide anything from me. Please let me explain what happened to you and Rohen."

Galen shook her head. "Semino…"

"It's all right, Firefly. You don't have to say or listen to anything if you don't want to," Rohen said. "Terra, what do we do to keep this from happening again?"

"You must not get angry with each other. Small quarrels are harmless, but if it leads to a true fight…"

The two young necare exchanged a worried look.

"Just keep a good grip on your temper, and be aware of your emotions when you are together," Terra continued. "Anger is the trigger to your power. Is this the first time it has happened?"

They both nodded. "Don't spar anymore. And if you get in an argument, walk away from each other. That should suffice."

"All right," Galen said, jumping to her feet. "Can we go now?"

"There is much more I think we should talk about."

"No. Please, I don't want to know any more." Galen took a step back. Her face was green again. Terra knew she was going to do more harm than good by forcing her to listen.

"All right. But if either of you need someone to talk to, I am here. Please remember that, especially you, Galen."

She nodded, but did not look at her. Terra watched as Rohen followed her out the door.

She dropped her head on her desk once the door closed. What would Humo have done had he realized that Galen was not the one who had almost lost control? And how long before he realized that he had two necare at his Academy?

"Firefly, you don't have to do or say anything you don't want to. You know that, right?" Rohen asked as they walked down the stairs. He knew how she felt.

She nodded.

"But she does have a point. There is much we need to know. What we are—"

"We are a couple of Espies students. That is all," Galen interrupted.

"Galen, please, let's go somewhere and talk about this. I am as upset as you are."

"No." She stopped at the landing leading to the entry hall. "Not yet. This is something no one was supposed to know."

"You can trust me." He prayed she would believe him.

"I know that," she said as they crossed the hall. It was surprisingly empty for late afternoon. "But right now I feel I should not be with you."

He didn't feel that way. He did not want to leave her side. "Jamu showed me this little patio behind Espies. The one you discovered while you were both practicing in the wood."

"He told you about that?"

"He did. I will be there tonight. If you change your mind and would like to talk, you know where to find me." He opened the door for her, but held her arm before she could dash down the steps. "And don't be afraid, because I will protect you."

"Thank you, Rowy, but I don't think you would be able to." Her eyes seemed to cloud over. She pulled her arm free and ran over to where Jamu waited for her at the bottom of the steps.

Rohen watched them walk away together. He did not like the way Jamu put his arm around her shoulders. Jamu was her troop leader, but there was no reason for Galen to trust Jamu more than she trusted him. And since she really was one of the eight that Vitalia had told him about, they were going to have to stick very close together.

Humo sealed the last of the numerous order requisitions and pushed them into the basket on the floor beside his desk for Elin to pick up in the morning. He reached over to snuff out his candles—candlelight was much more soothing than the harsh globelights the mages loved to use around here—but hesitated as he felt something not quite right. Sure enough, Animis appeared before him, looking angry enough to kill and holding a piece of torn vellum in his hand.

"What now, Animis?" Humo asked, pretending to be annoyed. He knew why Animis was there, the shredded vellum the blue dragon held said everything.

"You tried to kill my ward!" Animis slammed the vellum down on Humo's desk.

Humo found his fellow dragon's rage quite funny. It was so unlike Animis not to think things thoroughly and rationally. "And if I did?"

Animis snarled and lunged forward, but stopped as Humo jumped to his feet.

"Good to see you have some speck of self control," Humo said.

"Why? Why would you attack her?" Animis looked close to losing control once again.

"Calm down, you are beginning to act like Semino. First of all, she is not your ward, so it is inappropriate of you to even react this way. Why you have yet to mark her is beyond me."

"It is her choice. I will mark her when she is ready."

"You won't get to mark her at all if Abeo gets to her first. Although I find it quite odd that he has not shown the least amount of interest in her. Could it be that maybe she is not the one?

Maybe Abeo knows something you don't?"

"If that is how you feel then why did you try to kill her?"

"That is my second point. I did not have her traveling group attacked. Whatever you may have found out," he pointed at the piece of scrap, which floated over to his wastebasket on the opposite side of his letter basket and fell in. "I did not plan or expect that to happen. And I am rather upset that it did occur."

Animis seemed skeptical. "Do I have your word on that?"

"I may be deceitful at times, but I do not directly lie to my Draca brethren, as odious as they may behave," Humo snapped. "You have my word as an Earth Dragon. Now get out of here."

"No. Tell me about the armies."

"What armies?" Humo smiled.

"Tell me, or I'll—"

"You will what? Destroy them? Kill them all? Something about not getting directly involved with the affairs of humans comes to mind."

"Fine. But you had better warn your precious Adfligere. Because the moment I find out who he is will be the last moment of his life." Animis smoothed his hair back and adjusted his hair tie, glaring at Humo as he waited for a reaction.

Humo only sat back in his seat. He would not give Animis the satisfaction. "Yes, well I suppose you could just kill him. Funny how the Pact will not allow you to stop an army from razing a village, but you can slay a single human for no better reason than just being annoyed. Whoever created this Pact was not an Earth Dragon, that is a certainty. So, are you officially back in Syntrea? If so, I can have Healer Stanis send you a nice bottle of raspberry wine. It does a wonderful job in calming the nerves."

"I'm not back. I have matters to attend to elsewhere." Animis tugged at the brooch holding his silly blue cape and disappeared.

"Go attend to your matters, Animis," Humo said cheerfully. "Go ahead and abandon your precious little princess. She is at such an impressionable age. But worry not, I will be more than happy to take her off your claws while you fly about chasing torn up pieces of paper." Humo snuffed out his lamp with a happy little flourish.

Galen stirred absently at her chowder, thinking about what Mage Terri had said. Jamu and the rest of her troopmates sat with her in the dining hall. They gloated about their win, but she ignored them. Questions were beginning to form.

"Gayly, you need to eat," Jamu said gently. "If you did not get into any trouble, why are you so upset?"

"I just wish I had never asked you to let me spar with Rowy," she replied. She hoped she had not hurt Rohen's feelings when she told him she did not want to be with him.

"We would have lost our rank if you hadn't," Rus said. "Why do you feel that way?"

"I don't like to fight with Rowy." She hoped that would suffice.

"Ro fights with Megan all the time, but they still love each other very much. It is not wrong to be angry with loved ones once in a while," Jamu said.

Galen pushed her bowl away with a sigh. "I'm going to see if I can find Ben, if that's all right with you."

"Fine, but you must eat something before you go to bed," Jamu told her.

Galen nodded and left the dining hall. Ben would understand what she was going through. She hoped Ben would be in his room. She needed to be with her brother.

He was not there. After knocking for the fourth time, she headed back outside, disappointed.

She walked slowly, her head down, letting her feet take her where they would. She felt horrible. She had to get her mind off this mess. What could she do?

She tried to keep Rohen out of her mind, but her thoughts kept coming back to him. He would be able to answer some of her questions. He seemed to trust Terra, and Galen knew she could trust him. He always knew how to make her feel better, too. He was as much a brother to her as Ben was.

She reached the Espies Wood. She should not have rebuffed him the way she did. He was probably as shocked and terrified as she. But he would never show it because he would want to protect her feelings. She suddenly wanted very much to be near him. She moved faster, but kept quiet.

She heard Rohen talking to someone as she approached. She stopped, curious. Jesi's voice drifted back to her.

She scooted up a tree and silently made her way over to peek. Did Jesi find Rohen here, or did he bring her? She smiled. Megan would probably blow a hole through Uncle Bilin's roof if she found out about this. Did he bring her here to...?

It seemed so. Daylight was fading, but she could still see the patio clearly. Rohen sat on the ground with Jesi on his lap and both his arms around her. They talked quietly, but their faces were so close together that they could whisper and still hear each other clearly.

"Are you sure no one will find us here?" Jesi asked him.

"I am sure," Rohen replied. "Galen might come, but I doubt it. She was very upset."

Galen settled herself down on the branch. She felt a fleeting sense of guilt, but dismissed it. Espies Wood was for spying, and nothing was sacred. Rohen knew that very well.

She watched Rohen and Jesi carry on for a while, wondering how far Jesi would let him go. Surprisingly, Rohen stopped and tried to stand up just when the kissing started to get heavy.

"No! Don't stop," Jesi begged.

"I think we should, before..." Rohen stopped as Jesi grabbed his belt and pulled him down to his knees. He tried to push her away, but she grabbed his head and pressed her face against his. After a while he stopped trying to get away and kept kissing her.

Somehow Jesi managed to pull his shirt off over his head.

Galen snuck away. She was not sure whether to be relieved that Rohen did not seem worried about the day's events, or upset because he had not given her a chance to show up.

She decided to be relieved. She had too many other things to be upset about. She had not even had a chance to get over Ben's revelation, and now Rohen, too, had a dragon watching over him. Why hadn't Semino told her about them? She was certain he had known. All this time she thought she was all alone with this secret. It was relieving to know she was not alone, but now she had to guard the secret of two others.

She heard a whizzing sound and jumped to the side. Something smashed into the tree beside her. She switched to her nightvision and looked around. Two figures stood nearby in the trees, one of them holding what looked like a sling.

"You missed." Why did they have to bother her now?

"You are not going to get away with what you did to Ro," Keran said. "I know you tricked him. He is too good to be beaten by you. I won't let my troop leader's reputation be ruined by some girl!"

"Worry about your own reputation, what little you have," she replied.

"You know, it's time someone fixed that mouth of yours," Sprit said. He took one step toward her, but Keran held him back.

"Beating a female is shameful and cowardly," Keran told him.

Galen felt her face heat up. "And trying to stone one while hiding is not? I think you are just afraid to fight me, Keran. Afraid of a female, now I think that would be the ultimate shame for a Sevilan."

"Why don't we get some sparring sabers out so I can show you how afraid of you I am?"

"Why don't we?" If she could hold her own with Rohen, Keran would be no trouble at all.

"Because I am telling you both not to." Jamu's deep voice

made all three of them jump. She felt a hand fall on her shoulder.

"Come with me, Galen. You are restricted to your cabin for the rest of the evening for trying to incite a fight," Jamu continued. "You two find something else to do." He led Galen away.

Galen chewed on her lip. What else was going to happen to her before the end of the day?

"I think you have had enough of an eventful day." Jamu gave her shoulder a squeeze.

She didn't answer him.

"I had forgotten that Ben would be out this evening, so I went to look for you to let you know." His hand slid down her arm and took hers. "I had a feeling I would find you roaming around here."

Galen rubbed at her eyes. She tried not to, but by the time they reached the cabin, she was crying hard.

"I'm sorry," she sobbed as Jamu closed the door behind them. "I'm sorry I'm being such a baby."

"That is all right. You can cry all you want," Jamu replied. He sat down on his bed. "I understand."

His words set off a flood of pent-up anguish. She sat down beside him and cried long and hard. He put his arm around her as she wept.

"You know, in my country, 'baby' is an endearing term, not a teasing name for someone who is crying," Jamu said when she finally began to calm down.

"So what do you call people who cry a lot?" she asked, wiping her face with her sleeve.

"We call them by their name, and ask them what is wrong, and if there is anything we can do to help," he answered, glancing at the window. Voices could be heard from outside. "Let us go somewhere where we can be alone."

"I'm restricted, remember?"

"I will have to sneak you out, then." He winked and grabbed a bag on the bench. "Would you like that?"

"Yes!"

Jamu opened the window, and they both slipped out unseen.

Follow me, Jamu signaled, running off into the dark. Galen chased him. They made their way through the woods, behind the library and around to the back of the Academy Tower. They climbed up the outer wall with their bare hands and through one of the windows.

"Is this your room?" she asked him.

"It is." He lit a lamp, and she shielded her eyes from the sudden glare. She looked around as her eyes adjusted.

"Your bed is so different from Ben's," she said. It was set directly on the floor, covered by a fluffy quilt with soft cushions and blankets piled on top. There was a smaller one in front of the fireplace.

"I had my sister send me these," Jamu replied. "Along with some other things from home."

Scrolls hung from the walls. A strange teapot decorated the mantle, along with five cups. Galen walked over to a varnished sword stand and ran her finger along the silk-wrapped scabbard it held. "If I had a room like this I would never go back to the cabins."

"I cannot let myself become spoiled, and I have to keep an eye on all of you," Jamu said. "Sleeping here reminds me where I came from. Sleeping at Espies reminds me why I am here. And sleeping outside during field training reminds me how much I love sleeping here."

Galen kicked her boots off and jumped on the bed. "So nice and soft."

"Here." Jamu threw his bag at her. "There is some food in the bag. Eat while I get a fire going."

Pulling out a sausage wrapped in bread, she climbed off the bed and sat down on the floor. She watched him work on the fire while she ate. She suddenly felt so much better.

"I thought you were going to spend the evening with Jai," she said.

"The fifth-year mages are planning something for Ben tonight, to make him feel better about being turned down by the Casters," Jamu replied.

"Oh." So that was why Ben was not in his room.

"Would you like to talk about it?" Jamu asked as he placed pieces of burning straw carefully onto the splintered log.

She did, very much. "I can't."

Jamu nodded. He seemed to understand. "Then tell me how you feel."

She looked at the piece of sausage she had left. "I am afraid." She did not feel like finishing it.

"There is no reason for you to feel afraid here," he replied, standing up. "Nothing can get to you in here."

She tossed the sausage into the growing fire. "I'm afraid of something happening."

"Anything in particular?"

"No."

"Do not be afraid." He found a washcloth and wet it. Galen let him wash her face and hands.

"My sisters would always come to my room when they were sad or upset. A week would not pass when I would not enter my room and find one of them asleep on my bed, with their faces dirty and wet from crying. They would never tell me why they were upset, either." He pulled one of the blankets off his bed and wrapped it around her. "When I would ask them why they always ended up in my room, they both told me that they felt safe being there."

Safe. "I understand what they meant. I feel safe here with you."

His blue eyes twinkled in the firelight. "Then there is no reason for you to be afraid."

"No, there isn't."

Jamu sat down next to her. Galen put her head on his lap and closed her eyes. The crackle of the fire and his hand stroking her head soon put her to sleep.

The wine Nelsen had managed to get was as sweet as fruit juice. Jania set her cup down carefully. The table was playing games with her. It kept moving up and down. She yawned, and the room began to tilt. How much wine did she drink?

Hedi's voice cleared her head somewhat. "Ben, you still need to allow your mind to accept what has happened."

"You have no idea how right you are," Ben mumbled to her. He looked a bit tired, but it was impossible to tell that he had finished two pitchers of wine and was working on a third.

"Well, I'm glad we are not losing you, Ben," Jai said. Jania noticed she had a hard time setting her cup down, too.

"We stand behind you in whatever decision you make, Ben," Seth slurred. "Don't we, guys?"

"Ben, are you sure you want to give up your dream?" Jania asked him. She could not understand why he would change his mind so quickly. He wanted so much to join the Casters. "Don't quit because you see it as a losing battle."

"You think I'm a quitter?" Ben asked her. He sounded hurt.

"Of course not. But you are acting as if someone has talked you out of it. Did Mage Terri tell you something?"

"She told me many things, but she didn't talk me out of anything."

"So why the sudden turnaround? Ben, I know you are upset, but—"

"You have no idea how I feel," Ben shouted. He tried to stand up, but thought better of it. "You have no idea what I've been through, or why I wanted to join the Casters, or anything like that!"

Jania decided not to say anything. Silence had always been a good tool for her.

Ben stared at her for a long time. The room seemed to turn behind him.

"Ever since I was a little boy, I have had to hide how I feel, keep it down, keep it under control," Ben finally said. "My mother taught me all these tricks on how to keep my anger and fear hidden inside me. I grew up never showing anyone I was anything more than annoyed or nervous, or maybe a little sad. Even when the Eastern armies came and took my home and my family away from me. My world came to an end, and I never even cried, except for the time a soldier beat me to make me tell him where Galen was. I cried, but I never told him anything. And I never even tried to fight back."

The room stopped spinning. Jania stood quiet. She had nothing to say anyway.

"I hated them for what they did, and I felt guilty because I hated them. So I told myself there was no need for me to hate them, because I was going to harm them ten times more than they had harmed me. And I was going to do that by fighting. I was going to join Gladia, and I was going to lead the army that would destroy the East.

"Then Mage Terri pulls me away from my dream and tells me I must become a mage. I almost panicked, but then Ro made me realize that it was all right. I was not losing my dream; I only had to go about it another way. I knew mages went to war. So I learned about the Casters, and what they wanted in their recruits. And I began to prepare. I will be eternally grateful to Mage Terri for dragging me to the owl banner, but Arcanum was just a path to reach the Casters."

"So that is why you lift those stone weights," Jai said.

"Right. I have worked all these years to be the perfect candidate. And now my dream is dashed again, because someone..." Ben paused. He seemed to arrive at some kind of realization. "Someone had the authority to make a decision affecting my life," he finished slowly.

Jania frowned at the wine. The room was shaking this time. She should have known better than to trust Nelsen to get some decent wine.

"You know, I was never good at anything," Ben said. "And my sister was good at everything. She shot her first rabbit when she was four. I never did. She learned how to ride in two days. It took me months to get comfortable on a horse. Galen and I learned how to read together. She was five and I was eight. I was capable of helping the metalsmith and working on sword drills with my father, but I can't say I was good. But I am good at spell-casting."

"Then be the greatest mage in history," Jai said. "Forget about avenging your home and family. In a way, Galen has already done so."

"You don't understand, Jai. If I do that, the hate will come back. Already it hovers, deep inside me." Ben took his cup and threw it against the wall.

Jania jumped as the ceramic cup shattered. She looked at Ben's angry face. "That felt good, didn't it?" she asked him.

"It did." Ben looked at the wall. The polished wood panel covering the wall was splintered. "I want to do it again."

"That is what you need, Ben, to let out all your frustrations," Nelsen said. "Father Cin's old church near Druid Bilin's cottage is empty now that he has moved into the new Monastery. I'm sure we can find some things for you to throw over there."

"But that's a holy place," Ben protested as Nelsen pulled him to his feet.

"Not anymore," Nelsen said, holding on to Ben to keep himself from falling. "It's just an empty building. Who wants to join us?"

"I wouldn't miss it," Jania said, getting up very carefully. At least the room was not shaking anymore.

Galen knelt beside Jamu's bed in the dim light of dawn, watching him sleep.

She stared at his lips, wondering what it would be like to kiss them. She wanted to, but she knew he would wake up if she tried.

She did not want to leave him, but she knew they could both get into trouble if anyone saw her leaving his room in the morning. She remembered the fight he had with Anton the year before. She would not do anything to shame him.

She felt an ache in her chest. Jamu would never see her as anything other than one of his troops, or maybe a little sister. That was too bad, because she would never look at Jamu in the same way again.

She was ashamed. Feeling the way she did would only bring trouble for both of them. But her feelings were her own, and no one needed to know. What was one more secret? She touched her lips, stood up and left his room through the window he had left open.

11

Morning

Galen found Rohen perched on the roof of his troop's cabin. It did not surprise her to see him there; he always woke up very early. She climbed up the cabin wall to join him.

"Good morning, Firefly," he said as she sat beside him. He stared eastward.

"Are you all right?" Galen asked him. He seemed upset.

"Sure," he said. "I'm a bit sorry you never showed up last night, though."

"I did. You were busy."

He looked at her, his eyes big. "How much did you see?"

"I left when she began taking your clothes off."

His face turned crimson. Galen was a bit surprised; she did not expect him to be embarrassed by something like that. Why would he have taken her to the woods otherwise?

"I wish you would have interrupted us."

Galen giggled. "I didn't think any boy would ever say something like that." She stopped laughing at the look on his face. "Did something happen?" she asked.

"Things did not go the way I expected them to," Rohen answered.

"Did she make you stop?"

"No. Quite the opposite."

Galen frowned as she thought about what he had just said. "And you are upset about that?"

"Yes! I did not mean to take things so far, especially in the woods where anyone could have seen us. Now she will never leave me alone, and she probably thinks we are a couple." His face grew even redder. "Where have you been? It is kind of early for you to be up and about."

"I slept in Jamu's room."

"You spent the night with Jamu?"

"Yes. No! Not in that way! He knew I had a bad day and wanted to cheer me up. He gave me something to eat and let me sleep in that little bed he has in front of his fireplace." Her stomach fluttered as she remembered him stroking her hair.

Rohen put his arm around her. "I was not there for you when you needed me. I am so sorry."

"Don't be. It's all right, really." She turned her head away so he couldn't see her smile.

"Do you think you could ever be angry enough to kill me?" Rohen asked.

Galen gave a start at his question. "No. Never."

"I think if you were about to strike me down, I would let you. I don't think I could ever hurt you."

"You sure didn't feel that way yesterday."

"Yes, well, I will know better the next time we have a fight."

"I don't want a next time to happen." Galen sighed. "What do you think Uncle Bilin is going to do to us?"

"We can worry about Papa's punishment once he gives it to us." Rays of light began to shoot up from behind the trees. "Right now let's just watch the sun come up."

Galen took his hand as they watched the sun rise. She could feel the pulse in his head, just like Ben's. "Concentrate on my hand. Can you feel it?" she asked him.

He nodded. "How did you learn to do that?" he asked.

She only smiled and looked back at the sky.

Ben groaned and sat up. He looked around, trying to remember where he was.

It took him some time to recognize the Winter Room. Jania, Hedi, and Jai were on the floor, all asleep. He glanced over at the pitchers and mugs on one of the desks.

"Did we really drink that much?" he asked himself out loud.

His voice seemed to make the whole tower shake. He sat very still, waiting for the buzzing in his head to subside.

The girls stirred, and Jania sat up. "I feel terrible," she whispered. "What the hell am I doing here?"

"Where are Nelsen and Seth?" Ben asked.

Hedi whimpered. "Don't talk so loud," she whined. "I think we left them at the church."

"Did we really go there last night?" Jai whispered.

"We sure did." Ben looked at his rumpled clothes. His throat cried out for water. He ran his hands through his hair. The girls would never stop teasing him, looking the way he did. He combed the tangles out of the lock of hair at the nape of his neck, hoping they weren't staring at him.

They were. "Your mage's tail is growing in nicely," Jania said.

The compliment made him feel better. He was proud that he was finally allowed to grow the tail now that he was a fifth-year student, but to know that it looked nice on him felt good. It was especially good that Jania liked it.

Jania was looking at him. His heart almost stopped. What she must think, seeing him all rumpled and sleepy! He must look a sight. He jumped off the couch and over the three girls.

"Would you like to do something after classes today?" Jania asked.

"No. I need some time to myself," he called out behind him as he ran out of the room. He had to get himself presentable and ready for class, before he was late.

Jania watched him run out. After all the talking they had done last night, she had sworn he was finally warming up to her. She was obviously wrong. She punched the carpet in frustration. "All the fun we had at the church, and all the talking, and he runs out of here like we're a bunch of strangers. What the hell do I do to get him to like me?" she cried out. Hedi whimpered again.

"You know, combing your hair, washing your face, and putting on some clean fresh clothes might help," Jai remarked.

Jania looked down at herself, and gave out a whimper of her own.

Keran climbed out of his cabin window and dashed into the woods.

It annoyed him that he would have to take the long way around to Somatica, but Rohen and Galen were on the roof, able to see half of the Academy grounds. They were the last two people he wanted spotting him.

What the hell was Galen doing there with Rohen anyway? She was supposed to be restricted. He toyed with the idea of telling Jamu, but that would mean explaining how he saw her in the first place. He wanted to keep this trip a secret.

He reached Somatica and made his way to the student's quarters. The covered walkways and numerous plants provided many places to hide, and he knew exactly where he was going.

He had been watching Megan for months. He knew her schedule, her free times, and what time she liked to go to bed. He even knew when she would sneak out of her room to meet Yar. He knew this was not a good thing to do, but he just could not help himself. She was the most fascinating female he had ever met.

He could not even think of a word to describe her. Wild was

the closest he could come to it. Everything about her, down to her long red hair, had such an untamed quality. Some of the things she did were frightening, and seemed to border on insanity at times. But her kindness shone through her uninhibited behavior so strongly that it was impossible not to like her.

He wished she would like him. Ever since his fight with Galen last year she had avoided him, even though she knew that he had been punished rather harshly. Rohen had even struck his name from the potential leadership list. Keran would never be a troop leader at Espies. Sure, Rohen had talked Jamu into doing the same for Galen, but that punishment was lost on her. No one would make a girl a troop leader, no matter how high her ranking score was.

None of that mattered to Megan, though. She saw Keran as a bullying oaf, and she had made sure he knew how she felt. But that had been almost a year ago. She must have mellowed after all that time. He would find out soon enough.

He reached her window and tapped on it softly. He waited.

It did not take long for her head to poke out. "Yar?" she asked.

"It's Keran," he whispered back.

Megan blinked sleepily at him. "What are you doing here?"

"I need to talk to you."

"No, you don't." Her dark eyes grew angry. "Now go away and let me get some sleep."

"Megan, please. I know you don't like me, but I really do need your help."

Her expression changed. Keran figured that would make her listen. He had never seen Megan turn someone away who needed her help.

"All right, talk," she ordered, folding her arms on the window-sill.

"You have to teach me how to control spiritual magic. Some-times things happen, and I'm afraid someone will think I am psychic."

"Keran, no one confuses psychic abilities with spiritual magic."

"Not yet. But you never know. Besides, what if I hurt someone by mistake?"

Megan stared at him thoughtfully. Keran waited patiently. He knew Megan wouldn't turn him down.

"All right, but on one condition. Leave Galen alone. Stop making her life miserable."

Did Megan forget who it was who humiliated her brother the day before? "I don't make her life miserable, and I have been staying away from her." Why did everyone have to defend her?

"Promise me you will not pick on her anymore."

He did not pick on Galen. She brought everything upon herself. "I promise."

It made him feel better to see her smile at him. "All right. Meet me at the north gate after classes today."

Jamu rolled onto his back and opened his eyes.

The sun shone brightly outside his window. He enjoyed the warm rays on his face for a moment before he remembered what had happened last evening. He sat up quickly, looking for Galen. He had meant to wake up much earlier. It would not look good if anyone saw her walking out of his room.

She was gone. Jamu sighed in relief and let his head fall back on his pillow.

He was so proud of her. Her fighting skills with the saber were awesome. Her speed was astounding, and her hits were sure and strong. The rest of her scouting skills were just as good. She was the best cadet at Espies right now, in his opinion.

He was going to have to think of a nice reward for her. She saved his troop from losing rank. She certainly deserved it.

He rolled out of bed. He would ask Jai what would be a good gift for Galen. She would probably have some good ideas. Jai was very smart.

Terra hurried up the stairs. She had left her scrolls in her study, and she needed them for her morning class. She opened her door, and froze.

She found Humo sitting at her desk, holding something. He looked up at her and cocked an eyebrow. Terra almost growled when she realized he held the paper Vitalia had given her.

Humo smiled at her. Terra crossed her arms and waited.

"Did you forget something?"

"My scrolls." She walked up to her desk and picked up the cases she had come for.

"I see. People forget things when they have too much on their minds. You seem to have plenty to worry about, too. Moreus was concerned when his scout head told him that he was unable to obtain the vellum he requested. It seems Autis had asked you where he could get it, and you neglected to inform him."

That damn vellum. "Autis did not hear me call out to him after he left."

Humo stood up. "It is not like you to be so forgetful. I think I have placed too much on your shoulders. I am relieving you of responsibility for the Mage's Guild at Trader's Pass. Deia can take over for you. Focus on your students. And stop worrying so much. Look, you are even collecting useless garbage." He held up the page in his hand.

Terra watched as it vanished in a puff of smoke. "I think you are overreacting."

"Right," he said, pushing past her and out the door.

12

A Concert and a Fire Spell

Jania cast a quick sideways glance at Ben as she flipped through the pages of her script. It had been almost two months since their drinking binge in the winter room, and things seemed to be getting worse between them. Their conversations when they were alone were always short and awkward, and Ben seemed to go out of his way to avoid her lately. At times Jania wanted to send him to hell and forget that he even existed. And yet...she thought of the beautiful water globe he had given her. *I won't give up on him. I might not be able to win his heart, but I will not lose him as a friend.* Her page skimming roughened.

Mage Mitzi mistook her frustration for something else. "So you disagree with what Nelsen says, Jania?"

Jania quickly tried to remember what it was they were talking about. "When do I ever agree with him?" The laughter brought her some time. *Yes, about whether we should strive to constantly improve and change civilizations and governments even though they are effective. Nelsen doesn't seem to think so.*

"All past civilizations that we know about have ended badly," she began, wondering how she was going to set her point effectively. Her mind was not on philosophy today. "We need to always respond to the needs and wants of the people, and if that means changing the way we govern them, then so be it. If they are not happy, they will not contribute to society. If they don't get what they need to live, they will focus their energies on getting what they need to survive. And if they are neither happy nor can get what they need to live, they will revolt."

"You don't know what you're talking about," Nelsen said. "If people are perfectly happy, they will not try to improve their lot in life. They will stagnate. The best works of art were during times people were not happy."

"Oh, Heavens, let's not make our people happy! We'll never get any good new art."

Nelsen glared at her as the rest of the class laughed. She was relieved to hear Ben chuckle, too. "Just what Syntrea needs, a funny future Queen. What are you going to do when your people come revolting at the gates to your castle because you decided to 'improve' something that worked well for them and ruined all their lives? Make them laugh until they forget what they were doing there in the first place?"

Their argument continued, but Jania's mind was only half in it. The other half was trying to figure out how to get closer to Ben.

"I really don't think he is avoiding you," Jai told Jania.

"Ben living over at the Tower doesn't make it easy for you two to just bump into each other during our free time," Hedi said, shaking the water globe to make the flakes flutter around. "And you don't have much in common. I mean, how much more different can you get than a Princess-Heir and an orphaned village boy?"

"It sounds just like one of those old classic love stories," Jai said dreamily, dropping onto Jania's desk chair in a mock faint.

"I'm not in love with him," Jania snapped at her, blushing. "I just want to be his friend."

Hedi and Jai looked at each other and laughed. Jania gave them a furious look.

"You're only fooling yourself, Princess," Jai said. "But let's say you just want to spend time with a friend." Hedi gave a most unladylike snort at her remark. "Find something you two have in common."

"What could we possibly have in common?" Jania asked.

"You are both fifth-year mage students, yes?" Jai picked up Jania's script from the desk. "You share a desk in philosophy class, yes?" She waved the leather bound sheath of pages in the air. "You both need to finish reading this by the end of the weekend, yes? You two have much in common." She tossed the manuscript up in the air and wiggled her fingers. "Ka!"

The manuscript erupted into a tiny fireball and a puff of smoke. As Jania and Hedi gasped, ashes floated to the floor, much like the flakes in the water globe.

"Jai, how could you do something like that?" Jania was appalled. Books were practically sacred; burning one, to her, was akin to murder.

"What a shame, me and my crazy fire spells. Now I've gone and burned your script," Jai said lightly. "You're going to have to make another copy. Now where can you get a copy from?"

Hedi stared at the ashes on the floor in disbelief.

"Hedi and I are going to Syntrea tonight for the weekend. That Oracle band is performing tomorrow," Jai said. "And you always had trouble understanding our handwriting, anyway. I wonder who would be able to help you out. Oh, wait, what about that nice boy who sits next to you in philosophy class? Doesn't he owe you a favor?"

"I wanted to go to that concert," Jania grated. "You've gone too far, Jai. What if Ben is planning to go?"

"He's not. I spoke with Jamu earlier today. Jamu is bringing Galen with us because Ben has a bad cold."

"Great, now I'll probably get sick on top of that," Jania muttered. She kicked over her chair, sending Jai sprawling to the floor. "Pray that your plan will work, or else I'm taking your script for myself!"

It took her three tries before she could finally gather the courage to knock on the door. She knocked four times, and waited.

This is madness. I shouldn't be bothering him if he's sick. But he looked fine during class. Besides, I need to get that manuscript done. She shifted from foot to foot, half of her wanting to run off, half of her looking forward to seeing him. Damn Jai! She really got me into a hole this time. Ben, please come to the door already.

The door swung open without warning. Jania took a step back, startled. Ben's sleepy face squinted at her. "Jania?"

"Oh, Ben, you really are sick," she said, disappointed. He looked terrible. His eyes had dark circles underneath them, and he looked even paler than usual, except for his nose, which was bright red. He had not looked sick earlier that day.

"So the word is out," he replied, rubbing his eyes.

"Jai was talking to Jamu, and..." she stopped herself to keep from rambling on. "Ben, I need your help. Jai burned up my manuscript with one of her stupid fire spells." Her words came stumbling out as he gave her a shocked look. "I need to make another one, and I need a copy. I can't use Jai's or Hedi's because their handwriting is so lousy, and they went to that concert, and I know your handwriting is very neat and pretty, so I thought I would ask you to lend me yours and maybe help me with the copy, but you're sick, so I guess..."

She did it. She just had to ramble on. Promising herself a good pinch once she got back to her room, she lowered her head and stared at the floor. "Can I please borrow your copy? I'll bring it back as soon as I'm done, and I won't bother you anymore, I prom..."

"I'll help you," he said before she could finish her sentence. "I don't…" a coughing fit interrupted him.

Stunned, and a little excited, she shook her head. "You should rest. I'll get this copy done in plenty of time." She hoped she sounded like she meant it.

"It took us three days to finish our scripts. Working together, we can finish it by this evening. And I only have a cold. Sitting down at the library won't hurt me any." He cleared his throat. "I didn't want to go to that concert anyway. The cold was a perfect excuse. Besides, being with you is much better than listening to a bunch of bards." He realized what he had said, and the rest of his face became as red as his nose. "That did not come out the way I wanted it to," he said.

Jania smiled. "No, I like the way you said it." The butterflies inside her began to settle down. "But I don't think Old Cow will let you in the library if she feels you are going to be sneezing and coughing all over her books."

Ben made a face to show what his feelings for the librarian were. "We'll go to the philosophy classroom. We won't be bothered there, and everybody's gone. Wait." He gave her a worried look. "You will probably catch my cold if I help you."

"If I get sick, then I get sick. Getting this copy done is more important than a cold." I'll make sure Jai catches it, too, if I do. "When can you meet me there?"

"We can go now, if you want. I need to change, though." He suddenly looked uncomfortable.

Jania looked him over. He wore a white cotton shirt and loose pants. They seemed to be made out of silk. "You look fine, Ben."

"Well, at least let me brush my hair."

"Ben, I said you look fine. This is not a date."

His face flared red once more. Jania felt her own face heat up. "I didn't mean to embarrass you, Ben. I'm sorry."

"No, you're right. I'm being silly." He smiled at her sheepishly. "Let me go get my things. I need to drink something, too. I'll be ready as soon as I can."

"Take your time. I need to get a few things together. I'll meet you in the classroom. Thanks, Ben."

"Sure," he said, closing the door.

Jania managed not to skip as she made her way back to Arcanum. Halfway there, she stopped, turned, and headed toward Somatica. It was very kind of Ben to offer his help. The least she could do was get him something for his cold.

Ben walked calmly up the tower stairs, keeping his excitement under a tight leash. He couldn't believe his luck. Spending a whole afternoon with Jania! Too bad he had a cold, but he wouldn't have even been around if he had been well. Funny how things worked out.

He stopped before the door to Mage Mitzi's classroom. He patted the pouch tied at his waist, stuffed full of soft cloth napkins for his nose. He grimaced at the thought of himself sniffling and blowing his nose in front of Jania, but he did notice that his nose was not running nearly as much as it had been back at his room. *Here we go. I'll either earn her undying gratitude, or totally disgust her to the point where she will not even want to sit next to me anymore.* He opened the door.

Jania sat in her seat, pouring something out of a round metal flask into a tiny cup. She looked up at Ben and smiled. "I got some medicine for your cold. And some cherry syrup for your throat, too. Sit down and drink up," she said cheerfully, pushing the cup over to his side of the desk.

Syrup for his throat. That was very sweet of her, to do that for him. "You didn't have to do that, Princess," he said, going over and taking his seat.

"Of course I did, and don't call me Princess," she replied in her haughtiest princess-like tone. "The least I can do is try to make you more comfortable." Her hand reached for his forehead. "Do you have a fever?"

He grabbed her hand before she could feel his head, and they both flinched back. "What was that?" Jania asked, staring at her fingers.

"Probably static," Ben said, shaking his own hand. "I was practicing a permanent light spell, but all that came out were these static discharges. I probably still have a few left." Grinning, he pointed his finger at her, waving it menacingly in front of her nose.

"I have a spell in my head that will make your hair stand up on end, so you better put that finger away." Jania raised her own finger.

"You're bluffing!"

"Try me."

"What are you two doing here?"

They both jumped to their feet and spun around. "Mage Terri! We're finishing up our philosophy assignment." Jania said.

"I thought you were both going to that concert." Her black eyes were expressionless. "They are only going to perform once."

"This is more important, Mage Terri. We had a setback and need to catch up," Ben answered. He was glad his voice sounded calmer than Jania's.

Mage Terri nodded. "I see. Well, keep the door open. I don't think it would be appropriate for the Princess to be caught alone with a boy, even if he is a classmate." She gave them a small, quick wave, and walked off.

Ben turned to Jania. "Is it all right for us to be alone like this?"

"It is perfectly fine," she said. "It's not as if you are going to try something inappropriate. Are you?"

"No! How could you even think such a thing?"

"It's that company you keep. Ro and Jamu are a pair of rakes. If I were to ask Jamu that question, he would ask me if I wanted him to do so, and I don't think Ro would even give me the courtesy of an offer."

Ben forced himself to smile. How annoyingly true. "He would

most likely kiss you, then ask if that was inappropriate." He drank the contents in the cup Jania had poured for him, and struggled not to spit it out. "This tastes awful."

"It's good for you," Jania said.

"I would rather stay sick."

"Sometimes you have to feel worse before you can feel better. You don't always enjoy things that are for your own good."

He had to ask. It had been bothering him for a long time. "You mean like having to date Jamu?"

Her mouth actually fell open. "Jamu is dating Jai. But how did you know about that?"

"Jamu is my friend, remember? He mentioned that he may have to court you, for political reasons." Why the hell did he bring this subject up?

"Jamu is with someone else, so I don't have to worry about that," Jania said.

Ben stared at the cup in his hand. He could not imagine being coerced into wooing someone he didn't like.

"If Jamu stops dating Jai, I just might have to start being seen with him, at the very least."

"Do you like Jamu?"

"Not in that way. But he is nice and I trust him, so I think a courtship with him would not be bad."

"But if Jamu stopped courting Jai, and you were dating someone else at the time, it would be the same as if Jamu were still with her."

"I suppose so. But who would have the courage to ask a princess for a date?" Jania turned to her papers and began spreading them out neatly on the desk with a small sigh. "We should start," she said wearily.

Ben's blood raced through his veins as he looked at her. "I've upset you with this. I'm sorry."

"You didn't upset me, Ben. My whole situation upsets me. Have some cherry syrup. I think the best way to do this is for me to read to you, and you copy it down. When you get tired, we will switch. How does that sound?"

"Sounds good." Ben readied his pen. "Let's begin."

Candles burned on the desk by the time Ben inked the last few words out. "There you go, Princess," he said, blotting the page and waving the page to dry the ink. Jania placed the other pages together between two stiffened leather covers. She took the last page, carefully bored three holes into it, and lined it up with the others.

Ben emptied the jar that held the cherry syrup. Whatever was in that flask worked wonders for his cold. He had not blown his nose once, to his immense relief. His throat was another story, though. After a few tries at reading aloud, he had settled to just writing as Jania read to him. He didn't mind. She had a nice, sweet voice. Her comments on some of the passages made him laugh, and her motherly attentions to his cold were almost endearing. All in all, the afternoon seemed more like fun than work. And he finally got his chance to spend time with Jania.

"Ben, please don't stop talking to me," Jania said, binding the pages together with a silk cord.

"What?" Ben peered into the jar. That cherry syrup was delicious.

"Don't stop. Don't be afraid to talk to me." Jania tied off the binding and turned to him. "You always distance yourself from me. I am your friend. I want you to treat me like your other friends."

"Jania, I call my friends names and smack them around. I think you might get tired of that after a while."

"Is that the only way you know how to treat people?"

"Why are you upset now?"

"Ben, I... oh, never mind." She began gathering her things.

This was not going to end well. Ben's mind raced for something to say, but came up with nothing. And he was supposed to be smart. He said the only thing that he could think of. "Jania, I don't want to stop talking to you." It was not the smartest thing he had ever said.

But it seemed to have worked. Jania's hands stopped moving.

"I do consider you a friend. I would do anything to prove it to you." He waited for her to reply, but she only looked at him, waiting.

He took a deep breath. It was a terrible risk, but... "What if I asked you if we could date?"

Her jaw dropped once more.

He had gone too far. He needed to say something before she ran out of the classroom screaming. "It doesn't have to be real. It could be like any other of these courtships for show. But you don't have to worry about dating someone you don't like. And we can spend time together as friends. I mean, if it is appropriate for a village boy to ask a princess such a thing."

"You are not a village boy anymore. You are a mage." Jania gave him a strange look. "I really have to think about this, Ben. But it is a very nice thing you are offering. Thank you."

Something strange flickered inside him. Consideration was better than a refusal. He spoke quickly, while he still had his nerve. "Think about it all you want. Listen, while we were doing this, I was thinking about a copying spell I can create for our year-end project. We can team up. What do you think?"

He kept himself firmly composed as her eyes widened. "You want me to help you? Do you really mean it?"

"You're the smartest student in the class. Of course I mean it."

She looked confused. "I'm not the smartest student. Far from it. You are the smart one."

"Being smart is more than books and spellcasting. You have common sense, and you know how to explain things very well. And you are nice to be with." That last sentence came out awkwardly. "I think we'll make a good team."

Jania gave him the most beautiful smile he had ever seen. "Let's try to get the laboratory assigned to us some day next week," she suggested.

Ben nodded. "Let's do that," he said.

13

Setbacks

Obitus drifted about lazily through the Astral Plane in his full dragon form, enjoying the gray fog that isolated him from the insanity that constantly surrounded him. He wanted so much to return home. This dimension was so rich in magic and fuel, and the human's planet was really quite beautiful now that most of the empty drab buildings that would pierce the sky were gone. The dark roads that had horribly scarred the land were also gone, leaving the planet in a much more natural state. But after several thousand years, Obitus was tired and homesick. He kept busy, and took very long naps when he was tired, but there was only so much a dragon could do while waiting for the perfect human to be born.

Thankfully, after several false alarms, it seemed the time was finally at hand. Megan had shown promise since the day she was born. And seeing how Caeles had decided to involve himself and pull the girl out of reach only convinced Obitus that she was the real thing. As furious as he was at his fellow celestial dragon, he could not help feeling just a bit pleased that the redheaded druid child had attracted another dragon's attention.

Obitus stopped his drifting. A circle of pillars emerged from the mist. The pillars moved to surround Obitus, and a floor that seemed to be made of copper appeared underneath his floating body. Obitus shifted to his human form and set his white boots on the floor. Only one dragon had big enough dragonstones to disturb him in this place. Everyone knew how irritable he would become whenever he was drawn away from his relaxed state.

"What do you want, Caeles?" He hated posing as a human, but it was the human's world, and it wouldn't do to have a dreamer stumble upon a dragon in its true form. The Draca could not afford to have humans learn of them. Except for a select few people, of course.

Caeles stepped into view from behind a pillar. "I want to know why you are meddling with mongrels," he said. He looked as grumpy as Obitus felt.

"What are you talking about?" No one was supposed to know. Abeo was the only one who did not find the concept of creating Draca hybrid monsters appalling. The Spirit dragon seemed to actually take some perverse pleasure in breeding various types of creatures. As a result, the other dragons, both Tueri and Debellos, kept their distance. Obitus found the monsters as distasteful as anyone else, but the one he made, his ugly little half-fox, half-Draca, was a necessary evil. He needed that tiny abomination to get his ward back. It was more than justified. Still, it was a bit of an embarrassment to find out that his plan was no longer a secret.

"I am talking about that harbinger of pestilence you have hibernating near Megan's cottage," Caeles growled back. "I can appreciate your desperation, but you forget your heritage. You are a Celestial Dragon. You are supposed to symbolize purity and spirituality, regardless of your worldly values and beliefs."

"That would be fine if we were back in our own world," Obitus snarled. His human form slipped for an instant, revealing a sharp, polished talon as he jabbed his finger at Caeles to emphasize his point. "We cannot be true dragons here. And we may be brothers, but here in this world, we are at war. There are no rules anymore, other than the Pact. And nowhere in the Pact does it forbid us from dirtying our claws in less than pure stuff to accomplish our missions."

"You risk losing yourself for this child?" Caeles asked him, unruffled by his angry outburst.

"That child is going to get me back home!" Caeles was his enemy here, but he was right. All Celestial dragons were kin, regardless of their parentage or their views. He could speak to him as a brother here. But only here. And maybe back home. "I am tired of this struggle. I want to move on already. I want to find a mate, and I want to raise hatchlings. I want to pass on my knowledge and my power to my children. I am starting to feel like this is all a waste of time."

"Then why are you sill here? Is this world worth the fight? Why do you insist on spoiling and destroying alien life just to have a place you can draw the energy and resources to keep you comfortable?" Caeles asked gently.

His question enraged Obitus. "Why can you not understand that we need this energy, that we need these resources? The Creator gave us the intellect and the drive to survive, and survive we must. We will run out of resources if we do nothing. And there are infinite dimensions out there. This world will not be missed. This world had its chance and the humans ruined it! There are other humans in other dimensions, and there are countless sentient lives in this dimension alone! Sentient life continues to evolve. We can live forever if we are responsible. But you need to accept that some worlds will have to be sacrificed. It is called survival of the fittest, and it was all part of the Creator's plan! I will not allow you tenderhearted Tueri to hold us back from doing what we need to do to survive. And if that means I have to pine away here in this wretched place, then so be it!"

Caeles shook his head sadly and gave Obitus a sad look. "And this is what you wish to teach your progeny?"

"Yes! Now tell me how you found out about my little fox!"

Obitus wanted to strike out at someone. Damn that Tueri for ruining his afternoon!

"It seems Sanguis discovered the mongrel while snooping around the Academy. She told Animis about it," Caeles answered.

"That stupid oath breaker! What the hell is she doing helping Tueri?" Obitus clenched his fists and projected back to his body.

His glowing white eyes opened, and he leaped out of his cozy den set underneath the ancient stone floor of his temple retreat. He stretched his wings and flexed his arms and legs, his eyes quickly adjusting to the bright sunlight. He took a deep snarling breath through his nostrils before taking to the air.

He circled once around the bone-white temple ruins that he had made his home, the deserted site perched high atop the highest mountain on the island, overlooking the harsh ocean waves that crashed incessantly against the base of the barren mountain. His circuit completed, he turned in the direction of the mainland, flying faster than any human eye could detect.

Sanguis made herself comfortable on the Eastern captain's seat. It was nothing short of pure luck that she had stumbled onto a private meeting between the captain and what appeared to be a high ranking Syntrean soldier while searching for a new hiding lair on the Mainland coast. A pigeon had delivered a message right at the meeting spot. The captain had the message, and after two days of scouting the area with his officers, he was due to return to his camp any moment. Sanguis heard a group of horses approach, and patiently waited for him to enter his tent. She would be discreet and whisk him away without anyone knowing. She smiled as the tent flap opened.

Of course he would not enter his tent unaccompanied. The four men stopped talking at the sight of her sitting in the most important seat in the tent. They stared at her in shock.

Sanguis jumped out of the chair and grabbed hold of the captain's shoulder. "I need to have a talk with your captain. Excuse us." She formed a quick mental attack, and the three lackeys fell lifeless to the ground. She phased away with the captain before he could even react. She took him to the place he had met with the mysterious Syntrean officer, a small but thick copse of trees not too far from the main coastal road.

"You have been discovered, Captain," Sanguis said as she ripped his sword belt off and spun him around to face her. "Who was that man you met with a few days ago? Where is he now?"

The Easterner was not fazed. "Who the hell are you? Who sent you?"

Sanguis was becoming tired of these uppity humans. If they only knew she could crush them like a beetle! It gave her an idea. The man was not long for this world anyway. She switched to her bipedal half dragon form, waving her blue-black talons in front of his face.

"Tell me!" she roared.

The captain gave her a slack jawed look, finally afraid. "I… he…it is…"

A flash of light made Sanguis look up. A white half-dragon appeared behind the terrified man. Before Sanguis could react, the dragon snatched the captain out of her grasp. Holding the captain's neck firmly in one claw, the dragon gripped his head with the other and gave it a hard twist. Sanguis could only stare in shock as Obitus tossed the captain's body aside.

"You traitorous bat! My pet monster is dead! How dare you help the Tueri?" He grabbed Sanguis by her face. "I will strike you dead before I allow you to ruin my plans!"

Sanguis tried to fight the Draca magic flowing from his talons into her body, to no avail. She felt herself shrink, and she was human once more. Obitus released her face and gave her a backhanded slap. Sanguis went flying. She hit the ground face first. As she rolled over, spitting out grass and dirt, Obitus leaped over to her and slammed his white leathery foot on her chest.

"You should have admitted defeat and left this world the day you broke the Pact and allowed Vitalia to mark that boy," Obitus said. He held his hand up. "You have become too troublesome to tolerate. Your actions harm the Debellos more than they help. It is time." A glowing sphere appeared in his hand. "Farewell, Spirit Dragon."

The glow intensified. Sanguis saw her demise at hand. Not knowing what else to do, she screamed. In her human form, her cry sounded weak, shrill and pathetic. There could not be a worse way to die.

There was another flash of light, this time behind Obitus. A claw grabbed hold of Obitus and dragged him off of Sanguis. The sphere vanished as yet another half-dragon, blue like her, slapped the white dragon's claw down. The blue half-dragon pushed the white back, pinning him against a tree with its forearm, talons gleaming.

Sanguis opened her mouth as far open as it would go and breathed in a huge gulp of air. She could not believe she was still alive.

"Pull yourself together. You are above this," the blue dragon hissed at the white.

"You would break the Pact over a renegade, Animis?" Obitus asked in disbelief. "I always considered you the ultimate strategist."

"The Pact allows for the defense of a fellow dragon," Animis replied. "It did not exclude renegades."

"I am sure it did not allow for them either," Obitus retorted. "And she is not even Tueri. Release me. I am calm now."

Animis complied. Sanguis sat up slowly, fixing her torn dirty dress to appear new. The others changed to their human forms, Obitus in his white druid garb and Animis in his Royal Official attire.

"If you phase away, I will find you again. And I will make sure this Tueri does not interfere," Obitus said to her. "Now explain yourself! My plans have been foiled! Why the hell would you tell Animis about my mongrel?"

"Why are you playing around with mongrels in the first place?" Sanguis asked. "They are disgusting things."

"I refuse to confide my plans to a renegade dragon who cannot keep her snout shut!"

"Obitus, I am sure she did not know it belonged to you. Caeles came to that conclusion. I was worried. Only Abeo tinkers with those abominations. I feared something other than Draca might be involved."

Obitus glared at Sanguis. "I demand reparation! You owe me something for this setback!"

"Calm down, Obitus. We have suffered a setback, too." Animis walked over to the dead captain. "You have ruined our own plans. That captain was the key to our mysterious General's identity, was he not, Sanguis?"

"He was," Sanguis said with a sigh. "But I had nothing to do with this plan," she added quickly.

Obitus still had his gaze fixed on Sanguis. "You owe this nature lover Tueri your life, renegade. That alone should shame you into leaving this place. But take heed, you are a marked dragon. So you had better keep out of my way. I doubt Animis will find it in his mushy heart to save you one more time if our paths ever cross again in this world."

"My heart is not as mushy as he believes," Animis said. "You have failed me. The only reason I do not kill you now is because I cannot bring myself to slay a dragon I have just saved." Animis turned to Obitus. "Maybe I do have a mushy heart. What do you think, Celestial Dragon?"

"I think Sanguis is an imbecile for still being here," Obitus replied with a scowl.

She was not an imbecile. She could recognize a cue when she heard it. She wasted no time disappearing. She had her own scheme she needed to follow up on.

Animis and Obitus stood alone in the thicket. Obitus turned his scowl on Animis. "So how did my pet perish?"

Animis smiled at his displeased expression. "Semino's ward and her troop leader stumbled upon it and hunted it down. I was nearby and able to sense the mongrel when it woke up, so I was there with Caeles to witness what had happened."

"The one living being in this dimension I hesitate to retaliate against, of course she would be the one to thwart me! It makes me wonder why those kids were there to begin with," Obitus growled.

Animis shrugged. "I had nothing to do with that. I had no plans to interfere with your pet. But realize that I will protect my ward and her city as much as I can."

Obitus shook his head. "You really should not call her that until you mark her. But do not worry. Megan is all I want. She is my Chosen. I care nothing for Syntrea."

"If that is so, then tell me who is causing all this strife between Syntrea and Massea. The commander's name is Adfligere. I am sure you know."

Obitus chuckled. "You must think me as dense as Sanguis. In any case, I do not know. I do not care. What makes you think it was not Sanguis herself?"

"She is not smart enough to pull off something this intricate."

"No argument here. Have fun solving your little mystery." Obitus gave Animis a mocking wave before he vanished.

14

A Spellcaster Discovered

"That was wonderful! Don't you think that was wonderful, Gayly?" Jai asked, holding Galen's hand tightly as they pushed their way through the crowd.

"It was," Galen agreed, glancing at the empty stage. The concert had been amazing, but it was the young drumskin player who had left her awestruck. He played it so well, even better than the lute he had started with at the beginning. But beyond the way she felt about his music, there was yet something else she had felt from him.

She slipped her hand away from Jai's and slowed until Jamu had led Jai out of sight. She made her way toward the stage.

It was not hard for her to make her way through the crowd, once she did not have anyone's hand dragging her along. Soon she was right in front of the raised stage. She circled around it and ducked under the ropes that closed off the street beyond.

The lanterns set to light up the street for the City Watch to spot trespassers only made more shadows for her to hide in. She grinned as she evaded the Watchers on the street, sometimes passing close enough to touch them. She was an Espies scout. Slipping past the City Watch was warm-up practice for her. She made her way to the inn where the performers were staying.

She slowed as she approached the inn, suddenly unsure why she had come here. The Watchers at the entrance seemed determined not to let anyone in. She could sneak in through one of the windows, but that was not the way one made a good impression on strangers. She chewed her lip, wondering if she should turn back.

She looked up at one of the windows on the side of the building. A head appeared, looking out the window. She recognized the boy from the band. Her resolve returned and she made her way through the shadows so he would not spot her and become alarmed. She had to meet him. The feeling she had during the concert returned, and she realized why she felt the way she did. He had elemental powers.

A hand grabbed her collar and hauled her off of her feet. As her back hit the ground, a knee landed heavily on her chest and a hand pinned both her wrists down. Galen switched to her nightvision. She recognized her attacker's face, and stopped struggling.

You should not be here, Jamu signaled with his free hand. Come with me. He released her and stood up.

Galen picked herself up slowly and let her nightvision fade. She glanced back at the window. The boy still gazed into the darkness, oblivious to what was happening below. She turned to Jamu, relieved that the boy had not noticed her eyes glow.

She noticed Jamu's eyes studying the window. He gave her an amused smile before running off.

She knew better than not to follow him. With one last regretful glance at the window, she jogged off before she lost sight of her troop leader.

The following morning, Galen sat in front of her bed, thinking about the boy from the concert while she oiled her drumskin. Her troopmates were off playing forts, but Jamu, Jai, Megan, Rohen, and Hedi were there, talking about the past evening. Galen ignored the conversation going on, but her ears perked up at her brother's name.

"I wonder if Ben is feeling better," Jamu was saying. "He did not look well when I left him yesterday."

"Oh, I am sure he is more than fine," Jai replied with a big grin on her face. She sat on Jamu's lap on the bench beside the door.

Hedi and Rohen sat on Laren's bunk. Megan sat on the floor in front of them. Rohen stopped thumbing through Hedi's spellbook and frowned at Jai. "What do you mean?" he asked.

"Didn't you notice that Jania was not at the concert?" Jai asked mysteriously. She leaned back against Jamu as he began to stroke her hair. Galen kept from making a face as she watched them. Jai had really irritated her at the concert. Her constant babying was very unlike the friendly Jai who always gave her sisterly advice.

"Jesi kept me from noticing much," Rohen said.

"Why are you dating a girl you don't even like?" Jai asked Rohen. "That is the most idiotic thing I have ever heard."

"Oh, so you don't listen to yourself talk, do you?" Rohen asked.

Galen rubbed her drumskin vigorously, wishing Jai would go away. It was bad enough she was with Jamu all the time, now she wanted to be her mother as well. That was why she acted the way she had at the concert. She was playing family, much like the way young girls played.

"Why was Jania not at the concert?" Jamu asked before Jai and Rohen got into one of their usual arguments.

"Let's just say I arranged a nice date for her," Jai replied with a secretive smile on her face.

"Say more," Megan said. "What did you do?"

"Go ahead, Jai," Hedi said. "Tell everyone what you did." She had a disgusted look on her face.

"Come on, Jai. Stop playing around," Jamu said.

Jai relented. Galen's hands slowed, then stopped as she listened to Jai's story. When she finished, the cabin was deathly quiet. Even Megan, who saw little value in books, seemed shocked.

Rohen finally broke the silence. "So what was it you were saying about idiotic things, Jai?"

"Jai, how could you?" Jamu asked. He stared at the back of her head.

"It was for a good cause. Everyone knows how they feel about each other. Something had to happen to get them together."

"I'm surprised Jania didn't have you arrested," Megan said, shaking her head.

"Well, she did kick me off my chair," Jai admitted. "But it was only a script!"

No one answered her. Galen wondered how Ben would react if he found out.

"Trust me, it will be worth it," Jai assured everyone.

Galen's hands shook as she slid the tension ring around the drumskin. What could be worth burning a book, even if it was a script? Jamu still stared incredulously at Jai's head.

"So you incinerated Jania's script with a fire spell," Rohen said, thumbing through the spellbook again. "Was it this spell?" he asked Hedi.

"Yes, it was," Hedi replied, surprised. "How did you know that?"

"I learned how to read symbol characters from a book when I was a little boy," he answered. He studied the page.

"Jai, what you did was terrible. Burning a book is a crime. And Jania worked very hard to make that manuscript," Jamu said.

"Oh, stop making such a big deal of it. There are plenty of copies of that thing, and Ben and Jania are working on replacing the one I burned." Jai seemed oblivious to Jamu's shock.

"Burned. Like the symbols. They feel burned in my head," Rohen mumbled.

"What!" Jai jumped off Jamu's lap and faced Rohen. Hedi snatched her spellbook away from him.

"What? Relax, it's not like I can cast a spell or anything. Watch." He waved his fingers in Galen's direction. "Ka!"

Galen raised her drumskin just in time to shield herself from the fist-sized fireball that flew her way. Her fingers burned, and she threw the stretched skin aside.

Jamu was suddenly beside her. "Are you all right?" he asked her, checking her face and neck.

"My fingers." She looked at her hands, resisting the urge to strike back at Rohen. Her fingers were an angry red color. Megan took her hands and began to Heal them.

"I'm sorry, Firefly," Rohen said.

Galen looked up at him. For an instant, she had felt the rage. That thick, burning rage that made her want to hurt him. But she was able to control it. Terra was right; it was just a matter of knowing where the anger was coming from. She could never hurt Rohen. "I'm fine, Rowy. It's all right."

"No, it's not," Jai said. "Rohen can cast spells! Why is he attending Espies?"

Hedi stared at Rohen. "Because no one knew. I was sitting right beside him while he memorized a spell, and I could not even tell."

"Ro was standing next to Ben when Mage Terri dragged him to Arcanum. I will never forget that day," Jamu said.

"She grabbed Ben and told him he would love it at Arcanum. He wanted to go to Gladia. I told her so. I faced her and told her, and she just smiled and told Ben he could not attend Gladia. She never gave me a second glance." Rohen stared at Galen, looking confused. Had he felt the rage too?

"Ben has very strong spellcasting abilities," Hedi said. "Maybe that overshadowed your talent, and she could not sense you. But I couldn't tell either. I still can't. But the way the spell executed, especially for your first try at casting, shows how strong you are.

Maybe your abilities are shielded, somehow."

"You will look quite fetching with a mage's tail," Jai said.

"No!" Rohen threw Jai a dangerous look. "This incident does not leave this cabin. Do you understand me?"

"You have to go to Arcanum, Ro," Jai exclaimed. "You have a rare gift. I cannot allow you to—"

"Jai, if you breathe a word about this to anyone, I will tell everyone about your little book burning scheme. Old Cow will be the first to find out, too. I am an Espies scout, and that is the way it is going to stay. Is that clear?"

Jai looked over to Jamu for support, but he kept his gaze on Galen's hands.

"If Rohen does not wish to attend Arcanum, we cannot force him to," Hedi said. "He is fifteen, not ten, and he is attending another college. Your secret is safe with me, Ro."

He gave Hedi a grateful smile. "Thank you."

Galen pulled her hands away from Megan and reached for her smoking drumskin. The center was blackened and stiff. She flicked her finger against it, and flinched at the sound. Its resonance was gone. There was a tiny hole burned in the middle as well.

"Firefly, we will go and get you another one," Rohen told her.

"Where are we going to find another one?" Her drumskin was broken. There was yet another secret to keep. So many secrets. What would happen to Rohen if Arcanum found out about him? She would never find out who that mysterious boy was, and Jai was always going to be with Jamu. She covered her face with her hands and began to cry.

"Do not cry, Gayly. Everything will turn out fine," Jamu said soothingly, hugging her.

She only cried harder. It was almost painful to feel his arms around her.

Jesi crouched down to take a closer look at her growing plant, but the tears in her eyes made everything blurry. She wiped them away with her sleeve and pulled a weed out of the ground, wishing she could pluck Seanna out of her life as easily as she had done to the unwanted seedling.

She wished she had never agreed to help that woman. Becoming Rohen's girlfriend had been easy enough, but manipulating him into trusting her was making things miserable for both of them. She had thought that her psychic powers would make it easy to influence him, but Rohen was psychic as well. And he was stronger than Jesi. He was not as skilled, probably because he did not use his mental powers for fear of being discovered, but Jesi could easily feel how much power he had. She did not dare touch his mind. She did not want him to know that she was also psychic. Not yet, anyway.

With her psychic options out of play and her spiritual powers of little use to her, she had to revert to mundane ploys to get him to do what she wanted. Threats. Nagging. Guilt trips. Rohen was such a sweet and patient boy, but he had too strong a will to give in to henpecking easily. Spending time together was no longer fun, and Jesi was all too aware that the only reason Rohen still spent time with her was because he feared that she would tell Healer Stanis about his mental powers. Her eyes watered once more at the thought. She liked him so much. She wanted him to like her back. She did not want to lead him by a rope. She wanted him to be with her because he wanted to.

She blinked the tears away, and remembered where she was. She immediately pushed her sad thoughts away and blocked her mind. If that woman appeared, Jesi did not want her to even suspect she was having doubts about Rohen.

She was glad she did. She heard footsteps not too far off. Rohen walked into view from behind the greenhouse. Jesi was thankful he did not catch her off guard. The tears still on her face blended in easily with the sweat on her face.

"What are you doing here?" she asked as he walked up to her.

"I wanted to see you." He looked troubled.

"Are you all right? Did something happen?" Jesi took his hand, expecting him to tense up or try to pull away from her the way he usually did. She was a bit surprised when he did not.

"I learned something today, and I am a bit shook up," Rohen admitted.

"Tell me what happened."

"No, I don't want to talk about it. Can we just go for a walk or something?"

Jesi opened her mouth to argue, but she had no words for him. She would not force him into confiding in her, not this time. She only nodded.

It almost broke her heart to see his relieved look. He gave her a grateful smile and took her arm. They strolled through the gardens without saying a word.

Finally Rohen stopped by a large stone bench set not too far from the entrance to the Healer's college. He offered her a seat and joined her once she was settled. The sun was low in the west.

"Ro, would you like to talk about it now?" Jesi finally asked.

"I can't. But I would like to talk to you about something."

This was it. The time had come. "About us?"

Rohen nodded.

She had expected this for a while, and yet she was still shocked, and a bit angry. "Is there someone else?" She said it before she could stop herself, and the bitterness she heard from her own lips was a shock to her.

"No, there is no one else," Rohen snapped back. "But this is not fun. We are supposed to enjoy being with each other. Do you really enjoy being upset and irritated with me? Because I do not!"

"I don't like it either. But that is not a reason to give up."

"Give up on what?"

"Our relationship! Let's work on our problems instead of running away from them. Really, Rohen, do you want to walk away from me? After all we have been through?"

"We have not been through all that much."

"We know each other too well to just go our separate ways."

Rohen glared at her. Jesi regretted her words yet again. She had not meant for that to sound like a threat, but how else did she expect him to interpret that statement? It was too late to take them back, though. She held his gaze until he finally looked away in resignation.

"I will leave it up to you," he said. "But let me tell you that I am not happy, and I know you are not happy either. I don't want to hurt you, but I am not sure this is worth it. Is it worth it to you?"

She was not going to cry in front of him. "It is. I will not let you go without a fight. We can change, if we try hard enough. I won't give up on you!"

"You are upset. I think you need some time alone to clear your head." Rohen stood up. "Think about what I said and meet me by the Mall later." He walked away without looking at her.

Jesi watched him go. Maybe he was right, maybe she did need to reconsider the entire situation. At the very least, she had to pull herself together. She headed to her room, trying to think of the right words to say so he could give her another chance. She reached her door without a single idea. She opened the door and walked into her room. Seanna stood waiting at the foot of her bed.

"Things don't seem to be going too well for you," Seanna said. The friendly pleasantness was gone from her voice. "It is time. Have him here tonight, fast asleep. He is very strong, so I would advise you give him something nice to drink to help you get him down. I will return later, once the moon is up. Do not fail!"

Jesi clenched her fists as the woman disappeared. She had neglected to block her anguish, and Seanna had felt it. But instead of being a friend and reassuring Jesi, she treated her like a failure. Seanna had shown her true colors, but Jesi still held a tiny shard of hope. If Jesi turned Rohen over to Seanna, he would never trust her again, and would probably hate her. But she would be with him, and she would have him all to herself. If she backed out of her deal, it would only be a matter of time before she lost Rohen. Jesi let her tears flow, but deep down, she knew she had already made her decision. She told Rohen she would fight for him, and she meant it.

Rohen trudged into his troop's cabin. He still could not believe what had happened. He could cast spells! Why had no one realized this before?

He walked over to his bed. Why didn't Terra say anything? He remembered what Hedi had said about not sensing his ability to cast. But Terra was a dragon. She must have known. But if she did, wouldn't she want him to attend Arcanum instead of Espies?

"Ro? Are you all right?"

Rohen looked up at Keran. "I'm fine." Seeing him reminded him of Galen. "So your cousin is one of the Oracle bards?"

"Yes, he is," Keran said, rather proudly.

"I need a favor from you, and your cousin."

"Anything, Rohen."

Rohen knew Keran was not going to like this. "Do you think he can help me find a drumskin?"

Galen opened the door to her cabin and walked in. She dropped the bundle of arrows she was carrying when she saw the two boys sitting on her bed.

"Galen, this is my cousin, Kade." Keran did not look happy to be there. "Kade, this is Galen. She is the girl all those stupid peddler stories talk about."

Galen stood stunned as the boy from the window stood up and offered her his hand. "It is nice to meet you, Galen."

She stepped forward to take his hand, and slipped on her arrows. Kade grabbed her shoulders before she toppled onto him.

A tingly shock ran through her body at his touch, and she gasped. Kade steadied her quickly and yanked his hands away. He had felt the shock, too.

"She has always been clumsy," Keran said. "Just because she is a scout doesn't mean she is graceful."

Galen dropped to her knees and scooped up her arrows. Her heart thudded with embarrassment and excitement at the same time. "I'm sorry. You are the last two people I would ever expect to find sitting on my bed. I couldn't help being a little surprised."

Kade's laugh made her feel better. Now if Keran would only behave himself.

"Keran told me that your drumskin is broken. One of the attendants that travels with us knows how to make them. Keran asked me to have a new one made for you." Kade gave her a kind smile.

Galen looked from Kade to Keran. How did Keran find out? And why would he do something nice for her?

"I'm doing this for Ro," Keran stated firmly.

That explained it. She looked back at Kade. "You are very kind. Let me get my drumskin." She put the arrows away and reached under her bed. As she pulled out her drumskin, her eyes caught Keran's.

She stood up and faced Kade. All Sevilans were not like Keran. That was a relief to know. "Thank you, Kade."

"Anything to help a pretty young lady out," he replied.

"She is not pretty and she is not a young lady," Keran said nastily. "She is just a little freak."

Kade looked at Keran, then back at Galen. Galen looked down at her burned drumskin. She had not expected Keran to behave himself, anyway. She kept her gaze lowered as she followed Kade out the door.

15

The Son of Aoiyama

Jamu gulped down a sigh of relief as he reached the top of the steps leading to Arcanum Tower and stepped in front of Jai to open the door for her. She had not stopped talking since they left the cabin. That is, except at the mess hall, where she would pause to shove some food in her mouth. Jamu opened the door. Funny how Jai's talking never bothered him before.

"You're not coming in?" Jai asked, a bit surprised.

"It is dusk," Jamu answered. "There are a few things I would like to do."

Jai leaned against the door and gave him a big smile. Jamu knew what that meant. He had no interest in spending any more time with her, however, and he did not even feel guilty about it.

Jai must have noticed something in his look. She stopped smiling. "Is it that important?" she asked.

Jamu smiled and gave her a kiss. He could not lie, and he knew better than to try and twist words with her. Jai could easily match wits with him even after downing half a pitcher of wine. "Meet me at the patio in the Espies Wood tomorrow after lunchtime. We will talk then."

She gave him a little frown. "Very well. But I must say you are not quite yourself this evening."

"I am still stunned by the incident at the cabin. That is all."

"Oh." She hesitated. Jamu expected her to ask which incident exactly, but she did not, to his relief. "I hope you feel better in the morning, then."

"I am sure I will. I will see you tomorrow. Behave yourself."

"Behave myself?" Jai giggled. "I always behave."

"Casting an irritant spell on Myelie's duster is not behaving."

"She was bothering you! You are my boyfriend. And she is a bit old for you anyway."

He did not wish to be pulled into another conversation. He gave her another kiss. "I do not bother with her, and you should not, either. I have to go now."

"Goodnight, Jamu." Jai closed the door behind her. Jamu waited by the door, listening to her footsteps echo throughout the Atrium.

Her admission to burning that script was an eye-opener for him. Jamu had seen Jai's sneaky side before; her vindictiveness toward the older Arcanum student was a perfect example. But any book, even a journal or scrip, was a worldwide symbol of what humans valued the most: knowledge. To burn a book was to bring back the travesty of those dark ages, where people burned up their books—and their knowledge—in order to survive. Jamu realized that Jai was the type who would trample over anything and everything to get what she wanted. She was kind to her friends and loved helping others, but Jamu had seen her dark side. He turned and rushed down the steps. He did not like that side of her at all.

Halfway down the steps a man in white flowing trousers and tunic appeared. He also wore what looked to be a druid's sash, except it was white instead of yellow. Twilight was almost gone, making it difficult for Jamu to make out the man's face. Jamu stopped in his tracks and looked around. The man had phased here. That in itself was surprising, but as Jamu glanced around and saw that there was no one in sight, his surprise turned to alarm. The man had planned this encounter. Jamu could not think of anyone who would appear to him in this manner. He frowned as a thought came to him. No, that was not true.

He leaped over the remaining steps to land before the man. It was quite a long way down, but no one was there to see. "You promised not to—" His words froze in his throat as he realized the man was not who he had expected.

"I promised what?" the man sneered. "The only promise I have made in regards to you is to make sure you pay for killing my pet!"

Jamu saw his hand go for his throat, and jumped out of his reach. He landed four steps up, staring at the stranger in shock. Those white eyes…

"Come here, brat!" The man leaped after him, too nimble to be human. Jamu rolled to the side, barely avoiding the fist aimed at his head. The marble step cracked under the force of the punch. Jamu scrambled up a few steps. There was only one thing he could think to do. Not caring whether anyone was around to see, he phased away.

He appeared flat on his back, tangled up in a thicket. He clawed himself out and jumped to his feet. He stood in the wild brushy area north of the Academy, not too far from the wall. No one would be around here to witness whatever was to happen in the next few moments. Jamu clenched his fists and squeezed his eyes shut. He was weaponless and alone. He needed help.

He opened his eyes again. The white druid-garbed man stood directly before him. The man's hands glowed white, as did his eyes. "You are Surian! That would explain how you knew about the hibrida and how to kill it. You should have left well enough alone, boy!"

Jamu had not made the connection until now. He was too shocked to react to the bony hand that finally caught hold of his throat in a viselike grip. His windpipe clamped closed as his feet left the ground. The dragon pulled Jamu's face up against his own, his teeth bared. Jamu did not have to use his nightvision to see his white eyes. He met the dragon's stare with an angry one of his own.

Those white eyes widened in shock, and Jamu fell to the ground in a heap as the hand released his throat. The dragon actually took one step back, growling.

Jamu heard a footstep behind him, followed by the sound of a pair of sabers being pulled out of their sheaths. A hand grabbed hold of his arm and pulled him to his feet. "My lord," a woman's voice whispered in his ear. "Hurt, are you?"

"I am fine, Shiko," he said, relieved to see her standing beside him. General Kuten stepped between Jamu and his attacker. Jamu took the saber Shiko offered him.

"Who are you?" Jamu asked.

"I would ask you the same question," the dragon replied.

"You know about my encounter with that hibrida, so you obviously know much more about me than I do about you," Jamu shot back. "What is your name and why did you drop me the way you did?"

"Hibrida?" Shiko gasped. The general stepped back, closer to Jamu.

"It is dead. It was a puny rodent of a mongrel, apparently designed to spread disease," Jamu explained to them, keeping his eyes fixed on the dragon before him.

"You have the brain of a dragon, boy," the dragon said in a surprising compliment.

"Answer my question!" Jamu shouted, causing his companions to jump.

The dragon glared at him. "Just because I did not slay you on the spot does not mean I fear you. I am Obitus. Now it is my turn. Why are you here? Who sent you?"

"I am here to become an Espies scout. I was sent by my King."

"You expect me to believe that?" Obitus pushed General Kuten aside as if he were a pestering child and towered over Jamu.

"Do you truly believe that? Do you know who you are? Do you know what you are?"

"Lord Jamu, second son of House Aoiyama, I am! I am the faithful subject of King Tohe of Sur, and that is all. I speak the truth as an Espies scout." Jamu gripped his saber tightly and switched to his nightvision. He was terrified, but it would be shameful to show fear.

Obitus tossed his head back and laughed, to Jamu's surprise. "You fool no one here, young Jamu. I would love nothing more than to slice open your throat like you did to my pet, but I must admit you have me intrigued. You are not really Aoiyama's son, are you?"

"Aoiyama's son he is," Shiko stated, her thin braids waving about as she tossed her head back proudly.

"The pride and joy of Aoiyama, Lord Jamu is," General Kuten added.

"You carry yourself as highblood," Obitus said. "Your subjects love you, well, at least these two do. Although it was poor judgment on your part to summon their help."

"It was," Jamu agreed. "Shiko, Kuten, you should leave. In danger, your lives are."

"At your side we shall remain, until your own life is safe," General Kuten said.

"Your Guardian I am. My duty it is, to guard your life," Shiko added.

"You are a beautiful Guardian," Obitus remarked. "You know, I may consider a deal. I will leave your beloved lord alone if you offer your head in exchange for his."

"That I would gladly do," Shiko said without hesitation.

"You will do nothing of the sort!" Jamu pulled Shiko's arm to have her stand behind him. "You wish for revenge? How about a duel?"

Obitus laughed again as Shiko and General Kuten yelled in protest. "Yes, yes, I truly like that idea. But the duel I am thinking about is a bit different from your funny saber fights. It would be most unfair for you, especially seeing as you are nothing more than a noble's minor son."

"The truth he speaks. His speed and strength you cannot possibly match," General Kuten said.

Jamu remembered the trick his mother taught him, just before he left to begin training at Espies. She had promised it would protect him if ever anything like this were to happen. "I know. But I think I know what he intends to do. Perhaps we should call it a test rather than a duel."

"That sentence alone betrays you! But call it whatever you must." Obitus lifted his hand.

"You will strike me once, and then you will leave. That is the deal," Jamu said.

"Very well." The dragon's hand began to glow. A white flame sprang up from his palm.

"Stand away, both of you," Jamu warned his companions.

"Lord Jamu," Shiko cried out fretfully.

"I said stand away!" Jamu turned to face Obitus. He cleared his mind, protecting it with a mental shield just in case. He did not use his mental powers very often anymore, but he had been so well trained at Sur that his mind had no trouble responding quickly, despite months of respite. He changed his stance and held his hands up before his heart. He switched to his normal vision. The flame gave out quite a bit of light. "I am ready, Draca!"

The flame Obitus held thickened and circled over his palm to form a sphere. The glow burned Jamu's eyes, and he could feel the promise of death, deep within the hot whiteness. He pulled the energy he needed, up through his feet. It was a cooling force that calmed him and kept the panic at bay even as the dragon pulled his arm back and hurled the sphere at Jamu's chest.

Jamu cried out as the sphere slammed into his hands and enveloped him in white flames. The flames did not burn, not on his skin, anyway. He doubled over in agony as the fiery pain squeezed his muscles into painful knots and burned the very air out of his lungs. His mind shield kept most of the fire at bay, giving Jamu the chance to draw more cooling energy to help him fight off the death strike. The coolness warred with the fire, draining all of his strength. The flames around him brightened as he dropped to one knee. He heard Shiko sobbing.

"Enough of this," General Kuten said. "Survived the attack, he has. His suffering you must stop."

"There is nothing I can do. He must survive this on his own," Obitus replied.

Jamu pulled air into his lungs and closed his eyes. He was too weak to pull more life-saving energy. He willed the white fire on his skin to disperse. He focused the pain toward the center of his chest and breathed out through both his mouth and nose, pushing out some of the sphere's power with his exhale. He opened his eyes in time to see a faint glow in front of his face. It floated up and vanished like smoke. The pain coursing through him became bearable. Shiko's sobbing stopped.

"Victorious, Lord Jamu is," General Kuten said.

"I am," Jamu wheezed. He stood up and used his nightvision to catch the look on the white dragon's human face.

Obitus stared back at him impassively. He gave Jamu a slow nod. "I see. I will tell you this. Whatever you wish to call yourself, whatever reason you have for being here, you had better not cross me again! Stay away from the wards! Complete your training here, and go back to your country to live out your life in pampered comfort the way a true lord's son should."

And then he was no longer there. Jamu dropped back down on the ground, stunned. A dragon tried to strike him down. And he was still alive!

"My lord!" Shiko rushed over and held his shoulders steady as she sat him up and pressed her forehead against his temple. The remainder of the pain immediately vanished, and strength returned to his limbs.

"Thank you, Shiko," he whispered.

She responded by hugging him. Jamu rested his head against her shoulder; grateful she was there with him.

"My lord, to your ship you should return to rest," General Kuten suggested gently.

Jamu shook his head. He reached for Shiko's hand and gripped it tightly. As an empathic psychic, Shiko was able to sense Jamu's feelings. He did not really want her to know how he felt right then, but there was no way he was able to keep that from happening. He waited for her reaction.

"My lord, these feelings you must not have," Shiko chided him. "A brave, strong young man you are! The pride of Aoiyama, you are."

"Brave and strong, yes, if a bit stupid," General Kuten added.

"A brave, strong man would not have survived that attack, stupid or not," Jamu said.

"These dark thoughts of yours you must dismiss," Shiko said sternly. She grabbed his shoulders and turned him to face her.

"Shiko, you just saw what happened! This is why my mother never wanted me to come here. She feared something like this would happen. And now what? Am I going to have to face another one? What if they all want me dead? I will be exposed for the freak that I am!"

"No! A freak you are not!" Shiko shook him hard. "A rare and wonderful gift, you have. Your true self you must see, and not the picture you see now. Shocked and frightened you are, and so the truth these thoughts will not allow you to see."

"Our mental powers, a gift from the Creator, it is," General Kuten said. He pulled Jamu out of Shiko's grip and helped him stand. "A blessing for only a select few, this gift is. How much different is your gift from ours?"

Jamu used his nightvision to see the expression on the general's face. "How can you compare? Anything different is feared by most. My eyes, how many people shied away from me the very first time they took a close look at my face?"

"And how many Syntreans have stared enthralled at that same face? Compliments, do you not receive many of those?" General Kuten asked. "Many visits I have made to the city, and always I hear of the handsome Surian attending Espies. Very popular you have become, and your eyes are feared by no one here."

"And yet our psychic powers, terrorized this country is becoming of it," Shiko added. "The inhuman and the abominable, different, it is, for everyone. Inhuman you are not. A freak you are not. Never must you believe these things."

"I see now," Jamu sighed. He did, sort of. "Thank you. Thank you both."

Shiko smiled. "With General Kuten I must agree. To the ship you should return."

"I cannot. Do not worry, I am well, and that Draca will not bother me again anytime soon."

"Hopefully his word he will keep," General Kuten said. "Yet his last words I did not understand. Wards, what are those?"

"I wish I knew." Jamu grabbed at his hair, not really wanting to think about it. He could not help himself, however. "He said to keep away, and there are more than one. They have to be Academy students."

"Avoid your fellow students, you cannot," Shiko pointed out.

"No, I cannot. Wait!" Galen had been with him the day he killed that mongrel. "I must go back. I was with one of my troops when I encountered that hibrida!"

"In danger, you think the boy is?" General Kuten asked.

"The girl," Jamu corrected him. He reached out, sensing for his star troop.

"Many girls you have in your life, I see," Shiko giggled.

"Laugh about my girl troubles some other evening, please," Jamu told her. "She is in our cabin, unhurt, and a bit sleepy. If Obitus wanted to harm her he would have done so by now. So that is a relief. I should return, though. It may be a good idea to be near her, just in case."

"By your side I will remain," Shiko said. "Hidden, of course."

"No. Leave, you both must," Jamu ordered. "Difficult it will be to conceal you. And the light from the attack might have attracted attention. I will walk back to my quarters."

Shiko did not seem to like the idea, but she nodded. "As you wish. Good it is to see you, my lord, despite the circumstances. A true man you have become. Visit your ship more often, you must."

"I will try my best to do so," Jamu said, smiling. He turned to General Kuten. "Thank you for helping. In your debt, I am."

"Nonsense," General Kuten scoffed. "My duty it is, to keep you safe and comfortable. But foolish your duel was, I must say."

"We faced an angry dragon, and all turned out well," Jamu said. "The right decision, it was."

Shiko and the General exchanged a look. "Farewell, my lord," Shiko said as they both phased away.

Jamu reached out with his mind once more to make sure no one was nearby. Satisfied the area was deserted, he phased back to the Academy, just inside the northern wall. It would be a bit of a walk back to his room, but he did not dare phase anywhere closer. It was a dark moonless night, but the evening was still early. And it was a nice evening for walking.

Megan set the last of the planters on the ground beside the new greenhouse. She had been tasked with maintaining it until she graduated, part of her punishment for destroying the old greenhouse. Most of the shelves on the east wall were not strong enough to support the heavy pots, so she needed to pull the shelves off the wooden columns holding them against the wall and refasten them securely to the side of the greenhouse. She whispered a prayer as she walked inside. She stood before the shelves and held her hands out. The shelves detached from the wall, nails and dowels falling to the floor. The shelves followed her wave, floating out the door. They piled themselves in front of the pots. Megan followed the wooden planks to make sure they did not crush anything. Satisfied with the way the shelves were set on the ground, she glanced inside the greenhouse, wondering how she was going to complete this before bedtime. She gave herself until moonrise, and if she was not done by then, she would just have to endure her father's scolding. She brightened the glowspheres inside that she was using for light. As the three globes brightened, Megan caught a shadow she had not noticed before. She turned her head.

Jamu walked out of the dark. "I noticed the light in the greenhouse, and I just had to see who would be insane enough to work so late. It all makes sense to me now," he said with a grin.

"Sneaky scout! You walk too quietly. What are you doing wandering around Somatica, anyway?" She frowned at him, but she was actually quite happy to see him.

"Just walking and thinking. Today was a rather eventful day, was it not?"

"It was." He was being evasive. Living with two Espies scouts made it easy for her to tell. But she was not about to press him and scare him away. "You know, if you would like to take a break from thinking, I have some shelves I need to put up. I would love to grant you the honor of becoming my assistant."

Jamu hesitated. "Um, I… sure. I would be honored."

"You don't seem all that sure, scout. Is there something wrong?"

Jamu frowned and turned his head south, in the direction of Espies. Megan studied his face. His expression reminded her of Rohen.

After a moment he turned back to her. "Everything is fine. Come, let us get this done quickly."

Megan said nothing as she watched him pick up a plank and walk inside the greenhouse. She was quite sure she knew what Jamu had done. But she did not know for sure, and she did not want to find out. She followed him inside, rushing in front of him to gather up the mess on the floor. She fixed the nails with a hammer and a few spells. With Jamu holding the plank in place, she had the shelf securely fastened to the beams in no time. Jamu carried the second plank in, and she began hammering the nails into place.

"Meggie, can I ask you something a bit personal?" Jamu asked her.

"You are free to ask, but that does not mean I will answer it," Megan replied.

"During your first year at Somatica, when your spiritual energy was out of control and no one could really figure out why, how did it make you feel?"

She paused, trying to think of what to say. He did not know that her uncontrollable spiritual energy was really elemental magic. His question made her think of her days living at the commune. She remembered the tiny cyclone she had created the day the Penta questioned her.

"I will not feel bad if you do not wish to talk about it," Jamu said.

"No, no, I am fine. I was just thinking." She kept hammering. "I was worried for the most part. Not knowing what is going on with you, with your body, is pretty scary."

Jamu adjusted the plank to make it level. "I can imagine. But how did you feel about yourself? Did you ever feel different? Like there was something wrong?"

"I have always felt different," Megan answered. "Look at my hair. I was teased by the other kids at my commune when I was little, and most of the stories they would tell us had red-haired villains. The old druids would say that red hair was the mark of one who can wield forbidden magic."

Jamu tensed, letting the plank slip slightly. "Forbidden magic? What kind of magic is that?" he asked.

"I have no idea. It was an old tale, and probably just a story.

The grownups would avoid talking about that in front of me, but kids like to hurt other kids' feelings." Megan finished the second nail quickly before Jamu let the shelf slip again.

"I am sorry you had to endure that," Jamu said.

"It was not that bad. My mother was always there to make me feel better." She hammered two dowels into place, whispering a prayer to help drive them deep in the wood. "And then she begged Daddy to take me. She told him my secret, the secret only we were supposed to know about, and she…" Her eyes began to burn, and she stepped back and looked up at Jamu. "You know, I don't want to talk about this anymore."

Jamu nodded. He stepped back to allow Megan to put in the remaining dowels. "There is no worse feeling. To have your mother believe you are not normal, it feels like she has turned her back on you. You feel abandoned. It matters nothing that there are others who love you for who you are. How can your own mother shy away from you like that?"

His words were shocking. Megan turned around slowly. "You know how it feels. Your mother did the same to you?"

"You could say that. Surians do not have blue eyes like mine. Druids might not like red hair, but at least it is not unheard of. How do you explain to others an eye color that has never been seen before? Mother never wanted me to play with others, she never wanted me to attend Espies."

"Why?"

"She never explained to me why. But I remember one night she argued with my father. My sister and I were trying to sneak into the kitchens to help ourselves to some freshly picked grapes. We passed the door to their suite in time for me to hear her tell Father how tired she was having to watch people cringe and keep their distance from me. She said she refused to sit by quietly and allow my King and my Father to force me to endure the scorn of the people."

"Oh, Jamu!" Megan could hardly believe what she was hearing. Jamu was such a handsome boy. And he never seemed troubled about anything. He was always smiling, and it was so easy to make him laugh. "How does someone handle that?"

"Well, my Father did much for my self-esteem. I never felt unloved. And I have a Guardian. She is kind of my bodyguard. She has been with me since I was five. She knew what to do to keep me from hating Mother, and there were times when I really came close to hate. Are you going to finish setting up that shelf?"

"I suppose I should." She turned back to her hammering. Jamu had returned with the third plank by the time she was done. "I have never hated myself, even when all kinds of crazy things would happen around me. But I think that is because during the worst of days, someone was there who loved me and did not care what I looked like or what I could do. And to be honest, the only time I truly felt bad about my crazy powers was the day you guys wouldn't take me to the market after I almost killed Ben with that tree."

"I know you felt bad, it was plain on your face. I am sorry." Jamu hefted the plank for her.

"That's fine. I knew why you left me. I forgive you," Megan said. She finished the third shelf without saying anything else. Jamu was also quiet. They finished the rest of the shelves with still no moon in sight. Jamu even helped her clean up and replace the pots.

"Jamu," she said as he pushed the last pot in place on the lowest shelf.

"Yes?"

"I do not think your eyes are strange. I think you have beautiful eyes."

Jamu's olive-skinned face darkened as he blushed. "Thank you, Meggie. It really feels nice to hear you say that."

"Just don't tell my boyfriend I told you that. And don't tell him about this, either." She kissed him on the cheek. "Thank you for helping me."

"You are very welcome. It was more than worth it."

Jamu eased open the door to the cabin he usually shared with his troops. The cabin was dark, except for a faint glow behind Galen's curtain. From where he stood, he was unable to make out her silhouette to see what she was up to. He could tell that she was still, so she was probably reading. Satisfied she was safe and sound, Jamu quietly closed the cabin door and carefully backpedaled down the steps.

He was certain Obitus would leave her alone, but he did not understand why. Maybe he did not know Jamu had a companion that day. Or maybe Obitus was just focused on the one who slit the monster's throat, rendering it unrevivable. It did not matter. Obitus was gone and Galen had been left alone. He could relax.

He sat on the ground beside the steps and got into his usual meditation pose. It was time to reflect on all that had happened that day with a clear and focused mind. His mind was not as clear and focused as he would have liked it to be, but he knew that at right that moment his mind was as clear and calm as it was going to be tonight. He closed his eyes. He would seek out his father tomorrow night.

16

Vitalia's Ward

"Rohen, you are quite good with that flute. Maybe you should take a break from Espies and travel with us for a while," Kade said, pushing strands of hair out of his face.

Rohen put his flute away, much to the dismay of his troops. "I am tempted, but I have to keep your cousin out of trouble."

"There is no way we are going to let our troop leader go," Keran said. His troopmates voiced their agreement rather loudly.

Rohen grinned proudly at his group. He loved working with them, even Keran. He could not quite understand what the issue was between him and Galen, but although they still did not get along, the separation had worked wonders for both of them. They were both exceptional cadets. Sprit, Tuck, and Chet were also good, but Keran was clearly his star troop. "I know it's hard for you guys to be away from me, but I must take my leave now."

"Already?" Keran's face fell. "Come on!"

"I have things to do. Sorry."

"Well, can Kade stay with us tonight?" Kade's eyes lit up at Keran's question.

"I don't mind, as long as you all stay out of trouble. I will see you boys in the morning." Rohen put his flute case inside his trunk. "It was wonderful meeting you, Kade. I owe you a huge favor."

"It was my pleasure. It was great to meet Galen after all the stories about her," Kade replied, blushing a bit. Rohen noticed Keran's expression change, but ignored it. There was nothing he could do about Keran's feelings. And as Keran's troop leader and Galen's sponsor, he could not get involved in their discord. He left the cabin to go meet Jesi.

He found her near the Academy Tower. She sat by herself on a bench, holding something. Rohen walked over to her, dreading what awaited him. However, that dread vanished once he took one look at her face.

"Jesi?" He could tell that she had been crying, but she looked terrified now. She clutched a flask between her hands as if her life depended on it. "Did something happen?"

Jesi looked up at him and shook her head. "No. Not yet, anyway. Ro, I have to tell you something." She held out the flask. "I made you some fruit juice. Would you like some?"

Sanguis phased over to the Healer student's room, licking her lips in anticipation. After all these years, she was finally about to get her claws on Rohen. Finally. The girl Jesi stood in a corner, waiting anxiously for her arrival. Sanguis indulged her with a smile, but her happy excitement evaporated in a flash. Her bed was empty. "Where is he?" she snapped.

"I'm over here, Sanguis."

Sanguis spun around. Rohen leaned against the wall, his arms folded across his chest and his gray eyes smoldering eerily in the candlelight. He had no weapons, but that did not mean he was powerless. Sanguis snarled angrily.

"Sanguis? Her name is Seanna," Jesi said.

Sanguis turned back to her, unleashing all her fury. "You little witch! You betrayed me! Is that how you treat your friends?" She took one step forward and reached out to grab the little traitor, but Rohen grabbed her hair and forced her to turn back to face him.

"You have gone too far this time, Sanguis," Rohen said. A tiny glow flickered in his eyes. "You made a big mistake by bringing my girlfriend into this."

"It is noble of you to try to divert my attention away from your little plaything," Sanguis replied, thrusting her palm against his chest. He flew back, hitting the wall hard. "But I have a score to settle. No one betrays me!" She gestured with her other hand, and Jesi gasped as her body rose in the air and floated toward Sanguis.

"Leave her alone!" Rohen shouted. "I'm the one you want!"

"I will get to you in a moment," Sanguis said, grabbing Jesi by the throat. She felt Rohen try to touch her mind, but easily pushed him out. Jesi's face reddened as she squeezed. Her arms flailed in the air. She felt Rohen probe at her mind once more.

"Get off!" Jesi croaked. Her fist slammed painfully into Sanguis' jaw, just before Rohen unleashed a disorienting mental blast. Sanguis reeled, dropping Jesi. The room spun, but she shook her head and quickly regained her bearings. She stood between Rohen and Jesi in the tiny room. Jesi was enveloped in a soft white glow.

"What the hell?" Rohen stared at Jesi in shock, but not because of her white aura. Sanguis had felt her psychic surge, and realized what had shocked Rohen. She had placed a shield on his mind. Sanguis chuckled as she saw her opportunity.

"Didn't you know your girl is psychic?" she asked him. "Not nice, Jesi, to hide such a thing from your beloved. I know that having him as your boyfriend was part of our plan, but you should be a bit more trusting." She saw Rohen's reaction to her statement, and made her move.

Her mental strike was ruined by Jesi's own mind blast. It was as powerful as Rohen's. "What plan? To drug him and whisk him away while he was passed out? You lied to me! I would bet that you never planned to take me with you, either."

"Sanguis, your plan failed, and you are at a disadvantage,"

Rohen said. He had recovered from his shock, and was now completely focused, his hands up before him to counter any attack she should throw his way. "You may be able to take us by force, but we will put up a fight, and others will notice." His eyes glinted triumphantly. "I don't think you want anyone to know you are here, or do you?"

Sanguis gulped down an angry growl. The little bastard was right. Galen was probably running over right that moment. And if Animis or Humo caught wind of this... "I am not done with you yet, whelp!" She turned to Jesi. "And you will get what is coming to you!" She could not waste any more time. She phased back to her hideout nearby.

Galen pulled on her boots as fast as she was able to without making any noise. Her troopmates were all asleep, and she did not want them to wake up and see her leave. She struggled to keep calm. This panicky feeling had happened before, and all had turned out well. Still, she had to see what was making her feel this way.

She slipped through her curtains and made it out the door without making a sound. She jumped over the entrance steps, landing soundlessly.

"Where are you going?"

Galen almost choked on her own tongue as she whirled around. Jamu sat deep within the shadows on the ground beside the steps, his back against the cabin wall. His eyes turned red as he switched to his nightvision. Unable to come up with a suitable answer that was not a lie, Galen could only stare at him.

"I did not mean to startle you," Jamu said after a moment. "That was quite skilled of you. I did not hear a sound, and I almost did not see you jump down. But you really should be in bed. It is late."

She saw her opening. "I was restless. I need some fresh air. Why are you out here?"

"Same reason." The red glow in his eyes faded. "Enjoy your stroll. Do not get into any trouble."

"I won't." Galen turned and walked away. She was glad she had decided not to grab her bow on the way out. As soon as she was out of sight of the cabin, she sprinted off.

She did not even make it out of Espies when she realized that the panicky feeling was gone. She stopped, wondering if she should keep going. She had been meaning to go north, towards… Somatica? She was not sure anymore. She should return. Jamu had seen her leave, and…

She realized she had just passed up a wonderful opportunity. Jamu was by himself, not busy, and she had stupidly walked away. She would not have a better chance to spend some time with him. She ran back to the cabin, hoping that Jamu had not decided to go back inside to bed, or even worse, back to his room at the Tower.

He was still there, meditating. Galen stood still, watching him. She did not think she could ever get tired of looking at him.

He opened his eyes after a moment. "It is hard to concentrate with you standing right there," he said.

"I'm sorry. Can I stay with you for a while?"

Jamu shrugged. "If it will make you feel better. Come meditate with me."

Galen gave him a grateful smile and dropped down on the ground beside him. She closed her eyes and pushed all thoughts out of her head. She focused on Jamu's calm breathing. It felt so good just to be near him.

Rohen let his arms fall limp once Sanguis vanished. He could hardly believe she fell for his bluff. He looked over at Jesi, his heart pounding. "Sanguis lies about pretty much everything," he said. "Did she lie about you?"

Jesi's aura vanished. Rohen recognized the spiritual shield; Megan would practice summoning it often during their weekends at home. "Rohen, I have wanted to be your girlfriend since the day we met. Seanna...Sanguis had nothing to do with that."

"Why didn't you tell me about all this before?"

"How could I, Ro? Would you have told me? She told me that we were special, that I was destined to be in your life and that she would train us both!"

"She lied to you."

"I know she lied to me! But I believed her then! I believed that we would be together, that we would be great together. I am such an idiot! Ro, I am so very sorry!"

"It's all right," Rohen said. He put his arms around her and hugged her close. "It is not your fault."

"It is."

"I don't blame you. It's over now."

Jesi looked up at him and shook her head. "No, it's not."

Rohen did not like the way she said that. "What do you mean?"

"Kiss me and I will tell you."

He put his lips on hers. Despite their rocky relationship, he did love kissing her so. His worries melted away, and he relaxed. His eyes grew heavy. He heard her voice in his head.

Sleep now.

He touched her mind, not really meaning to. And he realized what she was doing. He pushed her away. "No! Why?"

"This is my way of making amends," Jesi said. "I will not have you worrying about keeping me safe. I know you. You will be afraid about Sanguis getting revenge."

"Jesi!" Rohen shielded his mind the way Jesi had a few moments ago, but the damage had been done. Jesi's sleep spell was spiritual, cast while he was distracted with their kiss. His legs felt like tree trunks, and the room began to sway. "Don't do this! I can't protect you if I don't remember!"

"I can protect myself," Jesi replied, guiding Rohen gently to her bed. "And I cannot have you knowing that I am psychic. It is best you forget this night."

He could not stop her from easing him down onto the bed. He fought the spell instead, but it took all his concentration just to stay awake. His mind shield melted away. "I can keep your secret. Think about this, we can start over! We know so much about each other now, Jesi. I understand you so much better. We can work on our relationship, just like you want. And what if Sanguis comes back tonight?"

"She is not coming back," Jesi said, putting her palm on his forehead. It felt very cool. "Ro, please understand. I want to be the person you enjoy being with more than anything. I want you to not have a care in the world while you are with me. You will always be worried about me if you remember. Worried about that woman attacking me, or worried about Healer Stanis finding out about me. This way you will not have that burden. And with that monster no longer hovering over my shoulder, we can finally be happy and have fun. I will be a model girlfriend from now on, you will see. Now close your eyes."

"Jesi, no, please! There is something about Sanguis you must know. I have to remember this night!" He was losing his fight. Jesi was using both her mental and spiritual powers to force him to sleep. He was no match for her. He suddenly realized that he didn't really care anymore. He stopped struggling, looking deep into Jesi's eyes as he drifted off. She did seem to be sorry.

Jesi took her palm off of Rohen's forehead after what seemed to be half the night. She had wanted to peer further into his mind, to explore his deepest thoughts and feelings, but she was drained after all that had happened. She gently pushed him over and climbed into bed beside him. She also needed to conserve what little energy she had. Rohen had a good point; Sanguis, Seanna or whatever that woman's name was, she might decide to return. She stiffened as a sinister presence snaked through her head.

Do not worry, you little twerp. I am done with you. You have brought about your own punishment.

Jesi tried to push Sanguis out of her mind, but she just did not have the strength.

I know what you did, and I must thank you. You see, he will not remember our nice little encounter, so I still have a chance with him. You, however, are a different story. He will only remember the bad times you had. He will not remember what you did for him. He will cast you aside, never knowing how you saved him, never knowing how you are the one worthy to be at his side, the one whose power can match his. You just threw that all away. Too bad, child. It will be a bitter pill, trust me.

She was gone as suddenly as she had appeared. Jesi held Rohen close to her, silently praying that Sanguis was wrong. She prayed until sleep took over.

17

Prelude to War

"So are you going back to the inn this morning?" Keran asked Kade as he pulled his boots on. They were alone in the cabin. Everyone else was off having breakfast. "You can have breakfast here in the dining hall if you want. No one will mind."

"I don't know. I really don't feel like going back there yet. It was fun staying here overnight with you and your troop," Kade replied. He finger-brushed his hair into place as he talked. Keran always hated when he did that, but today he was so happy to see his cousin he did not even feel annoyed.

"It was fun having you. My troop leader especially enjoyed it. That was very nice of you to show him new tunes for his flute. I've never seen him so excited." Remembering the happy look on Rohen's face made Keran feel warm inside. Rohen had not been his usual cheerful self these past few months.

"I'm supposed to entertain people, cousin. I'm glad he had a nice time last night." He smiled at Keran. "You look up to him, don't you?"

"He is the best troop leader a scout can have." Keran stamped his boots to get his feet in. "Jamu is good, but he is so strict and serious. Ro makes you want to follow his orders, and he never

makes you feel bad when you make a mistake or get in trouble."
He gave Kade a big smile. "I love it here."

"Now aren't you glad I made you come with me all those years
ago? Look at you now, you're top cadet in your troop, and third
highest ranking of the second year cadets." Kade walked over to
the window to look outside. "I can't believe that Galen is top ranking. She looks like she should still be playing with dolls in some
village."

Keran did not reply. Galen was the last thing he wanted to talk
about.

"She is amazing," Kade continued. "She is good at the drums.
She must be good at everything she does. Do you think we will see
her at the dining hall?"

That damned girl! How the hell did she get everyone to like
her? And now she was working on his cousin. "Why are you so
eager to see that little freak? You are supposed to be spending time
with me!" Anger made his voice quite harsh, but he didn't care.

Kade gave him a surprised look. "What is wrong with you? I
am spending time with you. I only asked if we would see her."

"You would rather spend time with her than me?"

"Why are you acting that way? And why do you keep calling
her a freak? She seems quite normal to me. She's even kind of
pretty, even with her hair cut like yours."

Keran could not believe his ears. Kade was defending her.
"You know, if you like her so much, why don't you go have
breakfast with her?"

Kade's green eyes glittered. "You know, I think I will," he said
angrily. He walked out of the cabin and slammed the door behind
him.

Keran grabbed his pillow and threw it at the door. Galen was
going to pay for that.

Galen watched quietly as Jamu brushed his hair. He had

strange hair; it had a dusky blond look from afar, but his hair color was truly a blend of brown and white and yellow. It felt different, too. Galen had touched his hair the other day. It felt silky but stiff, almost like quills on a hedgehog, but not quite. Yet he could brush and trim it. She wondered why his hair was that way.

"When do you think you will start growing a beard?" Galen asked him.

"I have no idea," he answered, dropping his brush on his bunk. "Some men do not grow hair on their faces until they are almost twenty. Everyone is different."

"Rowy is starting to shave."

Jamu stared at the floor. He didn't answer her.

Maybe she shouldn't have mentioned that. "Ben isn't yet, but he has this fuzzy stuff on his face, so he might start soon."

"Fuzzy stuff, huh?" Jamu laughed. "I am going to have to start calling him fuzz-face from now on."

Galen giggled, relieved that Jamu didn't seem to be upset. "Do you feel bad you don't have any hair on your face yet, Jamu?"

"No. I hope I do not have to shave for a long time." He picked up his brush and put it in his chest at the foot of his bunk. "Why have you not gone to breakfast yet?"

"I don't know. Do you want to come with me?" She hoped he would say yes.

"I am not hungry. I have some things I want to do today, and I am going to see Jai soon."

"Oh." She looked out the window so Jamu wouldn't see her face.

There was a knock on the door. Galen kept looking outside as Jamu opened it. She wondered why she kept trying to be alone with Jamu as much as she could. He always ended up running to Jai. And she always ended up wanting to cry.

"Good morning. I was wondering if Galen was still here."

Galen spun around. Kade stood at the doorway. He saw her and smiled.

"Good morning, Kade." Why was her heart beating so fast? "Why are you looking for me?"

"Well, Keran is angry with me for some reason, and I was looking for someone to take me to the dining hall. I don't really want to go back to Syntrea just yet. Would you like to have breakfast with me?"

"Sure." She could not believe one of the Oracle bards was asking her to breakfast. And Keran's cousin, no less. The look on Jamu's face told her that he could not believe it, either.

She skipped over to Kade, ducking under Jamu's arm. "Let's go. I am starving."

Humo licked his lips as he began sawing his knife into the roasted pork shoulder before him. He considered tossing manners out over the terrace and ripping into the juicy meat with his fingers.

His hand stopped sawing as Sanguis appeared before him. She was in human form, and she looked upset.

"What the hell are you doing here?" he growled at her. "I told you to stay away from the Academy!"

"I know, but you must listen to what I have to say. Please, Humo," Sanguis pleaded.

He studied her as he tasted the roast pork. "Your demeanor is unusually humble. Where's the demanding dragon I have grown to despise?"

"Humo, you have to help me. Animis is hunting for me. He wants me dead."

"I see. I wonder why he feels that way."

Humo marveled at her restraint. She barely frowned at him. She must be desperate. He kept his smile hidden as he waited for her reply.

"Humo, Animis ordered me to find out who Commander Adfligere is."

Humo set his knife and fork down. "He did? Obviously you failed, because you are running from him."

"No. I did not even try to obey him."

"Right."

"You don't have to believe me. I did not find out, and now he is looking to kill me. I need protection."

Humo thought he had taken care of that threat once he stopped Terra from meddling with the mages at Trader's Pass. And that was extremely stupid on his part, because Animis had made it clear to him that he would continue to search for Adfligere. No wonder he had been out of sight for so long.

Sanguis drew back at the look on his face. "Will you help me, Humo?" she asked.

He looked at his roast. It looked greasy and unappetizing now. Damn that spirit dragon for ruining his supper! "Fine. Do as I say. You will lay low and keep away from Syntrea. I want you to observe events at Trader's Pass and keep me informed. I will protect you from Animis, and if you do a very good job helping me, you can have Rohen once he graduates from the Academy."

"Humo, thank you," Sanguis said. "You will not regret this." She gave him a grateful smile and disappeared.

Humo looked at his roast again. "I should just kill that bat myself," he grumbled. He stood up and walked over to his terrace. How was he going to keep Adfligere's true identity hidden?

First he needed to put Moreus in a position where he would never be seen as someone who would wish harm to Syntrea. How could he make the Scout Chief look like a true patriot? He was of noble blood; that had to help somehow.

Of course. Noble blood made him eligible to be a suitor for Jania. What better way to commit Moreus to the well-being of Syntrea? Humo snickered. Jania had the right to chose, being the Heir, but he had her little princess ear, and she swallowed every word he said. One good talk with her, and she would be throwing herself at Moreus' feet.

He would wait for her to come to him. That would make it look better once he broached the subject. He went back inside. That pork shoulder was beginning to smell good once again.

Rohen sat up and stared at Jesi's window. How late was it? The sun was well up in the sky. He never woke up after the sun. Jesi must have given him something. He looked around. The room was empty.

He had just finished dressing when the door opened. Jesi walked in, holding a tray with food. "I got you something to eat," she said brightly.

Rohen remembered the juice they shared the night before. He had met up with her after leaving his troops, and she had invited him over to the Mall to share some of her drink. "What the hell did you give me last night?"

"You were so upset yesterday. I wanted to make sure you had a good night's sleep," she replied, putting the tray down on the small table next to the bed.

"In your bed? How could you do something like that?" Rohen headed for the door.

"Ro, wait. You need to eat." Jesi grabbed his arm and pulled him back.

"Don't tell me what to do," Rohen replied, yanking his arm away from her.

"Don't you dare walk out of here," Jesi threatened.

This had gone too far. Ever since that evening at the patio, he had complied with her every wish, hoping to keep her from talking. She knew he was psychic. He had no idea how she discovered his secret. He must have let something slip that night. He had hoped that dating her would keep her tongue from slipping, and it seemed to be working, but now she was becoming too demanding, too bossy. And now this.

Let her blackmail him if she wanted to. He had a few secrets on her, too. He doubted that she would want to send him to a place where she would never see him again. And maybe girls would leave him alone after hearing whatever spiteful things she might have to say about him. "I am leaving. And I want you to stay away from me. Don't come looking for me after classes anymore. Goodbye." He took one last look at her shocked face and rushed out the door.

He froze as the door thumped shut behind him. Maybe he should have listened to her after all.

He let go of the door latch. Megan, Florie, and Healer Stanis stood frozen before him, staring at him much like Jesi had stared at him a moment before.

Galen guided Kade through the trees. Galen carried her drumskin, and Kade had a small lute tucked under his arm.

"Too bad Rowy isn't around. He plays the flute. He would have loved to join us," Galen said.

"I heard him play last night. He is quite good. Where are you taking me?"

"There's this patio nearby. We can play our instruments without bothering anyone," she replied. "Are you sure you don't want to find Keran? He is your cousin after all. You shouldn't fight with him."

"He should not have acted the way he did. If he wants to spend time with me, then he should come looking for me, not the other way around. I'm the guest here," Kade said.

"I suppose you're right," Galen said. As they walked, she wracked her brain trying to think of a way to bring up the subject of his elemental abilities. Did he know he had elemental powers? Could he be a member of the Coven that Widow June often spoke about? But what if he didn't know? He was leaving very soon; what was the right thing to do? Maybe she should take him to meet Megan.

Voices up ahead made her stop. She gently pushed Kade against a tree. "Someone is there. Wait here," she whispered.

He nodded. Galen made her way to the edge of the patio and climbed the same tree she had when she looked in on Rohen. She eased herself onto the same branch to look down at Jamu and Jai.

"You are shallow and heartless," Jai told Jamu. She sounded as if she were crying. "How can you turn your back on me because of something like that?"

"It is not that hard, really," Jamu replied. "What you did shows what kind of person you are. And I do not like what I see. Jai, nothing can justify what you did, and you could have gotten Jania in big trouble. I do not wish to give myself to a person like that."

"So now I am not good enough for the noble Surian hero," Jai cried out. "I burn things, I destroy precious stuff. And I hurt my friends with my scheming. It didn't stop Jania from going through with it."

"She did not have much of a choice!"

"She didn't have to go running to Ben!"

"Stop that! I am not going to blame her. This whole thing was your doing."

"So I do one thing you don't like and you wish to cast me off?"

"You have done other things."

Jai let out a choked gasp. "I confided things to you. I trusted you. And now you judge me?"

"I think you should go now."

"You are overreacting. And I think you are using this as an excuse to stop dating me. You are going to regret spurning me!"

"Watch yourself, Jai."

"Are you threatening me? What can you possibly do to an Arcanum mage?"

"I can tell that mage's classmate the horrible thing she did. Not only will he be quite disgusted, it might even destroy the relation-ship that you tried to forge in the first place. Not to mention your relationship with one of your best friends." Jamu folded his arms across his chest. "I can also scheme, when I have to."

Jai turned around without another word and ran into the woods. Galen watched to make sure she did not run in Kade's direction, then turned back to Jamu.

He stood still for a moment, listening to Jai run off. Then, with a sigh, he sat down against a tree and pulled his legs up against his chest. He folded his arms on top of his knees and rested his head on them.

Galen watched him for a while. She wanted to run over to him and hug and kiss him until he felt better, but Kade was waiting for her. She finally climbed down and made her way back.

"Is it all right to go?" Kade asked when he saw her.

"No. We have to find another place," she said.

Kade gave her a tiny frown. "Why are you smiling?"

Galen looked into his green eyes. They were almost as green as Jamu's were blue. "I'm just happy, I suppose." It was definitely not a lie.

Jania hopped down the steps. Ben was waiting for her in the Winter Room to discuss their year-end project. She was looking forward to classes tomorrow. Now she could finally enjoy sitting next to him.

Jai appeared on the landing. She rushed up the steps, almost knocking Jania down. "Jai, stop! What is wrong?" Jania asked, grabbing her shoulder and stopping her.

"I hope you're happy," Jai exclaimed. Her eyes were red and teary. "I hope you are very happy with Ben!"

"What are you talking about?"

"Jamu doesn't want to have anything to do with me anymore! He thinks I am some kind of monster because of what I did." Jai pulled away from Jania and ran up the stairs.

"Jai, wait," Jania called out, running after her. She tried, but could not catch Jai before she ran into her room and locked the door.

"Let me in," Jania called out as she rapped her knuckles on the door.

"No!"

"Jai! Let's talk about this. I'm sure Jamu did not…"

"Shut your bloody mouth! Don't say his name!"

"Jai, please. You need to calm down. Let me come in."

"Jania, please go away. Ben is waiting for you downstairs. Don't mess things up with him the way you always have. That would make this even worse."

Jania was about to ask her how it was that she messed things up with Ben, but thought better of it. Jai was distraught. Jania knew very well just how deeply Jai loved Jamu. She was going to have a word with that boy. Did he realize how much he had hurt her?

"All right, Jai. I'll leave you alone." Feeling sad and angry at the same time, she walked back to the stairway to meet Ben.

"So how does it feel to be the only female at Espies?" Kade asked as Galen drummed out a beat that he had just taught her.

"It depends. Some days are harder than others." She stopped playing. "I was almost turned away. If Jamu had not asked for me to be in his troop, I would have had to leave. Rohen is my sponsor, so he could not ask for me, and none of the other troop leaders wanted me. And even afterwards, many of the scouts felt uncomfortable having me around. But now that I have proven myself, it is not so bad. And Jamu is the best troop leader anyone could ask for. But there are still a few people who don't want me around."

"Like Keran?"

"Yes. Why do you think he hates me so much? I thought it was because he was Sevilan, but you are so nice. I don't understand him."

Kade scratched his head. His black hair looked soft and shiny. It made Galen want to touch it. "I don't know, Galen. Maybe he gets that from his father. His father was very strict, and his mother was not even allowed to speak out of turn. But Keran never liked the way his father treated his mother."

"So what is it with him?" Galen asked. She looked up, and saw Keran walking toward them.

She didn't say anything when he reached them. He looked angry enough to kill her. This time, however, she could not really blame him.

"It's time to head back to the city, Kade," Keran said. "You need to get ready to travel."

"You're right." Kade stood up. "Thank you for letting me spend the day with you, Galen. I am so glad to have met you. You are quite famous, you know." He took her hand and kissed it.

"Thank you, Kade," Galen said. She did not dare say anything else. She did not want to make Keran any angrier than he already was. On the other hand, it did feel good to get one over on him.

Keran's eyes promised some sort of payback. He walked off, followed by his cousin. Galen waited until they were out of sight, then made her way to the north gate to go home for some clean clothes for the week.

She jogged through the woods as she headed back to the cottage. She could not remember ever having such a wonderful day. She had a great time with Kade, and she had Jamu all to herself once more! Summer break was almost here. She hoped Rohen would plan another camping trip with everyone the way he did with Uncle Bilin a few summers ago.

She heard Megan and Rohen yelling at each other as she approached the cottage. Everyone wanted to have an argument with someone that day, it seemed to her. She hesitated at the door, debating whether to go back and just forget about her clothes.

"You couldn't be discreet and take her to your room in the

Tower. You had to spend the night in Jesi's room. You are disgusting!" Megan sounded extremely upset.

Galen rushed inside. She could not have possibly heard right. She knew Rohen was dating Jesi, but he would never spend the night in her room. She sat down on the bench next to the door. Rohen and Megan stood facing each other. Uncle Bilin sat in his chair, far away from them. They barely noticed her come in.

"It was not what it seemed. Meggie, she gave me something and took me to her room to sleep it off. Why can't you believe that?" Rohen looked like he very much wanted her to believe him.

"Because it is just not believable, Ro! Now stop lying to me," she shouted back at him.

"Scouts don't lie!"

"That is obviously a lie, as well. I didn't know my brother was such a liar. I guess you want me to believe that she knows about your psychic ability as well?"

Galen bit her lip. So that was why Rohen was upset that morning. She could not understand how Jesi would be able to find out, but... "It's true, Meggie," she said.

Megan gave her a skeptical look. Uncle Bilin frowned. "How do you know this, Galen?"

"That day we fought, I saw him with Jesi that evening." She glanced at Rohen. He rubbed his forehead, purple-faced. "They were...friendly. But early the next morning I saw Rowy, and he was upset. So I know he's not lying. And if he says she gave him something to drink, then I believe him. She would do something like that."

The room was quiet for a long moment. Rohen finally spoke. "I don't need to explain myself to a silly Somatica student. I will go see Healer Stanis for my penance tomorrow." He left.

Megan stared at the door. "I hate her," she said. "I hate her for doing that to him!" She stamped her foot, and a chunk of earth flew up out of the floor and through the ceiling of the cottage.

Galen looked up at the hole above them. She really did blow a hole through Uncle Bilin's roof!

Megan did not even seem to notice. She ran out of the cottage, slamming the door behind her.

Bilin did not seem to notice the hole, either. He smiled at Galen. "My children are growing up," he said, a bit sadly. "Galen, promise me you will stay eleven forever."

"I'm twelve now, Uncle Bilin."

"Oh. Well, that shoots that wish dead. Maybe you should follow them to make sure they don't get into any trouble. I will take care of the roof."

"But I want to go back to the Academy. I only came here for some clothes."

"I think you should keep an eye on them. They are both quite upset, and you know the kind of trouble those two can get into."

"All right." Galen stood up and went outside. So much for trying to spend the rest of the day with Jamu.

Jania stared at the scroll Ben held between them, but she was not reading the words. She barely heard what Ben said. She still could not believe what Jamu did to Jai.

"Well, what do you think?" Ben asked her.

"What? Oh." He had been talking about the spell they were going to create. The little that she heard sounded feasible. "I think we can create this, Ben. When do we start?"

"How about now? We can use the laboratory until bedtime. Everyone else is taking advantage of what is left of the weekend break."

"I would love to, but I can't." Jania stood up. She hated having to turn him away, but… "I have to talk to Jamu."

"Why?" He looked wary.

"Jamu and Jai are no longer a couple."

"You must be joking. Are you sure?"

"Jai told me herself, just before I came downstairs to meet

you."

Ben stared at the scroll, much like Jania had. He looked bothered. "Let us both go and talk to him."

"Ben, I think I should speak with Jamu myself." She heard footsteps coming from down the hall, and turned to see who would pass by.

Jamu stopped at the doorway. He saw Jania and gave a little bow. "I heard you say you wanted to speak with me. Good, this is, because I wish to speak with you as well."

Jania gave him her sternest look. Why did he look angry? He was the one who hurt Jai. "Let us go to my room, then. Ben, will you excuse us?"

Jamu shook his head. "I am not going anywhere near where that girl might be."

Ben stood up. "You mean Jai? What is going on? Jamu, why are you playing games?"

"I am not playing games. Quite the contrary. And I am tired of both of yours!"

Jamu's outburst made Jania take a step back. She stared at Jamu. What did he mean by that?

She frowned at him, but he only held her gaze with his angry blue eyes. "Fine, Surian," she finally said. "Where would you like to go and talk?"

"My troop's cabin is empty at the moment," Jamu replied. "We can go there. Ben, I apologize. But I do need to speak with Jania in private."

Jania expected Ben to get angry. It did not take much to offend him. He looked worried, instead. "I suppose you won't tell me what this is about," he said.

"This is about many things," Jamu replied. He offered Jania his arm. "Will you come with me?" he asked her.

"Of course." She turned to Ben. "Can we continue this after classes tomorrow?"

He gave her one of his rare smiles and nodded. "Of course."

Relieved, Jania took Jamu's arm and left the winter room. She managed to keep her composure until they reached the cabin. Jamu shut the door.

"Do you realize how much you have hurt Jai?" she asked him.

"I do. But I believe it is for the best. There is more to my decision than how I feel about her destroying a book," Jamu said. "But I do not wish to be with a person who would do such a thing just to get two people in the same room."

Jania sighed. How was she going to argue with that? "You are just shocked right now. I am sure you will see things differently in a few days."

"Maybe. Maybe not." Jamu dropped down on his bunk. "So was it worth it?"

"What?"

"Your afternoon with Ben? Was it worth it?"

Was it worth Jai's heart being torn to shreds? "Why did you tell him that we may have to date?"

"We were talking. I wish I had not. It really bothered him." Jamu grinned. "You know why, do you not?"

"Of course. It bothers him that someone would have to date a person they didn't want to date. He even offered to date me if I wanted to avoid a forced courtship."

"He said that?" Jamu sounded incredulous. "Are you sure he was not propositioning you?"

"Of course he wasn't! He was being a friend."

Jamu covered his face with his hands and shook his head. "You are both fools," she heard him say.

"Why don't you look at me and say that to my face!" she yelled at him.

"I will! You are a fool. You do not see the obvious. And Ben is a coward. He should have told you straight out that he wanted to date you."

"You are the one who does not see the obvious. Ben feels uncomfortable around me because of who I am. And he is jealous because I compete for his friends' time. Who would be attracted to someone who always puts him in an awkward spot?"

"Oh, please. Did Master Humo tell you that?"

Jania's eyes narrowed. "Where did that come from?" she asked.

"Does it surprise you? Seen you, I have, taking walks with the Headmaster, listening to everything he has to say. This is the man who wants to discard your throne, Jania. Why are you listening to him?"

"He is Headmaster for a reason. It behooves me to listen to whatever wisdom he has to impart. I will not close my mind to other views and beliefs."

"Nor to brainwashing! You have changed. You used to care about relations between Syntrea and Massea."

"I still care! It just isn't an important issue right now."

"With border skirmishes threatening trade? Do you really think so?"

"Humo says…"

"Oh. So he is just plain Humo to you now." Jamu jumped to his feet and grabbed her by the shoulders. "Open your eyes, Jania. Your throne and country are on the line here."

"No. You are overreacting." Jania pulled away from him. "He sees how advantageous it will be for Syntrea to have me as Queen."

"Advantageous for Syntrea or for him?" Jamu asked.

Jania stared at the Surian. She suddenly felt unsure of herself.

"Tell me, Princess, how do you feel about the graduating scouts having to go to Trader's Pass for their first assignment? Yar tells me that the Gladia soldiers might have to go as well."

"I didn't know about that." She should have, though.

"I see. So Humo did not inform you about that little decision of his."

"No, he didn't." Jania turned away, suddenly angry. There was no reason for her not to know. Was Humo stringing her along? Did he really believe she would be gullible enough to be brainwashed? Was she?

She jumped as a loud whistle sounded. Three long blasts, and a pause. Three more long blasts, and another pause.

Jania's mouth went dry. Never in all her years at the Academy had she heard that whistle. And the dreaded pattern was one she had never hoped to hear. "Jamu, that is…"

"A call to arms," Jamu finished for her.

Galen stared at the pile of rubble that had been the old church. She always went to the church at the Academy, but it was shocking to see Father Cin's old home leveled to the ground. Only the bell tower stood.

She knew they were both here. She had tracked them here; Rohen had not even bothered to take care to hide his trail. She walked around until she found the entrance to the stairs, and walked up to the belfry.

She found them sitting before the arched opening. Megan had her arms around Rohen's shoulders.

"Did you do this?" she asked them.

"No. We found the church this way," Megan said. "We were wondering what could have happened to it."

"We haven't been around here for so long," Rohen said. "It's impossible to even tell how long the church has been like this. You would think a bunch of drunken mages had a party here."

Galen sat down on Rohen's other side. "Uncle Bilin is worried. He sent me to keep an eye on you two."

Megan and Rohen looked at each other and laughed. Galen smiled. Everything was going to be fine.

"Daddy is always afraid that we are going to end up killing each other one day," Megan giggled.

"Now why would he think such a thing?" Rohen asked.

Galen laughed.

"Gayly and I are going to have a nice talk with Jesi tomorrow," Megan said.

"No, Meggie, let it go," Rohen said. "That will only cause more trouble."

"She is not going to get away with what she did."

"Meggie, I said let it go. We have much more important things to worry about."

"Like what?"

"Like the druids coming after you again. And what am I going to do about my spellcasting ability."

"Are you going to tell Ben and Jania about it?" Galen asked.

"Yes. I wonder how their afternoon went. I hope it was worth burning a book."

Galen bit her tongue to keep from telling Rohen about Jamu and Jai. She was not supposed to know about that.

"You know, this is nice," Megan said, looking around the belfry. "We should make this our special place, for just the three of us."

"Oh, I like that," Galen said. "We should come up with a kind of signal to send, and when we receive the signal, we always come here."

"Our special place," Rohen repeated. "I like that too."

"So what will the signal be?" Megan asked.

Three long whistle blasts sounded in the distance. There was a pause, and three more sounded.

"What the hell?" Rohen helped Megan and Galen to their feet.

"A call to arms? How can that be?" Megan asked.

"I don't know, but we better hurry. We need to make sure Papa Bilin heard the call."

Terra stood at the edge of the Mall and watched as all the last year students, Gladia soldiers, Arcanum mages, Somatica Healers and Espies scouts, lined up on the plush grassy area. They all carried travel bags. The Academy rule about carrying bared arms was waived. Terra looked at the group of young men and women, barely children. There would be no graduation ceremonies this year.

In a hasty ceremony, honors that were usually bestowed to graduates upon completing the Academy were given to the last year students. Healers sported their bright yellow and orange armbands. Scouts had tiny golden hoops poked into the tops of their ears. Mages wore their hooded robes, and soldiers were donning the bronze helmets and gauntlets that distinguished them as elite Gladia soldiers. They all wore their badges proudly, waiting for the next step.

Humo walked by her. He only gave her a quick passing look, but Terra still caught the triumphant grin on his face. He had done it. Somehow, he managed to get Massea to pull back all their forces, leaving Syntrea vulnerable to Eastern attack. Now, every resource available was to go and reinforce their suddenly weakened troops. The mages and Healers were going to Trader's Pass, the only place in Massea that Syntreans were allowed to venture freely, to be better accessible to the defending forces.

Terra turned and headed back to the Tower. She did not want to hear Humo give the orders to move out. At least none of the wards were in that group.

Jamu watched the last of the students march out of the inner gate. He was numb. How did the situation deteriorate so quickly? He knew that the skirmishes were making Massea angry, but they seemed to understand that the disputes were condemned by King Raimo. And what would drive them to risk the security of their coasts?

People began moving. The call was done, and it was time to prepare for the next day. Jamu walked over to Rohen, who stood nearby.

"This is awful," Rohen said as he approached. "Did Jania know this was going to happen?"

"She would not have let it happen if she had known." Jamu wondered if his words were true.

"She must feel terrible about this," Rohen said. "Well, there's nothing left to do but go to bed. I need to see Healer Stanis in the morning."

Jamu looked around to make sure none of his troops were still running around. He didn't see any of them. "Good idea."

"I wonder what happened with Ben and Jania that afternoon," Rohen said as they walked to the Tower.

"Wonder no more," Jamu replied. He told Rohen about Ben's offer. Rohen laughed.

"Oh, Ben! How can such a smart person be such an idiot?"

"Lack of common sense seems to be a mage trait," Jamu said. He went on to tell him about Jania and Headmaster Humo. This time Rohen did not laugh.

"We can't let Master Humo corrupt her," Rohen said. "She is too important. Humo could take over Syntrea if he had the Princess under his control."

"What can we do?" Jamu asked. "Why would our words carry more weight than the Headmaster's? We can only hope that this incident has opened her eyes."

"Opened her eyes how? Do you think Master Humo had anything to do with this?"

"You know something? For some reason, deep down inside I hope he did. And I hope someone will find him out." He had to speak with his father about this.

18

The Princess-Heir of Syntrea

Jania sat quietly at the foot of the steps leading to the Academy Tower, fighting back tears as she watched. Jamu's words echoed over and over in her mind.

You used to care about relations between Syntrea and Massea.

He was wrong, but he was also right. Humo had convinced her that the rift between Syntrea and Massea was not something she should spend too much time worrying about. She was ashamed. Jamu must think her such a fool.

She did not move once the students were out of sight and people began to move on. No one noticed her as they walked by. They would move aside but no one realized why. Jania congratulated herself. She had concealed herself, but she had not used a spell.

Jamu and Rohen approached the steps. Jania forced herself to keep calm. This would be the true test. They knew her well and might see through the illusion. Especially Rohen. She remembered the day they met, and the risk he took by asking her about psychic abilities. She looked straight ahead as they passed her by. They spoke in low tones, but she was able to hear them clearly.

"We can't let Master Humo corrupt her," Rohen said. "She is

too important. Humo could take over Syntrea if he had the Princess under his control."

"What can we do?" Jamu asked. "Why would our words carry more weight than the Headmaster's? We can only hope that this incident has opened her eyes."

The thought of Rohen believing that she could be led by a string was unbearable. She looked around. Suddenly nothing seemed the same. She felt as if she had been living in one of those old children's adventure stories Dara would read to her at bedtime. Only the evil villain was actually her Headmaster. She caught sight of Humo, walking towards the Academy Tower. The sight of him cut into her train of thought and gave her pause. Humo's words had affected her reasoning. She had to make sure that Jamu and Rohen's words did not do the same. Her eyes might have opened, but she needed to see for herself.

She watched Humo walk by her, also oblivious. She stood up and followed him up the stairs. Don't worry, Ro. No one will ever have control over me.

Moreus walked into Humo's office without knocking and closed the door behind him. Jania stood nearby, still concealed, but hidden within the shadows cast by the torchlight beyond the curving corridor. She was a bit surprised when Humo had the Scout Chief summoned, but she knew that this meeting would give her the answer she sought. Was she really being fooled by the Headmaster? She silently made her way to the door. She had to see for herself. Or rather, hear. She pressed her back against the wall and listened. She was not worried about anyone catching her. She would hear the lightest footstep in plenty of time.

It was difficult to make out what they were saying. Jania took a deep breath, grateful she was wearing a simple cotton blouse and comfortable silk leggings under her Arcanum duster instead of a restricting corset. Proper breathing helped her immensely whenever she used her mental powers. Her hearing sharpened. And then she heard her name. That was all she needed to hone in on the conversation.

"She will be the crowning touch, literally," Humo was saying. "But keeping you in a positive light is what is most important right now. You must make a move for her hand. Begin wooing her."

"You want me to court the Princess-Heir of Syntrea?" Moreus sounded as appalled as Jania felt.

"The Princess can consort with anyone she chooses to," Humo said. "There is no age limit. You are an excellent prospect for her. Plan this well, and you might even end up sitting on a throne beside her."

"Sounds quite enticing," Moreus said. "If a bit farfetched."

"Worry not, she trusts me, and will follow through with whatever I advise her. We only need you to show interest in Jania right now. It is all about appearances. We cannot have anyone suspecting." Humo's voice faded as Jania's shock set in and spoiled her concentration. She tiptoed away, breaking into a run after passing several doors.

She ended up before Jamu's room a few floors down. She raised her arm to knock on his door, her arm trembling furiously. But she could not make herself knock. She pulled her hand back and wiped her eyes instead. She wished she knew which room belonged to Rohen. She would have no problem asking him for help. Rohen would never think any less of her, even after learning about her and Humo.

An idea came to her. She could sense for Rohen and find him that way! It was a bit risky, but getting caught using psychic powers was the last thing she was worried about. Still, it might cause trouble she could not foresee at the moment. No, she couldn't bother him either. She had to deal with this on her own.

She heard someone on the stairs. The footsteps reached the floor she was on, and continued downward. Jania rushed to the landing and peeked over in time to catch a glimpse of the Scout

Chief's head. Jania quietly followed him. She had to end this fledgling plan of Humo's before it even began. Using almost every mental trick she knew, she shadowed Moreus all the way back to his cabin quarters at Espies without being detected.

She watched from behind a tree as Moreus closed his door shut. She looked around to make sure no one was nearby before sprinting over to the Scout Chief's quarters. She considered mind-blasting the door open, but thought better of it. She unlocked the inside latch with her mind and entered, slamming the door shut quickly behind her. Moreus spun from where he stood, an empty glass goblet in his hand.

"I am sorry to bother you at this late hour, but this is rather important," Jania said as she walked over to Moreus. His shock was so complete he did not even struggle as she grabbed his face with one hand. Her attack was quick, focused and piercing, the way Animis had taught her to do in order to grab control of an opponent's mind.

"What are..." Moreus gasped in fear as Jania raised her other hand. She snapped her fingers, and his expression went blank. Pulling on his face, she tugged him over to a nearby chair and pushed him into it. She glared at his rugged, bearded face in disdain. How dare he even think she would be interested in someone so much older?

"Listen to me, Moreus," she began, keeping his gaze locked on her eyes. She hoped she looked as infuriated as she felt. It would make the hypnosis much easier. "Humo may have given you an order, but he does not realize that it will be impossible for you to accomplish. And I will tell you why. You are not worthy of my time. I am the Princess-Heir to the most powerful country in the world, and I am a powerful spellcaster as well. You are powerless compared to me. You are meaningless compared to me."

She felt Moreus protest slightly, but his struggle against her will felt like a worm trying to pry open her closed fist. It was quite pathetic. She continued. "Remember where you stand when it comes to me. You will not look me in the eye, ever! You will not speak to me unless I address you first. You will realize that you are not capable to meet my expectations and I would never consider you for a suitor. You will fail at this if you try, so do not even bother." She released his face and stepped back.

The goblet slipped out of his hand, but Jania caught it before it hit the floor. She set it on the mantle as Moreus slowly emerged from the trance she had placed him in. She walked over to the door, but waited until he sat up straight and turned to her. Their eyes met.

Jania grinned as he immediately dropped his gaze. "I am glad we understand each other, Chief Moreus. Thank you for your hospitality, but I must take my leave now." She slipped through the doorway and closed the door.

Her blood rushed angrily through her veins. An idea bloomed in her excited mind. Without hesitation she rushed back to the Academy Tower. Her idea was insane, but if she could overpower the Scout Chief so easily, she should be able to do the same to the Headmaster. He could not possibly be much harder to overpower. He was a powerful mage, but he was still a man.

She reached the Tower steps and sprinted to the top. Nearly giddy from the adrenaline fueling her, she reached the front doors and pulled one open.

Rohen stood at the entrance.

Jania felt her courage slip away. The way he stared at her made her feel like she had been caught doing something wrong. "Ro! Why are you just standing there?"

He did not answer. He took her arm and led her over to the top of the steps. He took a seat at the top step, pulling her down to sit beside him.

"What are you doing here?" he asked.

"I have to see Humo," she answered.

"Why?"

"None of your business."

"I disagree. I saw you."

"Saw me where?" She knew they had to be careful with words. Anyone could be eavesdropping, and they did not have to be nearby.

Rohen only sighed. "I saw you," he repeated. "You heard us talking, I am sure."

She wanted to leave and finish her business with Humo, but she wanted Rohen to keep her company even more. "Jamu was right. But my eyes are open now. So I have to go and—"

"No!"

Jania was taken aback by the look on Rohen's face. "I have to. I can't let him get away with treating me like a fool."

"Jania, you say your eyes are open now. You have already beaten him. You risk unnecessary trouble if you confront him."

"But he tried to use me! He deceived me, and I fell for it. I need to redeem my honor!"

"Honor? How did he dishonor you?"

Jania felt the tears return. How could she explain to him her humiliation, and how far she must have fallen in Jamu's eyes? "You wouldn't understand. Jamu, he would understand."

Rohen shook his head. "No, you're wrong. I think I do. You are embarrassed. You think Jamu will see you as someone who can't handle powerful people. You feel as if he lost confidence in you."

"How? How do you and Jamu do it? You are so smart, so... so much smarter than I can ever be." She put her head on his shoulder and whimpered. He put his arm around her waist and held her against him for a moment.

"Pull yourself together, Princess. We are outside, and people are still walking about. Do you have any idea how scary it feels to have a Princess crying on top of you?"

And he always knew how to make her laugh. "I can...hide us."

Rohen nodded. "I know," he said with a smile. "But no. Let us avoid any more trouble. May I escort you to Arcanum?"

"Yes, please."

He helped her to her feet and took her arm. Jania was grateful for having such a friend. They walked slowly towards Arcanum Tower.

"There is one more thing I should tell you," Rohen said. "Jamu does not think any less of you. He is worried about you, but not because he thinks you are not capable. He knows that the Headmaster is more cunning and experienced than all three of us combined. And yet you saw through his scheme. He will be awed when he realizes you are too smart to be manipulated by Humo."

Jania's shoulders eased, and her knees wobbled just a bit. "I have no choice but to believe you, scout. Thank you."

"You can thank me by promising me you won't do anything to antagonize the Headmaster."

"I promise." She owed him that much. He had very likely saved her soul that night. What would have happened if she had confronted Humo?

"You are going to be a great Queen. I wish you were my princess."

"Then let me grant you that wish." Jania kissed Rohen's cheek. "I am your princess. And your princess I will always be."

Jesi walked slowly, keeping close to the trees and bushes as she made her way to the Academy Tower. Hardly anyone was about, few people wanted to be out and about after having to witness that shocking departure, but Jesi did not want to have to acknowledge or greet anyone. The only person she wanted to talk to was Rohen.

So that wretched woman was right. It was horrible to see how true her prediction had been, in the span of just hours. She had expected him to be upset, but she had not anticipated her own reaction. She thought she would be different, she thought her demeanor would change. And yet she had threatened him right be-

fore he left her and walked into a heap of trouble. It was over. After enduring the shame of facing Healer Stanis, Healer Druce, and
Druid Bilin, she could not even imagine what they had in store for
Rohen. But whatever it was, she knew that it would irrevocably
destroy what little was left between the two of them.

But even though Rohen was lost to her, she needed some kind
of closure. She needed to know how he felt now. She could not
bring those memories back. She did not know how, and even if
she did, she was not sure she wanted to. Even after everything, she
still felt the same way she did when she first put him to sleep.

She stopped in her tracks. Rohen was walking across the Mall,
with Princess Jania clinging to his arm. Jesi's knees began to
shake. She leaned against a tree to steady herself and watched
them walk by.

Not even a day had passed and he was already hovering
around other girls. Seanna's hateful thoughts echoed in her head.
It was a bitter pill. But what could she do?

Rohen's head turned in her direction, his eyes glowing red. The
Princess chatted on, oblivious. Jesi stared back, waiting to see
what he would do.

His nightvision faded, and he turned away. Jesi then realized
that there was something she could do after all.

She was not sure whether she was mostly angry with Rohen,
Seanna, that prissy princess or herself, but what she was sure of
was that someone was going to answer for her loss. Someone was
going to suffer the way she was suffering right then. She glared at
Rohen and Jania as they walked out of sight. Yes, someone was
going to pay.

Epilogue

The black fountain that materialized within the mist spewed grimy smoke instead of water or mist. Obitus sat at the edge of the fountain and watched the smoke blend in with the gray astral fog. It reflected his mood perfectly. Waiting for the other Draca to appear was not cheering him up any, either. Even Humo, who always prided himself on promptness, had not yet arrived.

As soon as he thought of the cranky Earth Dragon, Humo walked into view, his plain black shirt and breeches slimming him to the point where he looked gaunt and spindly. Combined with his human black hair and eyes, his skin looked ghostly. The scowl on his face made him the perfect picture of villainy. Obitus could not keep a smile off his own human face.

"Find something funny?" Humo snarled. He was in an even worse mood than Obitus.

"Yes. How is it that your students do not run away screaming in fear at the sight of your face?" Obitus asked.

"I am still working on that. Most humans are too stupid to recognize danger when it jumps out at them," Humo grumbled back. He took a seat beside Obitus.

"I would say humans are just too stupid to know when to run from danger when they are faced with it," an unexpected voice said. Obitus turned his head to see an ancient man, bald except for a clump or two of wispy hair on his spotted scalp. The man sat hunched, but his glowing blue eyes were sharp and clear as he looked at Obitus. "I would say the same for some dragons."

Obitus recognized the threat. Sandwiched between the two other dragons, Obitus struggled not to squirm. He kept his seat, however. He would not let Abeo intimidate him, even if it meant facing his disgusting ancient form up close.

Abeo's hoarse, trembling voice kept talking. "It is a beautiful day over at Sur. I planned to bask in the sun, but of course I would never dismiss a call from a fellow Debellos. We may not always work together, but we must always respect each other. It could mean very bad luck if we didn't."

"Abeo, what?" Humo cried out in exasperation. "Why the veiled threats? Tell me what is going on."

"You have not been paying attention at the events unfolding at your school, have you, Earth Dragon?" Abeo asked, leaning forward to look at Humo. "Your Surian scout seems to have caught the attention of our fellow Debellos here."

Humo glared at Obitus. He was obviously not pleased.

Obitus shrugged. "Abeo, the fact that you know tells me that he has attracted your attention as well."

"He is the son of the most powerful House in Sur! Of course he has attracted my attention!" Abeo said.

"What are you doing snooping around my Academy?" Humo snarled. "If you are interested in one of my students, all you need to do is ask me about it."

Obitus let out an exaggerated sigh. "You are both making too big a deal out of this. Humo, you have all these powerful whelps in your school. It is hard to ignore sometimes. The young Surian seemed to be a possible ward. I investigated, and discovered it was not so. And that is all. Abeo is upset because he probably never thought to take a closer look a the boy." He turned to face Abeo, daring him to say something contradictory in front of Humo.

The elderly human backed down. "If that is how you want to phrase it," he said. "What I find curious is how you noticed him. You belong far west, beyond the Freelands. What were you doing in Syntrea?"

"The answer to that is the reason I called this meeting," Obitus replied, glancing up as the mist shifted overhead. A black dragon and a red floated down to land before the fountain. The dragons quickly shifted to human forms, the black dragon becoming an impossibly buxom woman covered in skin-hugging black leather from neck to feet. The red dragon turned into a small lithe woman, much less curvaceous but beautiful nonetheless, dressed in a simple black sleeveless gown adorned with flowers made out of red and white flames. The mist became still once again.

"Where is Aboria?" The raven-haired dragon asked. She waved some astral mist over and made herself a comfortable seat. Obitus noticed how she avoided Humo's gaze. The flame-haired dragon hooked her hands behind her back and began to pace in circles.

"I don't know, Tabesis. I do not believe she will appear," Obitus answered, glancing at the mist once more to make sure. "She is furious with me for losing Poli."

"Yes, I forgot to thank you for ruining the one advantage we had against the Tueri," Abeo muttered. "You should be chasing after her instead of young brats you cannot even mark as your own."

"She knows all your plans now, and you did not benefit one bit from her ability to detect the wards once they were born. Abducting her was by far the biggest miscalculation you have made since we arrived here," Humo added contemptuously.

"Enough already!" The redheaded dragon stopped pacing. "It is done, and it is a waste of time to throw accusations. There are two wards left. We should work together to find them before Poli!"

Trust Senui to always come to his defense. Obitus gave her a tiny smile of gratitude. She pretended not to notice.

"Yes, sure. Found yours yet, Senui?" Abeo asked with exaggerated innocence.

Senui hissed at Abeo. Her hands clenched into fists and erupted in flames.

"Why are we here?" Humo nearly howled, interrupting the near confrontation.

"Shouldn't we wait for Sanguis?" Senui snarled back, resuming her pacing.

"No. That is why I called you all here," Obitus said. "Sanguis has foolishly broken the Pact, with no advantage gained. Her ward has been marked by Vitalia, and Sanguis is becoming desperate. Her plans to get hold of the boy, if you can call them plans, have made the situation worse for everyone. She has already ruined my plans, and I am sure she has inconvenienced at least some of you."

Tabesis shrugged. "So?"

"So she has become a liability. She has helped the Tueri dragon Animis."

Humo snorted angrily at that last statement, but he said nothing. The others seemed less upset.

"What do you propose?" Abeo asked. "You wish to send her back home? There is no one to take her place."

"That is not really an option. She refuses to leave. We would have to take more drastic measures."

"You wish to slay her?" Tabesis asked incredulously. Senui's foot froze in midstep.

"It is something I strongly believe we should consider. She is hurting our cause. She is allowing her ego and her failure to guide her actions." Obitus glanced at the others, and knew immediately what their decision would be. He turned to Humo. Humo held the most rancor. "Humo, you know the damage she has caused. She no longer has the competency to fulfill her duties."

"We are still short by one," Humo replied sourly. "There has to be a way we can use her to achieve our own ends. We must see her renegade status as an advantage, not a disadvantage. I cannot condone your suggestion."

Obitus hid his disappointment and addressed his closest ally next. "Senui. You understand my position."

"I do," she admitted as she set her foot down. Her blood red eyes met his. "But it is too drastic. I would love nothing more than to burn all life here to ash and build this world back up to the way it should be, but even we Debellos must behave the way a civilized species should. We are not evil, even though humans may believe we are, as well as some Draca. If we cannot indiscriminately exterminate an entire species, then we certainly cannot exterminate one of our own. Even my bloodthirsty brother would agree with me." She lowered her head in regret. "I cannot condone this either, Obitus."

"We are not evil," Abeo cackled softly. "An inferior species believes us to be evil, but just because we wish to do away with their way of life and steal their home out from underneath them doesn't mean we are. Ha! Could you possibly make a more ridiculous statement than that one?"

"Mock me one more time, cretin!" Senui shouted.

"So you agree with me," Obitus said to Abeo, more to distract him from Senui than anything else.

"No, I do not agree with you," Abeo spat. We turned his head to address Senui. "We do what we must to survive. Good and evil is all in the mind, not dictated by a set of rules. It is no different than beauty and ugliness. Who are we to say we are not evil? We come to terms with our souls and our values, and to hell with what anyone else thinks! You think we are not evil even though others believe we are, Senui? I think that counts as being evil."

"You see yourself as evil, and you do not care," Senui retorted. "That makes you the evil one of the group."

Abeo shook his age-spotted head and rolled his eyes. "Obitus, Sanguis is my sister. This evil dragon would never agree to have another Spirit Dragon slain. Let her be, she will most likely get herself killed sooner or later, just like Gravesco."

Obitus could almost feel the rage emanating from Humo. Tabesis smiled at him from her misty perch.

"Need I say anything? I believe I will pass on the explanatory speech." The mist she sat on enveloped her, and she was gone.

"I have things to do," Humo said. "I shall be more than happy to have you visit the school as an honored guest, you need but ask. Otherwise, stay the hell away from my Academy." He pushed himself off the fountain ledge and walked into the mist.

Abeo stood and stretched, his bones creaking loudly. The thought he projected at Obitus was strong and fierce, nothing like the powerless frailty the Spirit Dragon displayed.

Jamu is mine to deal with. Leave him alone!

Obitus waited for Abeo to hobble away into the mist. "This group is a disaster. No wonder we have lost most of the wards," he said to Senui, who had resumed her pace once more.

"At least we all agree on what is important," Senui said. She walked over to the fountain and sat beside Obitus. "You are allowing your anger to influence your decisions. Did you truly believe we would all agree on killing her?"

"She is dangerous, Senui. I saw it."

Senui took his hand. "It was a divination you saw?"

Obitus nodded. He could let his guard down around Senui. "If we leave her be, she will bring disaster down on all of us."

"Come now! We make our own destinies. These predictions are only warnings, not prophecies set in stone. So Sanguis is a nuisance. Deal with it." She leaned forward to kiss him.

Obitus turned away from her. He would not make the same mistake Gravesco made. Love and courtship always muddled the brain. "I will deal with it. But you cannot blame me for trying to prune the weed before it grows."

Her face was still right next to his. "Just remember why you are here." Senui whispered in his ear. "And once this is all done, we can go home."

His shoulders tensed involuntarily. Senui always knew what to say to get a reaction out of him. He turned to face her, wanting to take in her human beauty that still was able to reflect her true self. He was fooling no one.

But she was gone. He sat alone by the fountain. He had to get Megan back. The druid child was the key that would open the gate to go back home.

Obitus stared at the patch of earth before him. The mongrel's body was long gone, but he still sensed some of the pestilence left behind once the body dissolved into nothing.

He dropped to his knees and thrust his human arm deep into the ground. He felt around for a bit before pulling it back out. He had not fished out much, not enough to infect more than one person, maybe, but that should be all he needed. He stood back up, frowning at the stains on his white trousers, and took a stroll over to Galen and Megan's home.

He pushed the door open with his elbow. Everyone was at the Academy, so he could move freely about the cottage. He walked from room to room, stopping at what was surely the room the girls shared while they were here.

There were few items in the room, but Obitus was able to distinguish Megan's clothes from Galen's easily. He had observed them for only a few days, but their size difference was obviously apparent. He picked up a blouse that was too big to fit Galen, but something in the corner of the room caught his eye.

He walked over to the folded up drumskin. He knew Galen would play often during her free time. He glanced down at his hand. He would have to choose.

He would have other opportunities with Megan, but Galen grew more dangerous by the day. And she had killed his little fox. It would be ridiculous to ignore this chance.

He ran his soiled hand over the drumskin several times, tapping the drumskin lightly to knock loose the small clumps of dirt. He blew the dirt away with a brief gust. It might take some time, but the disease would not die off on the new skin. Sooner or later she would succumb, and once she did he would make sure she would not recover.

Obitus glanced down at his soiled trousers. It was time to get cleaned up. And to come up with a new plan to get his Chosen back within his clutches.

The Draca Wards Saga

Continues in…

COMING OF AGE

Whether princess or peasant,
Healer or warrior;
Their destinies are intertwined.
They just don't know it yet.

The evil headmaster and his allies have been thwarted, but the teen wards still have some growing up to do. Studies become harder, romances begin to take hold, and war begins to touch their lives as Humo shifts his evil plans for world domination into full gear. And Humo is not the only threat the wards face…

From illness to fireballs, the Debellos use every trick they can to vanquish the wards. And when the two powerful countries of Syntrea and Massea stand at the brink of war, the alliance keeping the eastern invaders at bay is all but lost. But the Princess and Jamu have joined forces, and Jamu has a plan. Can they defy the Headmaster's will and live to tell the tale? And will their partnership kill any chance Ben has left to win over Jania's heart?

For more details and information,
visit www.SilverLeafBooks.com

Also available from Silver Leaf Books:

CLIFFORD B. BOWYER

The Imperium Saga

Fall of the Imperium Trilogy

An evil tyrant weaves a tapestry of deception as he plots to conquer the Imperium. Only a few heroes are brave enough to uncover the mystery and face Zoldex directly. Follow the adventures of the heroes of the realm as they try to preserve the Imperium and confront Zoldex's forces. Their hearts are true and their intentions noble, but will that be enough to overcome such overwhelming odds? Find out in the *Fall of the Imperium Trilogy.*

The Impending Storm, 0974435449, $27.95
The Changing Tides, 0974435457, $27.95
The Siege of Zoldex, 0974435465, $29.95

The Adventures of Kyria

In a time of great darkness, when evil sweeps the land, a prophecy fore-tells the coming of a savior, a child that will defeat the forces of evil and save the world. She is Kyria, the Chosen One.

From the pages of the Imperium Saga, *The Adventures of Kyria* fol-lows the child destined to save the world as she tries to live up to her destiny.

The Child of Prophecy, 0974435406, $5.99
The Awakening, 0974435414, $5.99
The Mage's Council, 0974435422, $5.99
The Shard of Time, 0974435430, $5.99
Trapped in Time, 0974435473, $5.99
Quest for the Shard, 0974435481, $5.99
The Spread of Darkness, 0978778219, $5.99
The Apprentice of Zoldex, 0978778227, $5.99
The Darkness Within, 0978778243, $5.99
The Rescue of Nezbith, 0978778251, $7.99
The Responsibility of Arifos, 1609750217, $7.99
Full Circle, 1609750233, $7.99
and more to come!

Ilfanti

Known as an adventurer, the dwarven Council of Elders member Il-fanti is one of the most famous Mages in the realm. Everyone knows his name, and others flock around his charisma. But even Ilfanti is at a loss for why the Mage's Council is ignoring the fact that Zoldex has returned and none are safe as his plans go unchallenged.

The Empress has been kidnapped while in the midst of trying to unite the races. Her true whereabouts are unknown, but her return is vital to the survival of the Seven Kingdoms. The Mages are doing nothing, and Ilfanti can no longer condone avoiding the obvious signs that are plaguing the realm.

Follow Ilfanti as he returns to a life of an adventurer and battles against time to save the Imperium. Experience the adventure and learn if the charismatic adventurer can complete one last mission in time to save the realm.

Ilfanti and the Orb of Prophecy, 0978778278, $19.95
and more to come!

Tales of the Council of Elders

Tales of the nine Mages who form the Council of Elders, the leading body of the Mage's Council. Some of the most charismatic, influential, and powerful characters in all of the Imperium at last reveal parts of what has led them to be the Masters of all magical beings. Follow the adventures of the Council of Elders from the dawn of Mages straight through to the aftermath of the *Siege of Zoldex*. Written by Imperium Saga creator Clifford B. Bowyer and other Silver Leaf Books authors, including Brandon Barr, Stuart Clark, Mike Lynch, B. Pine, and Brittany Westerberg, and introducing Karen Aragon, Ben Mitchell, and Robb Webb.

Tales of the Council of Elders, 1609750276, $19.95

The Warlord Trilogy

A prequel to the epic fantasy saga introduced by Clifford B. Bowyer in *The Fall of the Imperium Trilogy* chronicles the upbringing and development of the boy who is destined to become a legend. A young Braksis must learn how to survive in a world that threatens to overwhelm him, from the devastating battlefields of the Troll Wars, to the ultimate betrayal of the throne, to finding himself alone and unprotected in a world fraught with peril. Follow the adventures of Braksis as he seeks to survive, forge new alliances, reclaim the Kingdom that is rightfully his, and become the Warlord that he is destined to be.

Falestia, 1609750411, $29.95
Falestian Heir, 1609750438, $29.95
Falestian Legend, 1609750454, $29.95

CLIFFORD B. BOWYER
GEN-OPS

In the not-too-distant future, a catastrophic event decimates much of the surface of the Earth, but also presents an amazing discovery that drew scientists from around the world to work in secrecy of the marvels that it could unlock. Genetic manipulation, enhancement, and augment become the key to evolution, leading to test subjects the surpassed even the most optimistic expectations. Seeing the potential for financial gain, a handful of the scientists betrayed the government by contacting foreign powers and selling the technology to the highest bidders .

The technology is out there, the secret of the GENs is on the open market, and the government agency that had been tasked with recovering the technology or destroying all evidence of its existence has been targeted for assassination. Only one man, former Shadow Recon team leader Logan Stone, can be entrusted to take on this vital mission with any home of containing the situation and erasing all evidence that it ever even happened.

It is a race as Stone and his team fights to keep the true secret of the discovery from coming out and recover that which had been stolen. Gen-Ops combines military, espionage, intrigue, and strong character development in a fast-paced and dangerous not-too-distant future world where the fate of humanity hangs in the balance.

Gen-Ops, 1609750373, $24.95
and more to come!

CLIFFORD B. BOWYER
CONTINUING THE PASSION

Continuing the Passion follows the story of Connor Edmond Blake, a best-selling novelist who, after suffering the tragic and unexpected loss of his father decides that the best way to honor the memory of his father is by carrying on the legacy that his father left behind.

Connor's father, William Edward Blake, a Hall of Fame High School Baseball Coach had led his team to numerous state championships. Most of Connor's memories and moments he shared with his father have something to do with and revolve around the sport of baseball. Connor decides to at least make the attempt to coach a High School team in attempt to honor his father.

Continuing the Passion is seen through the eyes of Connor Blake as he experiences the tragedy of the loss of his father, and his pursuit to help his family find a way to overcome the loss.

Continuing the Passion, 097877826X, $18.95

BEYOND BELIEF

Damon Burke had strong family values, a good career, money, friends, and the foundation for a successful life. But he still wanted more than just success in business, and craved the love of a woman and a family of his own. While he had numerous romances, Damon had always prioritized his career over his personal life and failed to find the elusive one to share it all with. That was until he came across the profile of Cassie Caniglia through an alumni network.

Cassie was gorgeous, exciting, enticing, and rich. With a renewed vigor to find personal happiness, Damon could not help but be allured by her and find himself dreaming of a future together. She was everything he had always been looking for, and more. Accepting that, he knew he had to tread carefully to make sure that his dreams did not wind up rushing and sabotaging reality.

But tragedy began drawing Damon into a most dangerous game where everything and everyone he loved was at risk because of his connection to Cassie. While she fights for her very survival to escape the torment of her mob-connected brother-in-law, Damon finds himself desperately trying to help her even knowing that doing so makes him a target. *Beyond Belief* is a romantic suspense that will lead you down a path so dark and twisted that you will begin to question just what is real and what is mere illusion.

Beyond Belief, 1609750357, $24.95

STUART CLARK

PROJECT
U·L·F

Imprisoned for a crime of passion, Wyatt Dorren is given a second chance at life on the Criminal Rehabilitation Program. Dorren becomes the rarest of breeds: an ex-convict who has become a productive member of society, trapping U.L.F.'s—Unidentified Life Forms—from newly discovered planets and returning with them for exhibition at the Interplanetary Zoo. Dorren inspires loyalty and courage in his team members, but nothing from his dark past, or his years trapping dangerous aliens, can prepare him for what's in store now.

Project U.L.F., 0978778200, $27.95
Project U.L.F.: Reacquisition, 0978778286, $19.95
Project U.L.F.: Outbreak, 1609750470, $21.95

MIKE LYNCH & BRANDON BARR

SKY CHRONICLES

Since the dawn of time, an ancient evil has sought complete and unquestioned dominion over the galaxy, and they have found...us.

The year is 2217 and a fleet of stellar cruisers led by Commander Frank Yamane are about to come face to face with humanity's greatest threat—the Deravan armada. Outnumbered, outclassed, and outgunned, Yamane's plan for stopping them fails; leaving all of humanity at the mercy of an enemy that has shown them none.

Follow the adventures of Commander Frank Yamane and his crew as they struggle to determine whether this will be Earth's finest hour, or the destruction of us all.

Sky Chronicles: When the Sky Fell, 0978778235, $18.95
and more to come!

MIKE LYNCH & BRANDON BARR
AMERICAN MIDNIGHT

Tania Peters had it all—a loving, supportive family, and a future that seemed all but set. But when her mother is killed in a plane crash in the jungles of Ecuador, her world comes crashing down around her. As a result, she adopts a live for today philosophy. Throwing herself into the arms of her boyfriend, Tania seeks all that society says will bring satisfaction and meaning into her life. But she soon realizes this is a lie, and begins to fall under the spell of the Unity Party, a political movement that has swept Robert Allen into the White House. But such allegiances come at a price: complete and unquestioned loyalty to the Party. Despite all the "good" the Party does for society, Tania's devotion to the movement is pushed to the limit when her own father, the Pastor of the Calvary Community Church, is arrested and jailed when he refuses to compromise his religious beliefs. Forced to decide between her past and her future, Tania rediscovers the faith she has long since abandoned, even though such a decision could cost everything she holds dear, including her life.

American Midnight, 1609750195, $19.95

B. PINE
The Draca Wards Saga

In a universe where dragons are supreme sentient beings, it is believed that eight humans will be born with extraordinary supernatural abilities that will give them the power to challenge dragons. Divided into two factions—the Draca Debellos: conquerors of worlds to fuel their powerful magic, and the Draca Tueri: protectors of the worlds and their sentient beings—they tirelessly search for these gifted children to train and bond with to help in their eternal struggle and attempt to end their tenuous deadlock.

Follow the adventures, struggles, and development of these humans who have their innocence shattered at a tender age while trying to learn to live under the influence of powerful beings wishing to use them for their own ends, and growing up in a world of tragedy and horror, betrayal and deception.

Familiar Origins, 1609750314, $21.95
Plights, 1609750497, $19.95
Coming of Age, 1609750519, $19.95
Glimpses of Destiny, 1609750535, $19.95
and more to come!

T.J. Perkins
SHADOW LEGACY

Growing up ninja in a modern world with ancient customs is difficult, but the Japanese government still has need of them. Training in the Chaio village, home of the best ninja, Duncan Kimura dreams of one day being chosen for the elite special forces-the Black Dragon Squad. But his dreams won't become a reality if he can't control his destructive rage that threatens everyone around him.

Turmoil threatens to tip Duncan's balanced world; rivalries, disputes with other teens, competition, and a beautiful kunoichi-a female ninja. The plague of emotions fuels his anger and an entity hidden deep inside him threatens to surface-it wants out. Follow Duncan through his trials and challenges as he will either lose himself to his rage and become a threat to all he knows and loves, or triumph and become the ninja his people expect of him.

Art of the Ninja - Earth, 160975039X, $19.95
Power of the Ninja - Fire, 1609750551, $15.95
and more to come!

Justin R. Smith
CONSTANCE FAIRCHILD ADVENTURES

"*I was twelve when I realized I was a ghost.*"

So says Constance Fairchild, an eccentric poetess who is heiress to a fortune—and a girl who, from an early age, has believed that she had been reincarnated.

Orphaned at the age of 14, Constance finds herself in life threatening encounters, a victim of vast conspiracies, and under public scrutiny. With her vast fortune, an unforgettable cast of close confidants, a maturity beyond her years, and a desire to turn around unscrupulous and unethical business practices of her ancestors, Constance desperately tries to find a way to survive her ordeals and experience the adventure that is her life.

The Mills of God, 097443549X, $24.95
The Well of Souls, 0978778294, $19.95

CHRISTOPHER STOOKEY
TERMINAL CARE

Emergency Physician, Phil Pescoe, becomes alarmed by a dramatic increase in deaths on the Alzheimer's Ward. The deaths coincide with the initiation of a new drug study with an experimental and highly promising treatment for the disease to half of the patients on the ward.

Mysteriously, the hospital pushes forward with the study even though six patients have died since the start of the trial. Pescoe teams up with Clara Wong—a brilliant internist with a troubled past—to investigate the situation. Their inquiries lead them unwittingly into the cutthroat world of big-business pharmaceuticals, where they are threatened to be swept up and lost before they have the opportunity to discover the truth behind the elaborate cover-up.

With the death count mounting, Pescoe and Wong race against time to save the patients on the ward and to stop the drug manufacturer from unleashing a dangerous new drug on the general populace.

Terminal Care, 1609750292, $19.95

BRITTANY WESTERBERG
INTO FIRE

The fifteen year old Leora had always planned her entire life around working with her brother and father in their gemsmithing shop. She enjoyed it, she was good at it, and she wanted nothing more than to do it. But fate had other plans for Leora.

On a day like any other, Leora's life was turned upside-down when two strangers visited her and informed her family that she had the power of a Mage—abilities she had always been raised to fear. As they seek to whisk her away and train her in her abilities, Leora must decide whether to remain in the family business, or explore these amazing abilities, and, a potential link to her mother.

Deciding to embrace the adventure, Leora learns that there is a lot more in the world outside her home than she thought. With new allies, challenges, experiences, and problems she never knew even existed, Leora must accept the person she was meant to become or lose everything that ever meant anything to her.

Into Fire, 1609750330, $19.95

And available electronically:

JARED ANGEL
ENDLESS WAR OF THE GODS

In the world of Seibu, an endless war between the gods of Light and Dark threatens to destroy all life. Crevahn, mother of creation, struggles to save her newly created world and all life. Without the help of Vyas, a mighty jiva, and Malla, a humble human, Crevahn will fail. Will Vyas survive and maintain his sanity long enough in his battle against the God of Dark? Will Malla overcome her subordination and inevitable execution in her battle against the God of Light? Find out if the world will end or be saved in this high adventuring tale by debut novelist Jared Angel.

Betraying the God of Light, 1609750616, $9.95
and more to come!

BRIAN BANDELL
mute

Officer Monique "Moni" Williams, has never lived an easy life—with an abusive ex-con father, a two-timing, pistol-wielding ex-boyfriend and a racist boss—it's hard to see how things could possibly get more difficult for her. After she meets a child that she bonds with, Moni must protect the girl from a mysterious threat stalking everyone near the Indian River Lagoon.

A serial killer is on the loose on Florida's Space Coast, and Moni has been put in charge of the key witness in the biggest case of her life: an eight-year-old girl called Mariella. The child has gone mute after losing both her parents one harrowing night. Now, Moni struggles to protect the child and break her silence, while more reports of inexplicable deaths and animals with eerie purple eyes pile up. Her bond with the child is tested by a police force demanding answers. What does the lagoon's rotten stench have to do with a mute little girl? Can Moni save Mariella from what lurks along the water? Who is really facing the most danger? Find out in this suspenseful, page-turner that will keep you guessing until the very end.

Mute, 1609750594, $9.95

CLIFFORD B. BOWYER
SNAPPED

Alex Adams has always had a flair for excitement, the thrill of the moment, and pushing things to the edge. He is, always has been, and knows he always will be, a winner in everything that he does. His competitive nature has always driven him, pushing him to succeed in everything he does. Whether it's the sports he excels in, the academics that come easy to him, the charisma of his social life, or the career that he embraces, Alex only knows how to thrive.

Most who knew him felt he lived the perfect life. Everything came so easily to him, he always seemed so happy, and he even married his high school sweetheart. He had the perfect house, a perfect wife, and a perfect job. Or was it? Alex's world it turned upside-down when a cruel new manager, Maria Thompson, is promoted and becomes his boss. Alex finds himself pushed to the limit, acting in ways and doing things he never thought possible, and beginning to see all aspects of his life unravel all around him. Spiraling out of control, he seeks to find something to cling on to, trying to save his position at work, save his marriage, and save himself as his despair leads him to violence, an affair, and self destructive behavior. Alex knows that, for him, failure is not an option. So, the question becomes... how can one get away with murder?

Snapped is a psychological thriller that challenges even the most sane and successful of individuals and threatens to unleash the darkness locked deep within one's soul when pushed beyond one's limits.

Snapped, 1609750578, $9.95

ROB GULLETTE
THE APOLLO TRILOGY

"We choose to go to the Moon in this decade and do the other things, not because they are easy, but because they are hard...", stated former President Kennedy on September 12, 1962. These words inspired a nation in the initial race to the Moon. Now over half a century later these words are moving the world to action once more.

A terrorist attack on the National Air & Space Museum in Washington, DC ignites a new and more deadly race to the Moon than ever before. Too bad the United States has allowed its manned space program to fall apart. The space shuttles are museum pieces and the International Space Station now belongs to the United Nations.

When intelligence reports reveal China's plan to establish a permanent base on the Moon, former astronaut, U.S. President Olivia Kane is faced with a challenge she must confront: Will nuclear weapons soon be aimed at the United States from above, or will the Moon be the site of the next great war? Find out in this suspense-filled thriller.

Waking Apollo, 1609750608, $9.95
and more to come!

LINDA MCCUE
DARK DESTINY

Lisa Melton is a typical college student: she studies at the campus coffee spot, stresses over tests and even goes to parties with her friends. But when she wakes up one morning with no memory of the night before, looking like the victim of an brutal assault, and starts seeing a giant black dog in her dorm room—everything around her starts to spiral wildly out of control. Suddenly, Lisa's life isn't so humdrum anymore as she meets a mysterious and handsome man who seems to know more about her than she seems to even know herself. Who is this man: is he simply a supernatural stalker or is he something more? Lisa has little time to decide what to think of him, before she is tangled up in a web of kidnappings, brutal murders, a pack of strange giant black dogs, and an ancient family feud that takes her overseas and within inches of her own sanity.

Dark Destiny, 1609750586, $9.95

To order any Silver Leaf Books title, check your local bookstore, order through our website at www.SilverLeafBooks.com, or mail a check or money order to:

Silver Leaf Books
P.O. Box 6460, Holliston, MA 01746

Please include $3.95 shipping and handling for the first book and $1.95 each additional book. Massachusetts residents please add 6.25% sales tax. Connecticut residents please add 6.35% sales tax. Payment must accompany all orders.

B. Pine is an award-winning fantasy and science fiction author who keeps her days full by writing, gardening, reading, and raising her little ones. She is an avid reader of fantasy, science fiction, and vampire novels, particularly stories with backgrounds based on medieval culture from Western Europe and England, where she lived for four years. Her passion for writing was born after taking a college course in creative writing. She graduated from the University of Maryland and Wilmington University with degrees in Business Management and Accounting, respectively.

Her debut novel, *Familiar Origins*, has won two Royal Dragonfly Book Awards, and her Draca Wards series will be continued in 2013. She also has a short story published in The Imperium Saga: Anthology with fellow authors from Silver Leaf Books, LLC. She is currently working on the next installment of her fantasy saga.

CPSIA information can be obtained at www.ICGtesting.com
Printed in the USA
BVOW010730040213

312274BV00004B/12/P